REQUIEM

REQUIEM

Providence Trilogy (Book Two)

Jamie McGuire

Requiem

Providence Trilogy (Book Two)

Jamie McGuire

Edited by Theresa Wegand

Table of Contents

To Eden and Hailey, my little beacons of light

My sunshine eternal

1. THREE

I was back. Surrounded by darkness, two blurry forms crouched before an open safe, hidden behind a large hinged bookcase. They breathed heavily, working at a feverish pace to find what they had searched for the past months. One of the men froze and all movement stopped. He leaned further into the safe, using both hands to pull out a thick leather-bound book.

"That's it. Dear God, that's it," Jack whispered.

Every corner of the room held a warning. Lit only by the moonlight filtering through the blinds of a single window, antique swords and axes hung on the walls, bordering hand-painted landscapes of war and death. The air was stale, lacking human lungs to circulate it.

I had been there many times before, but my hands still trembled, knowing the panic would begin soon. It was coming, but I couldn't stop it. It would play over and over as if I were stuck in time, in a bad dream, or in Hell.

Jack's fingers ran over the branded seal in the center and looked to his friend.

"Are you sure you want to do this, Jack?"

"Are you sure it's her, Gabe?" Jack replied. Gabe nodded slowly, and Jack continued with a sigh, "Then you know the answer."

Hearing what Jack's human ears couldn't, Gabe's head jerked to the side. "It's too late," he said, his eyes twitching back and forth as he listened. "They're here."

They shoved the documents, artifacts, and jewels back into the safe, and the fair-haired man effortlessly pressed the heavy bookcase flat against the wall in an attempt to conceal any evidence of their presence.

"Don't worry about that now, Gabe! Let's go!" Jack growled.

"I'm trying to buy us some time!"

Their shadows glided over the wooden floor as the men fled the room, and I stepped aside, watching them in silence, knowing their fate.

Gabe ran ahead, gun in hand, accustomed to Jack falling behind. He waited at the end of the hall for his friend, calculating a way out.

"The roof," I whispered in his ear. "You always use the roof."

A large, warm hand reached out, and Jack was pushed against the wall.

"What are you . . .?" Jack began.

Gabe lifted his finger to his mouth and then pointed to the upper floor. Jack nodded quickly, pushing his tired body from the wall. They bolted down a corridor, tightly rounded a corner, and then launched themselves up the stairs. Both men took two steps at a time, their hands gripping the banister to pull them along with each leap.

"The roof!" Gabe called as many voices echoed below them, none of them human.

Jack's eyes widened when a terrifying shriek came from below. His stride grew longer as he streaked through another door, climbing a second stairway. He heaved a breath of relief. The narrow walls of crumbling concrete meant the roof was just a few steps away.

Already at the top of the stairway, Gabe shouldered through an outer door and ran across the roof to the edge. He looked down four stories to the road below and then at his friend. "We've still got two minutes, Jack. Are you sure?"

"Do I look ambivalent to you?" he shouted, tightly grasping the book to his chest. "I have to find a way to stop it!"

I frowned. In the past, I had begged my father to leave the book behind. Dozens of trips to this place taught me that Jack and Gabe's plight would replay exactly the same way. Each time I attempted to change the outcome, it just made the end harder to watch.

Gabe sighed in submission and then jerked his head to the north, gauging the distance of their escape. "Then it begins."

The shrieking grew louder, and Jack closed his eyes. "I have to save her," he said in a low, grieved voice.

Jack's body jerked forward. His tie slapped against his neck, and the wind howled past his ears as he flew through the night sky. It seemed as if the second he took flight, he had landed on another roof four buildings away. Jack lurched forward with the sudden stop, bending at the waist, making a loud grunting noise as the air was forced from him with the sudden impact. Gabe released him then.

"I'll never get used to that," Jack smiled, smoothing out his jacket and tie.

"I could have let you take the fire escape, brother, but with those beasts on your tail, only parts of you would have made it to the street," Gabe said with a smirk. His grin quickly faded when he looked up. "They are drawn to it. We need more distance."

Jack nodded. A door identical to the one they escaped from was a few yards away. He yanked open the door, and Gabe followed him down the stairs. After three flights, Jack slowed his pace; his chest heaved.

"Come on!" Gabe growled.

"I'm coming!" Jack snapped, taking another deep breath before descending the last two flights.

Just as their exit came into view, the shrieking and snarling grew louder. Jack looked over his shoulder and saw that Gabe had stayed behind, his firearm held closely to his face.

"We're not going to make it. They're too close." Gabe breathed.

"GABRIEL!" An animalistic hiss cried above them. It was one voice, but it was also many.

Gabe cocked his gun and narrowed his eyes. "Go, Jack. I'll hold them off."

"Gabe."

"If you want to save your daughter, then go!" Gabe yelled.

Jack clutched the book to his chest and made his way outside. He burst from the door and then grasped his knees, unable to catch his breath. He leaned against the door and lifted his face to the heavens, closing his eyes.

"God, help me," he whispered.

The shrieking stopped momentarily before piercing the air again.

For the first time, Jack looked into my eyes. He was afraid, something I'd never seen before. It felt strange at first, as though he shouldn't have been able to see me. I watched a familiar look of resolve paint his face. "I'm going to save you, Nina."

As if he'd never spoken to me, Jack's eyes darted in every direction to determine the best route of escape.

Just as he had made his decision to flee, the wood splintered behind him, and dozens of long clawed hands exploded through the door. Jack's eyes widened in terror as demons grabbed at his chest, his legs, his neck, and face. The sharp nails shredded his shirt, and sunk into his skin, blood spilling from his open wounds.

"Nina!" he screamed. His flesh ripped under the pressure of the long talons grating across it.

His arms and legs were thrust forward, and then his body bent in half and disappeared, sucked into the hell that awaited him inside.

"Daddy!" I screamed into the darkness.

Hands held my outreached arms, and I slapped them away. "No! No! Daddy!" I wailed, trying to get away. I wasn't strong enough.

"Nina, stop! It's me!"

As reality sank in, I stopped fighting. Jared sat next to me in our bed, holding my wrists against his chest.

"Nina?" he said, leaning over to flip on the lamp.

My eyes squeezed shut, rejecting the light. Sweat soaked my cotton gown, and damp hair matted against my forehead. With trembling fingers, I wiped the wet strands from my face. It always took a few moments to calm myself, but it wasn't fear this time. I was angry.

"They're getting worse," Jared said, concerned.

I had to clear my throat. "They're so real," I whispered. I could still smell my father's cologne, and the screeching still rang in my ears. Returning to the same place almost every night to watch my father die felt like torture. Resentment replaced the fear, and that was a good thing; I felt better equipped to handle rage than the overwhelming helplessness that normally woke me.

"Nina?"

I licked the salt from my lips. "I'm okay."

"That's the third one this week. I don't think you're okay," Jared said, his face tense. "Same one?"

Reluctantly, I nodded. Jared worried obsessively each time he had to wake me from a nightmare. He was tormented by the screaming, the trembling, and the inability to stop it. The frustration and concern he felt was only exacerbated by our unique link. Jared was half human and half angel. As a hybrid, he was sensitive to small changes in my body such as blood pressure, hormonal changes, and my pulse. Because I was his taleh—the human he was charged with protecting—he felt my feelings as if they were his own.

He watched me for a moment before pulling me onto his lap. "Maybe you should talk to someone."

"I don't need a shrink, Jared. They're just dreams," I said, more to myself than to him.

He pulled me with him, resting his back against the headboard. I worked to relax. My days without him the previous spring had been good practice when I didn't want to bother him with my ridiculous human fears and feelings. But I struggled after the nightmares, even after months of perfecting my talent.

I tried to think of anything but the terrifying image of my father being torn to shreds so that I could settle down and fall asleep. Jared's feverish chest against my cheek was comforting, and I breathed in his amazing scent. Any other time I would have instantly felt at ease, but after the three-peat of the worst nightmare I'd ever had, it didn't work.

"I'm going to take a shower," I said, abruptly peeling off the blankets tucked around me.

"It's three o'clock in the morning, Nina. You have to get up in three hours anyway for work. Why don't you just try to sleep?"

I scooted to the edge of the bed and planted my feet on the floor with my back to Jared. "Have you slept?" I asked him.

After a short pause, he let out an exasperated sigh. "Yes."

"Then there's no reason for me to go back to sleep. I don't want to sleep, anyway. It's the same thing every time I close my eyes." I waited a moment, and when Jared failed to argue, I pushed myself off the bed and walked into the bathroom.

The pipes whined when I turned the shower knobs, and I stood in front of the sink in quiet thought, waiting for the water to warm. Visions from my dream flashed in short, loud scenes—the screeching and the sound of my father's shoes running up the stairs—it wouldn't stop. I closed my eyes tightly, willing the memories away. Were they even memories if it was just a dream?

"Nina? Are you okay in there?" Jared called.

I leaned over, cupped my hands together under the running water of the sink, and then splashed my face. I let the drops of water fall from my nose and chin into the basin and watched as they followed each other in a trail down the drain. Concentrating on masking my emotions was easier when I focused on something trivial.

"I'm fine," I said, righting myself to stare in the mirror. My features had changed from the time when Jared and I had first met. Spending much of the summer indoors while my leg healed had left my skin pale and lifeless, and I was sporting a matching pair of purple circles under my eyes.

Our near-death experience in the restaurant seemed like a lifetime away. Aside from the occasional news story about the police department's finest meeting untimely ends in bizarre and unrelated accidents, our days went by as if Graham, Shax, and the book had never existed.

I let my nightgown drop to the floor and then stepped into the shower, sighing as the stream of water poured over my face.

Jared walked in and leaned against the sink, crossing his arms across his chest.

"Everything okay?" I asked.

Jared shifted uncomfortably. "It's you I'm worried about."

"The fall semester is getting ready to start. I have extra classes, and with my internship, it's probably just stress."

"I don't understand," Jared said. "It's been months since any of *them* have come around. This is the least I've seen of them in my entire life, and yet you're . . ." Jared rubbed his neck. "It doesn't make sense for you to be having these dreams now."

"Jared, people have nightmares all the time without demons present. It doesn't mean anything," I said, scrubbing shampoo into my hair.

"That's what you think."

I rolled my eyes. "Oh, c'mon. You're blowing this out of proportion. If I promise to quit having the dreams, will you promise to quit freaking out about them?"

"You'll promise to quit having the dreams," Jared repeated, his voice thick with sarcasm.

I poked my soapy head from the shower curtain, lather dripping down my face. "Okay, I can't promise, but you're giving me a complex. Unless you know something I don't, they're *just* dreams."

Jared smiled and wiped the line of soap from my forehead, promptly kissing my lips. "Okay. They're just dreams."

I nodded in approval and then closed the curtain. "I have to stop by the office today. Do you mind?" I asked, knowing he would.

"You mean more than any other day?"

Escorting me to Titan Mercantile was just another day at work for Jared, but as often as I asked him to come in, it had become an inside joke between us. Every day I asked, and every day he politely declined. For years, Jared's father, Gabe, walked the halls of Titan Mercantile. Jared didn't talk about it, but I assumed his refusal to go in had to do with unresolved feelings concerning his father.

The hours before dawn crept by slowly, and after my shower, Jared and I spent the remaining moments of twilight at the breakfast table. When the morning sun finally poked through the blinds, I smiled at the glowing light painting rectangles against the walls. I had spent hours staring at those walls, waiting for my leg to heal. Beth had visited infrequently, busy decorating her new apartment, Kim had taken her summer vacation on the road, and Claire was relentlessly eliminating any threat to us. Jared spent much of his time warding off loneliness and keeping me entertained. We had grown closer, and life had been more normal than ever. The only reminder of the night I almost died was the scar on my thigh.

Jared, working busily in the kitchen, caught my eye, and I listened to the pan pop and sizzle with our breakfast. He placed omelets on the table along with a small stack of mail.

"Anything interesting?" I asked as he thumbed through the envelopes.

Jared paused, eyes narrowing as he read over the handwritten address.

"What?"

"It's for you," he said, sliding it toward me.

The top left corner explained Jared's expression. It was from Ryan.

By Jared's expression, I knew it wasn't good news. "You already know, don't you?" I said, pulling out a single sheet of notebook paper.

"I have an idea."

"Something you should have told me by now," I accused, scanning the letter quickly.

Dear Nigh,

I wanted you to hear it from me, but didn't know how to say it, so I'm just going to write it. I'm not coming back to Brown. I talked it over with an Army recruiter, and I feel that it's the best place for me at this point. I know you better than you think I do, and right now, you're feeling guilty. Well, don't. You're happy, and that's all that matters to me. That's the truth. I'm sorry you have to find out in this stupid letter, but everything happened kinda fast and I didn't have time to call. Take care of yourself, Nigh. I'll think about you every day.

Ryan

The letter slipped from my hands and fell to the floor, quietly and slowly. The numbness was unexpected but welcome; I knew guilt would soon wash over me and that it would be unbearable.

"He left."

Jared touched my hand. "Claire called. He's doing well."

"Claire's *gone?*" I wailed, standing up from my seat. Once again, although the swing of emotions startled me, anger was always preferable to pain. Jared took a step toward me, but I stepped away from him. "You didn't even let me say good-bye to her! To either of them!"

Jared's eyebrows moved inward, creating a deep crease. "He wanted to do this, Nina. You couldn't have stopped him anyway."

"But you knew it was happening," I said softly. "You should have told me." The lack of sleep was already wearing on me, and my body felt heavy. I didn't have the energy to be angry. My eyes drifted to the letter on the floor. "This is my fault."

"Nina, no."

I nodded. "I did this. I broke his heart, and he couldn't stay here." I shook my head. "I should have left him alone. He's going to die out there."

"Ryan made his choice," Jared said.

His dry tone was hardly convincing. He had a right to be angry, watching his fiancée anguish over the man she was meant to be with. To Jared, Ryan being Claire's taleh meant that I belonged to someone else, and I used that to drive Jared away when I thought being with him meant putting his family in danger. My brilliant plan had been enough to drive Ryan to join a war halfway across the world. No matter what Jared said or how much he hated to see me upset, he wasn't sorry to see Ryan go.

As angry as I was, the only one to blame was me, and we both knew it.

I shook my head. "I have to get going. I have to get those documents faxed by eight."

Jared sighed. "If I had told you, what would you have done besides worry?"

I pulled my purse over my shoulder. "I don't know," I said, pulling out my cell phone. I scrolled through the address book until I found Ryan's number and then held the phone to my ear. As I expected, his voice mail immediately answered.

The sound of his voice made my insides wrench, but when the beep cued me to speak, my temper kicked in.

"I need you to call me. Call me right now. I mean it. I just got your letter and you can't do this. You just can't. You've got to call me so we can figure this out. Please."

Jared took the phone from my hand and let it slowly close. "He's not going to get that message, sweetheart."

"I had to try," I said, opening my purse for him to drop the phone inside. "Someone had to."

Jared touched my arm. "He's the safest enlisted man in the Army, Nina. He has Claire."

"And how is that going to work, exactly? Has Claire joined the Army?"

Jared smiled. "No. We've talked about this. She's keeps an eye on Ryan the same way we were allowed to train. We have connections."

"That's not the point."

"I know," Jared said, opening the door.

I didn't kiss him when I passed through the door or when he opened the passenger side for me as he always did or before he left me for the driver's seat. He didn't attempt to apologize, which he only did when he felt he was right, knowing that infuriated me further.

"I'm sorry you're angry," he said.

I glared at him. "That's lame and you know it. You didn't tell me Ryan had enlisted in the first place! You didn't let me say good-bye to Claire! Sorry I'm angry." I muttered the last words and crossed my arms, settling into an unyielding foul mood. When Jared didn't reply, I peeked at him from the corner of my eye. He was trying not to laugh.

"This is *not* funny, Jared!"

His mouth immediately flat-lined. "I didn't say it was. You're just," he shook his head as he pulled to the curb of Titan Mercantile, "trying to be angry, with a series of annoyed expressions on your beautiful face; it's amusing. I'm sorry."

"Stop being sorry and start being—I don't know—sorry!"

A corner of Jared's mouth rebelled and turned up slightly before he straightened it again. "Have a good day."

I slammed the door, beyond trying to have an argument with him. At times, it was maddening how in love with me he was.

I took a few steps toward the building and then stopped. I returned to the Escalade and opened the door. "Are you coming in?" I asked sheepishly.

"Not today," he smiled.

Jared had spent endless hours at Titan Mercantile as a child, and it was his least favorite place to go with his father. It didn't help that the other employees stared at him as if he were a zoo animal. They couldn't figure our relationship out; although, most of them knew that Jared was Gabe's son and my security.

In the days when my father walked the halls, seeing Gabe was just another day at the office. From the first day of my internship, it was apparent that I also needed protection, and my appointed bodyguard also happened to be my fiancé. Those facts alone began more than one string of rumors about my family.

One of my fellow interns in particular had an immediate interest in Jared. Sasha wasted no time with the saccharine-laced pleasantries; on the contrary, she was downright hateful to me on the subject.

"So Jared," she began as I walked into the office we shared. She eyed his Escalade from the window as she spoke.

"I have a lot to do, Sasha."

"He protects you?" When I didn't answer, she walked over to stand in front of my desk, tapping on it until I looked up. "From *what*?" she asked, dubiously.

I glared at her long nails clicking against the wood and then up at her. "I'm busy."

"But he's your boyfriend, right?"

"No."

"No?" she said, her voice an octave higher.

"We're engaged."

"Isn't that, you know, a conflict of interest?"

"Not really," I said, thumbing through a stack of papers.

"I just don't get it. I mean," she puffed an airy laugh, "I realize you're the princess of Titan Mercantile, but don't you feel a little ridiculous when you stand next to him? You're such an odd couple."

Recognizing what she meant, my head jerked up, and my eyes narrowed. "*Excuse* me?"

Sasha shrugged then, running her finger along the edge of my desk as she slithered around me. "Doesn't it make you self-conscious? Women must be throwing themselves at him all the time."

"Not really, no," I snapped as she walked toward the door.

Sasha smirked, backing away from my glare. "Hmm. Very interesting." Her long red ponytail flicked as she turned the corner, and I felt the heat radiate from my face.

On cue, my phone rang.

"Everything okay?" Jared asked on the other end of the line.

I covered my eyes with my hand, attempting to calm myself before I spoke. "Everything's fine. It's . . . Sasha was just here."

"Oh. That explains it. Is she leaving her coffee mug on your papers, again?" Jared chuckled. For whatever reason, it amused him that the woman got under my skin in such a way that I couldn't think straight.

I sighed. "No. She's . . . I can't say what I want to, so I just won't."

"You do own the company, you know. You don't *have* to work with her."

"Right now, I'm an intern, Jared. And," I sighed again, watching her flirt with the human resources manager, "don't tempt me."

"Think you could slip away a bit early today?" Jared asked.

"Probably. Why?"

"It's your first day back to Brown tomorrow. I thought we could get on the bike, head to the oak tree, and have some lunch."

"The oak tree?"

"The one I've wanted to take you to: where my father took my mother."

I smiled. "That sounds fantastic, but I have a meeting first."

"Right," Jared said, pretending he'd forgotten.

I straightened my skirt at the waist and then pressed the button for the third floor. My entire last day of freedom could have been spent with Jared, but Mr. Patocka asked that the interns come in for one last meeting before school began. Some of them were leaving, and he needed to redistribute responsibilities. I had looked forward to this meeting all week only because it was Sasha's last day. That alone was cause to celebrate.

"Interns." Mr. Patocka began looking through the papers in his hand. He always said "interns" as if it left a bad taste in his mouth. "Anna, Brad, and Evan will be leaving us, leaving Shannon, John, Nina, and Sasha with new responsibilities. I would like to say . . ."

Mr. Patocka's words blurred together after I realized he'd put Sasha in the wrong category.

"I'm sorry, Mr. Patocka?"

"Yes, Miss Grey?" he said, obviously irritated. I was well aware that had any other intern interrupted him he or she would have been promptly asked to leave the meeting, but everyone knew, including Mr. Patocka, that I wasn't just an intern.

"I think you've made a mistake. Sasha isn't staying," I said as professionally as I could manage.

"Still not paying attention to your briefs," Sasha snapped. "I'm staying on through the school year."

"*What?*" I said, my tone sounding more disgusted than I'd meant. I looked to Mr. Patocka, who nodded while looking incredibly bored with the turn the conversation had taken.

"I . . . She . . ." I stumbled over my words, trying to think of a way to save face after I'd made it so clear that I was shocked and dismayed at the news.

"It's okay, Nina. We still get to be office mates," Sasha purred. Her smile was that of a cat being polite to the bird just before she ate it.

"Moving on," Mr. Patocka continued. "Sasha, you'll be taking over Brad's duties, Shannon, you'll be taking over Anna's duties, and John will be taking over Evan's. I expect those departing to make sure those staying behind have exact instructions."

"What about Nina?" Sasha said, glaring back at me over her shoulder.

Mr. Patocka sighed. "Nina will be training with Grant during the school year, Sasha. Try not to make me feel as though I'm babysitting more than I already do, please."

"With Grant?" Sasha groused.

Grant was second in command at Titan. When Jack died, he assumed the management responsibilities until I was ready to take over. Working with him was not something I looked forward to; I had spent my teenage years watching Grant suck up to my father and, to Jack's amusement, shamelessly flirt with me.

Jack saw something in Grant that I couldn't—or wouldn't—see. Not only did he give Grant promotion after promotion he tirelessly tried to persuade me to go out with his up-and-coming, incredibly intelligent, star employee.

While being within five feet of Grant usually made me a bit nauseated, Sasha had been scheming to land a job as his assistant since her first day. Mr. Patocka's decision to place me in the very position she'd been working for all summer would no doubt push her beyond any irritation she'd had for me before.

I smiled at the thought. This would mean an all-out war.

"Is there a problem, Sasha?" I asked, trying to preserve a bit of respect from my future employees.

"Problem? Not at all," Sasha said with the sickeningly sweet laugh that liberated her from most awkward situations she'd created for herself. "I apologize, Nina. I didn't realize you were so sensitive." She smiled.

I looked to Mr. Patocka. "Are we finished here?"

"I'm finished with the meeting, but I need you to come to Grant's office with me, Nina. He needs to brief you on a few things before you start back next week."

The other interns filed out of the room, shaking hands and saying their good-byes. I nodded to each of them as they made a bee-line to the elevator, but not before meeting Sasha's cheap grin with one of my own.

Mr. Patocka escorted me down the hall and into the elevator, punching the button for the fourth floor, where my father's office still resided. Grant's office was on the opposite side of the floor, parallel to Jack's. Half of his walls were covered in degrees and pictures of polo ponies, and the other half allowed the sunshine to pour in from large windows that overlooked Fleet Rink.

Mr. Patocka knocked on Grant's half-opened door. "Er, Mr. Bristol? Nina's here to see you."

"Bring her in."

I walked into his office and sat in a puffy green chair, feeling amiable for a change. Grant had worked for my father for ten years, and, like every clichéd rise-to-the-top story, Grant started at entry level. The only thing that would have made his story any more boring would be if he'd begun in the mail-sorting trenches, had we kept a mail room. But Grant didn't begin his days at Titan as a mail boy.

He'd begun as an intern.

"Nina," Grant greeted me over his thin square glasses.

"Grant," I acknowledged with a nod.

Grant looked at Mr. Patocka and smiled politely. "Thank you, Eugene."

Mr. Patocka ducked from the door and shut it behind him. Even though I saw Grant as somewhat of a weasel, the rest of the employees regarded him as their personal savior.

"Okay, what's with all the formalities, Grant?" I said, crossing my arms.

"Give me a break, peanut," he smiled.

He sat in his chair, leisurely crossing his ankles on top of his desk. I frowned at his ridiculous argyle socks. They resembled the very thing I hated about Grant Bristol. He was handsome in an annoying, maddening way. His light brown hair and clean-shaven baby face made most women at our office swoon. He was well dressed and well spoken, and I suppose he was even funny at times. All of which made me want to plant my fist straight into his square chin. He reminded me of the typical soap-opera star. His words were fake, his smile was fake, and his very presence affected me like nails on a chalkboard.

"*Ugh!* You know I hate it when you call me that. If we're going to work together, you're going to have to stop that, Grant. I mean it."

"Anything you say." He smiled with his too-straight, too-white teeth. "I want you here when you're not in class. If I could do it, you can do it. No excuses."

Attempting to keep my temper in check, I stood and offered a small grin. "See you tomorrow."

"One more thing," Grant said. I turned and waited. "Nice skirt, peanut."

I stomped out of Grant's office, trying not to kick anything on my way out. When I pushed through the front door, I saw Jared's Escalade parked against the curb across the street as usual, only this time he stood against his door, looking extremely uncomfortable while Sasha leaned against his car with her shoulder not six inches from him. I could see that he was trying to be polite as he kept his arms crossed, careful not to react to her flirtation, but my eyes zeroed in on Sasha giggling and touching his shirt, chest, and arms with every other word.

"Nina! Hi, sweetheart," Jared said, my interruption a relief. He pulled me into his arms and made a show of planting a kiss on my lips.

"Hey, Nina," Sasha gushed. "I was just telling Jared that we should double date sometime."

"No," I snapped, my patience far beyond its limit. Jared walked me to the passenger side and opened the door. "I can get into the car on my own," I said acerbically.

"Nina." Jared smiled, amused at my mood.

"Don't 'Nina' me," I said, looking straight ahead.

"Well," Sasha called from the other side of the SUV, raising her eyebrows. "I guess I'll see you on Monday. It was nice to finally have a chance to talk to you, Jared."

Ignoring Sasha's final attempt for his attention, Jared watched me for a moment, trying to decipher my emotions. Finally, he walked around to his side and slid in beside me. He watched Sasha trot across the street and then shook his head. "You don't honestly think I was—"

"No. I don't think you were flirting with her," I grumbled.

Jared pulled away from the curb and nodded. "Good because that is completely ridiculous. Not only am I madly in love with you she's . . ." Jared shook his head, making a series of disgusted faces as he tried to think of the correct description. "She's something else."

"That's a word for it," I said, crossing my arms.

"How was your meeting?" he asked.

"You mean you don't know?"

"I kept tabs, but it was difficult to get the details with Sasha two inches from my face. Is Grant still a jackass?"

"Yes," I nodded.

"What's wrong?" Jared paused a moment and then his eyebrows shot up. "Oh."

"What is that supposed to mean?"

"Nothing. I didn't mean anything," Jared said, trying not to smile.

I shook my head, watching the trees pass by the window. Eli had once told us that when we made a commitment in a physical way, Jared's senses concerning me would be heightened. I still wasn't sure what that entailed. Jared never let on that anything had changed, but when his former urgent curiosity about the motives behind my moods or feelings had all but disappeared, I knew something was different. I cornered him on more than one occasion to explain his new attunement, but he always seemed to maneuver his way out of the conversation with an efficient and irresistible diversion.

"Do we still have lunch plans?" My attention focused on the passing landscape outside the window.

"Absolutely. I have a surprise for you," Jared said, taking my hand and pulling it to his mouth.

My mood quickly changed as the warmth from his lips shot up my arm. "I love surprises."

"I know," he said against my skin.

2. GONE

"Carved your name in a *tree*? That's so sweet!" Beth squealed.

"Yes, in a tired, done-three-billion-times kind of way," Kim droned, unimpressed.

I ignored her, smiling at Beth. "He brought me to a field that had a lone oak tree in the center. We rolled out a blanket for the picnic lunch he packed. It was perfect."

"You're up," Kim said, elbowing me.

"Oh," I said, briefly glancing to the menu hanging from the ceiling. "Large coffee. Black." The girl behind the counter nodded, and punched the buttons on the register, waiting for my check card. I nudged Beth. "Did you want anything?"

"Nah, not today."

I rolled my eyes. "She'll have a large skinny mochachino, please."

"I said I didn't want anything," Beth said, feigning annoyance. "And since when do you drink your coffee black?"

"We're not going to have our morning coffee talk on the first day of school without coffee," I said. "I know things are tight for you and Chad right now. Moving is expensive. It's not a problem."

"I'm not a moocher."

"Southern hospitality. Isn't that what you call it?" I winked.

"You're a Yankee," Beth muttered.

The girl turned to make our drinks, and Beth leaned in. "So the tree . . ."

I smiled. "The carving was amazing and brilliantly detailed. I've never seen anything like it. He walked me to the other side, and his parents initials were carved there, too, from, like, years ago."

"No way!" Beth shrieked. She looked around, settling down before her next question. "So have you guys set a date for the wedding?"

I looked down. "Er, no, But it was a nice lunch."

"A nice lunch?" Kim asked.

"He didn't mention it," I said.

"Well, that's a first," Beth teased.

It wasn't hard to guess why Jared's questions about a wedding date had tapered off. He was worried about the nightmares, and he didn't want to make them worse. I knew Jared wanted to set a date. As the weeks passed and I was still reluctant to discuss it, he had begun to get anxious. Once the sleepless nights began, the wedding was the furthest thing from his mind.

We took a spot by the window and updated each other on our summers. Beth and Chad had cut back on their hours at their jobs because of the fall semester. Money was scarce, but they were enjoying playing house. Kim had traveled to see family but returned early.

"My dorm room missed me." She smiled.

"How did you get them to let you in?" Beth asked.

"I have the gift of persuasion," Kim said, rubbing her fingers together.

"So you traveled most of the summer, didn't work, and you had enough money to bribe the powers that be at Brown University?" I asked. "Right."

Kim shrugged. "I robbed two banks and a liquor store on the way to Chicago."

"Nice," I said, taking another sip.

"So Ryan's in the Army?" Kim asked.

"Kim, geez," Beth said, shaking her head.

I nodded. "He wrote me a letter and just popped it in the mail on his way to war. Like it was nothing. Like a freakin' birthday card."

"Or a post card," Kim added.

"With soldiers on it," Beth said. She looked down, trying not to smile.

"With green and black faces and big guns." Kim smiled.

Beth waited a moment and then spoke again. "In camo speedos."

"Lying on a hammock on the beach with 'Greetings from the War' in big yellow bubble letters." I frowned.

Beth giggled before making a poor attempt at a straight face. "It's not your fault."

"It's completely my fault. I should have stopped him."

Beth's smile disappeared. She touched my arm. "Nigh, you didn't know to stop him."

"No, I sure didn't," I said under my breath, knowing Jared could hear.

We tossed our empty cups into the trash before making our way to campus. The walk seemed longer than the years before. I remembered walking down the same street, wondering if I would run into Jared, hoping I could steal another moment with him. A smile touched my mouth as I looked behind us. The Escalade was parked across the street, half a block away.

So much had changed since I had sat on the park bench. Life had gone from bad to worse to wonderful to unbelievable, and now my days were as mundane as any other college sophomore. If only I could close my eyes without seeing my father, but that was asking for too much.

Beth would steal a peek at me now and then. Finally my curiosity outweighed my aversion to her lengthy explanations.

"Okay, Beth, do I have something on my face?" I asked.

"A booger," Kim said without expression, pointing to my nose.

"I have a booger on my nose?" I gasped, my hand flying up to cover it.

"No," Kim said.

Beth smiled. "It doesn't look like you've had much sleep is all."

My hand didn't leave my face without wiping my nose a few times, and then I made a face at Kim. "I haven't, I guess."

"You guess?" Beth persisted.

"Bad dreams," Kim said.

"How did you know?" I asked.

Kim shrugged. "Just a guess. What are they about?"

"Mostly Jack."

Beth's mouth slipped to the side, and then she frowned at Kim with disapproval. Kim didn't flinch.

"What about your dad?" Kim said.

I scratched my head and watched for traffic—stalling, of course, uncomfortable with the direction the conversation had turned.

"Just the way he died. But it's different."

"Different how?" Kim prodded.

Beth stopped mid-step. "Geez, Kim! Knock it off already!"

"Sometimes talking about it can help, Nina," Kim said, ignoring Beth.

"Not today," I said, looking up the aged brick of the business building. "I'll see you guys at lunch."

Class was endless. My mind filled with thoughts of Sasha, Jared, and Claire waiting in the unforgiving desert sun to save Ryan from himself. As time wound down, I felt more and more angry. Guilt followed me everywhere I went, and the lack of sleep left me irritated. By the time class was dismissed, I pushed through the door, paying no attention to the flabbergasted looks of the students I shoved past.

Kim stopped me in my tracks. "Whoa!"

A few breaths were necessary before I could speak. "Sorry, I was . . . I don't know."

"Class was that bad, huh?"

"I don't remember," I said, rubbing my temple where it had met with Kim's bony shoulder.

Kim looked down the hall and then back at me. "Okay. What's going on with you? You're not yourself."

"I'm just tired," I said, sliding by her to escape down the stairs.

On the Greens, the closest bench took the brunt of my anger when I slammed my backpack into it before sitting down in a slump. My next class was in ten minutes, and I had no motivation to listen to the monotonous rules and itinerary.

The students passed, chuckling and chattering with the energy expected on the first day of school. The summer sun was already too warm for the early hour, and with no breeze, I could feel the beads of sweat forming between my clothes and the wood. Campus didn't feel like home, anymore. I felt years from the giggles and laughter I shared with my friends sitting at lunch and coffee shops and the pub. My mood grew worse, and I refused to budge from my bench.

And then he sat beside me.

"Warm day, huh?" he asked without looking in my direction.

"I guess."

"Did you miss the bus?" he asked, peeking at me from the corner of his eye.

I sighed. "I let it drive away so the love of my life could save me with a cab ride."

He smiled. "I'm going to make this okay, baby. Ryan . . . The dreams . . . We're going to figure this out." He took me under his arm and then pressed his lips to my forehead. I let myself melt into his body, and the anger gradually slipped away. Backpack in hand, he gently tugged my fingers. "May I walk you to class?"

A quick nod from me prompted a slow pace across campus. We walked in silence, but he squeezed my hand intermittently to encourage me along. It didn't feel right to be there without Ryan's smiling face. Everyone would be reminded of his absence and why he left when we were at the pub or in study group. It was discomforting to say the least.

The day was long, but I muddled through it. Jared drove me to the office after classes, and dealing with Grant, mountains of paperwork, and training took my mind off darker thoughts.

"We're moving you today," Grant said with his bright smile and deep dimples.

"Moving where?" I asked, wondering what else I could possibly train for. I had been in every department of the company and had just begun the managerial training. In truth, I had mastered everything Grant could do long before my internship and could do it better. I had excellent rapport with the clients, and because of my hard work over the summer, the employees had embraced me. Short of sending me overseas, there was nothing I hadn't seen.

"Over there," Grant nodded.

I didn't turn around. I knew where he was gesturing. He was moving me to my father's office, the one space in the entire building I had avoided.

"I don't need to do that yet," I said, trying to mask my unease.

"Nina, you're the CEO of this company. It's time you took the office."

"Why the hurry, Grant? Are you looking to retire?" I asked, fidgeting with my blouse.

"I'm not asking you to run the company, but you can't gain respect from the staff filing downstairs with the interns. Solidify your position with your employees before you graduate and take over."

The elevator opened and Sasha appeared, gliding a tube of lip gloss over her too-bright lip stick. "Grant, a package for you was sent to our office by mistake," she said, handing him the large paper envelope. "I saw a shirt exactly like that on a homeless woman this morning," she said, staring at me with repugnance. "There are better places to shop than the community thrift store, Nina, really."

I looked down and then back at her, suddenly open to the idea of changing offices. "Sasha, glad you're here. Grant wants me to take my father's office. I'll leave you in charge of transferring my things."

"Your . . .?" Sasha looked to Grant for indemnity, but he raised his eyebrows expectantly. Her expression scrolled through several emotions ranging from shock to anger to defeat, and then she finally turned on her heels. "I'll take care of that right away," she said through her teeth.

Had I slept the night before, my mood would have soared, but I simply looked at the door of my father's office and sighed.

Grant patted my shoulder. "You've earned it, peanut. And if it makes you feel better, I like the shirt."

"Thanks," I said, sliding from his touch.

Carl from maintenance exited the elevator and passed by with a tool bag, a bucket, and a squeegee. He stopped at my father's office door and peered at the black block letters on the glass.

JACK GREY
CEO

He pulled a box knife from his pocket and began scratching at the letters.

"Don't!" I yelled. Carl froze, and I hurried to the door, smoothing out the Y of my father's name. "Leave it," I said softly.

"Yes, ma'am," Carl said, clearly rattled. He shot a glance to Grant and then left the way he came.

"I'm sorry. I assumed you'd want your name on your door. I thought you'd like it," Grant said.

"They can both fit," I said, as I headed for the elevator. "Just put my name under his."

"You're the boss," Grant said, his expression matching his tone.

I pressed the button for the first floor and then leaned against the back wall of the elevator. "Too much for one day," I whispered.

Above the door, the number one was lit in a soft glow, accompanied by a pleasant dinging sound. The double doors spread open, and I squinted from the sunlight penetrating through the glass walls of the lobby. To my surprise, Jared stood at the revolving door.

"It has been a lot for you today. Let's go home."

I smiled, remembering my whispers in the elevator.

He let me lean against him as we walked to the Escalade hand in hand. The gulls seemed particularly loud, calling to each other along the harbor. The breeze brought in the sweet stench of fish and motor oil. The sounds and smells surrounding Titan always reminded me of my father.

"It's no wonder I'm having the dreams," I said.

"What dreams?" Jared teased.

I smiled. "Coming here every day, being around everything that embodies what I remember about Jack, I'm just surrounded by him. It's not some supernatural mystery."

Jared replied only with a thoughtful nod. He was careful to avoid the subject during the ride home, sticking to the weather and happenings at Brown. Once we reached the loft, he was all too eager to start preparing dinner, so I left him to his thoughts and ran a bath in the downstairs tub.

After lingering far too long in the cooling water, I wrapped my towel around me and opened the door, noticing only one plate of food. Jared was in the corner, dripping with sweat.

"You ate without me?" I asked, sitting at the table.

"I didn't want to disturb you," Jared said, grunting with the massive amount of weight above him.

Jared was hiding something, and his behavior told me it was probably something I didn't want to know.

I finished my dinner, started the dishwasher, and then made my way up the stairs. I slipped on my night gown and crawled into bed beside Jared. He was reading and put his book down long enough to kiss my forehead. I relaxed, trying to think peaceful thoughts. Wondering if I would wake up screaming wouldn't help to keep the dreams away, so I forced my mind in the direction of Jared and our oak tree.

"No studying tonight?" Jared said.

"Test is Monday. I'm too tired tonight."

Jared nodded. "Mom called today. Bex's coming home tomorrow."

A yawn interrupted my response, but I spoke in spite of it. "Oh?"

"I invited him over for dinner. I thought I could whip up a pot roast."

I smiled, drifting off. "Sounds good."

Just as Jared kissed me goodnight, I fell, dropping thousands of feet to a dusty wooden floor. Landing face down, my palms flat to the ground, I hesitated to move until I was sure of my surroundings. It was dark and quiet, except for the subtle disruption of the rustling papers. I turned my head, struggling to focus on two shadows on the floor, two hunched figures desperately searching.

I closed my eyes. "I'm not moving," I said, balling my hands into fists. "I won't watch."

The rustling stopped, and Gabe whispered the warning to my father. "It's too late."

"I won't watch you die tonight," I said, gritting my teeth.

Jack and Gabe escaped with their book, and I sat on my knees. The shrieking echoed through the halls, and my heart beat faster. I stood, determined to stay focused on the room I was in, trying to ignore the fiendish and frightening noises growing louder as they closed in. It was *my* dream. I would stay.

The room blurred, and time pulled me away. My stomach tugged, and then I was gone, violently thrust to the roof. Gabe took my father in his arms and leaped with transcendental strength to the site of my father's brutal end. Once again, I refused to move, locking my knees in place. The tugging began, but my feet remained on the ground.

Just then, countless shadows swept past, traveling with such momentum that my hair blew forward, as if two trains were passing at full speed on each side of me. The sounds that came from the shadows were indescribable, so loud that my hands automatically cupped over my ears. I screamed aloud to try to drown out the evil that saturated the space around me.

Then it was gone.

I waited. Sounds from the street below replaced the deafening roar of Shax and his minions. My knees buckled, letting my body fall to the ground.

"Please stop," I whispered, knowing no one could hear.

My breathing accelerated. The air seemed thin, and the tugging began again. "No," I pleaded, just as a hole opened up beneath me. I fell, landing on the wet cement of the alley.

A pair of familiar shoes stood before me, and I followed the tailored suit with my eyes to the face of my frightened father. His hands were wrapped around the book, his knuckles white. I closed my eyes, waiting for what would come next. The sounds of hands exploding through the door and the audible shredding of Jack's clothing and skin were much more vivid when I refused to watch. The bones of his spine snapped as demons yanked him through the hole in the door and into the building to his brutal death.

I cried out, not so much a scream as a low guttural moan, sobbing for my father. The alleyway quaked as if the earth below was trembling in the presence of such evil. Dark turned to dim light, and I focused as Jared's warm hands shook me awake.

"Nina?" he said, holding my cheeks in his hands, waiting for me to look him in the eye.

Once again soaked in my own sweat, I tore my nails from my palms, which were still clenched from trying to force myself to stay in one place. Jared looked down and then left for only a moment, bringing back two rags.

"Jesus, Nina," he choked out.

The white towels hid the four tiny, half-moon gouges in each hand but quickly revealed the damage as they began to turn red.

Jared placed another rag, this one wet and cold, on my forehead, wiping away the sweat and tears. My eyes felt swollen and tight. Although the dream was over, I couldn't stop crying. Jared's expression was heartbreaking. It was the same expression he had when he let go of my hand in the emergency room, as if I were dying before his eyes.

"I can't fix this," he said, his voice breaking. "I don't know what to do to help you."

"You're helping," I said, my voice raspy and faint. I left the bloody rag on the blanket and touched my hand to his face. I was too tired to hold up my own arm, so it fell to the mattress. Streaks of blood marked Jared's cheek, prompting me to turn my hand palm-up to see the oozing tears in my flesh.

"I'll take care of that," Jared said, reaching under the bed to fetch the first aid kit.

My head rested against the headboard as he tended to my wounds, kissing my fingers when he finished each hand.

"Jared?"

"Yes, sweetheart?" he said, his voice thick with agony.

"Would you make some coffee?"

"Yes."

He left me alone, rushing downstairs. I looked down to my red-stained hands and then to the clock. It read three thirty. Rubbing my eyes, I struggled to block out the shrieking that still rang in my ears.

Jared returned with a steaming mug of dark, bitter caffeine. He sat beside me on the bed with renewed hope. "Okay," he said, carefully passing the cup to me, "let's talk about this."

"No."

"No?" My answer caught him off guard. It took him a moment to recoup. "Nina, there has to be a reason for this."

I took a sip and sighed. "I told you. I'm at Titan every day. I'm surrounded by Jack and memories for hours at a time. Think about it. The dreams started shortly after I began my internship."

"That doesn't add up, Nina. You should be comfortable being there by now. The dreams should lessen, not get worse."

An attempt at rational thought proved futile. My mind was clouded by fatigue, and it didn't take long grow frustrated and give up. "I don't want to think about it, Jared."

"You must be exhausted. But let me try. Tell me about the dream." Jared smiled when I conceded with a sigh. "Please?"

"It was different this time. I tried to control it and let it happen without me being there to watch, but it kept pulling me back."

"What pulled you back?"

I shrugged. "I don't know. The dream? I would stand still and concentrate on staying in place, and then I would get pushed to the next scene. But once I stayed for a while, I saw something I 'hadn't seen before."

"Yeah?" he asked, anxious to find answers.

"The d—"

"Nina," Jared said, firmly interrupting me.

Nodding with understanding, I continued. "I stayed behind. Gabe and Jack jumped to the next building as they always do, but this time I stayed on the roof and the others . . . They surrounded me.

Dozens of them, hundreds of them—I don't know—they surged past me."

Jared nodded, still waiting for an epiphany.

"And then I fell through a hole, and I landed in the alley. I didn't watch this time. I kept my eyes shut."

"Did that help?"

"The noises were just as bad."

He waited for something to come to him. Thoughts were clearly racing through his mind as he methodically checked off each scenario, each possible explanation, and then went on to the next. Frustration scrolled across his face and he stood, walking to the railing that ran along the edge of our bedroom. He looked down to the lower level, squeezing the metal bar so tightly it complained as he twisted his hands back and forth.

Coffee finally made its way through my body, rushing through my veins. I kicked the covers away and planted my bare feet on the cold floor. "Movie?" I asked, but he was lost in thought. In the subdued light, I could see his mouth moving, but he made no sound. "Jared?"

His lips continued to move, and the metal still whined under his grip.

"You're going to break the railing," I said, walking the few steps to reach him.

He stiffened under my touch. "They won't answer."

"Who?"

"Eli. Samuel. Anyone."

"Maybe they're busy."

"Exactly," he said, his shoulders falling. "I can feel how exhausted you are, Nina. I don't know how you're still functioning. I can feel the way your body tenses and panics when you're having the dreams. I don't want to frighten you, but this is . . . If you want to believe it's Titan, okay, but I need to figure this out."

"What do you mean?"

"I'm calling Bex. I'm going to have him come in for a few days while I try to find some answers."

"You're leaving?"

"Just for a few days, sweetheart."

I grabbed his shirt, panic tightening my throat. We hadn't been apart for so long, and the thought of even a few days without him frightened me. I would feel naked, vulnerable. "But you promised. You promised you'd never have to go away."

"I did. I'm not going away," he said, touching my cheek. "I'm a phone call away."

"No. *No.* Send Bex."

"Bex doesn't have my connections, Nina, not yet. He doesn't know what he's looking for, and he doesn't know the right questions to ask. I have to do this."

I shifted my weight to one leg, trying to relax and play off my fears. "You can't go. You can't."

Jared touched the thin skin under my eyes with his thumbs, silently pointing out the darkened circles. Without another word, he pulled his cell phone from his back pocket and dialed. "Bex. I need you to stay with Nina for a while." He snapped his phone shut, keeping his eyes on mine.

"Don't do this."

Jared tucked my hair behind my ears. "You're overreacting."

"Please?"

"It's only a few days."

I frowned. "You don't know that."

"If I don't find anything, I'll just come back. Forty-eight hours and I'm right back here. I promise."

"You promised you'd never leave me."

He laughed at my stubbornness. "I'm not leaving you. I'm going to work."

One side of my mouth turned up and I sighed. Jared leaned in, kissing my forehead with his warm, soft lips.

The engine of a speeding motorcycle grew closer to the loft, stopping just outside. Within seconds of its silence, a quiet knock came from the door. My smile melted away, and Jared threw a few things in a duffel bag as Bex sprawled out on the couch downstairs.

"Mom wants you to call," Bex said, holding the remote in front of him, flipping on the television.

"Keep it down, Bex. Nina's going to try to sleep."

I crossed my arms, angry that he refused to compromise. "I can't sleep without you. You think I'm exhausted now? Forty-eight hours from now I'm going to lapse into a coma."

His arms encircled me, kissing me once more. "At least you'll get some sleep."

He was trying to keep the mood of his departure light. Jared didn't enjoy leaving me anymore than I, but he felt strongly enough about my recurring nightmares to break a promise. That realization only left me more unsettled.

Jared gently pulled each of my fingers from his shirt. Imprints from where I had crumpled it between my fingers remained in the fabric, and I hastily ironed it out with the palm of my hands.

"Come home soon," I whispered, trying to keep my voice from breaking.

Jared touched his lips to mine and then looked to his brother. "Bex?"

"Got this," Bex said, lifting his thumb in the air.

Before my eyes finished blinking, he was down the stairs and out the door.

For a few moments, I felt nothing, but the second air filled my lungs, an overwhelming sense of sadness came over me. Jared hadn't been more than a block away from me since I'd come to my senses and begged him back last May.

The bed seemed miles away, but I slowly made my way to it. The moment my backside sunk into the mattress, I heard purposeful stomping up the stairs. Bex ran at me full speed, jumping up and taking flight, landing precisely one inch away.

I didn't flinch.

"Hey," Bex said, elbowing me. "*Death Jungle* is on. Come watch it with me."

"Where is Jared going?"

"I dunno. Come on," he said. His voice was already deeper, and he had been taller than I was for several months. If I didn't know he was still a kid, I would have thought he was a fellow college co-ed. He still hadn't quite filled out—the only thing that gave him away.

He tugged on me to follow him downstairs, and I reluctantly agreed, resting my head on the arm of the sofa.

A ridiculous array of mutilation and mayhem filled the screen. Bex watched with unyielding focus, but my eyes struggled to stay open. Shifting to find a comfortable spot, I settled in and let my mind drift into oblivion. In the darkness, with the screams of dying jungle wanderers in the background, I somehow stayed away from the dark building and my father.

3. FOUR FEET

"Please?" Bex asked, holding open the passenger-side door.

I rolled my eyes. "Fine. Don't tell your mom."

"I won't!" he said. He took my backpack and threw it in the back as I collapsed into the seat. Within seconds, he was beside me, starting the engine.

"You're so cool," he said with a wide grin.

"The only reason I'm letting you drive is because you completed your driving course at Cleet. If you can out-drive cops, I'm assuming you won't wreck the only thing I have left of Jack's."

Bex frowned. "Buzz kill."

He pulled away from the loft, using his blinker and obeying every traffic law along the way. I watched the trees pass, the reds and oranges signaling the arrival of fall. Jared's whereabouts lingered in the forefront of my mind, but the wall I had learned to build around my feelings had long been routine. I didn't want Jared to make a mistake or get injured because he sensed my anxiety.

"Coffee shop, oh-seven-hundred," Bex reported, pulling behind Kim's dilapidated Sentra.

I shot him a look of disbelief. "Seriously?"

"Jared said you were to meet with friends, Kim and Beth, to be prompt, and to keep watch one block north with front door in sight."

"It's me, Bex. Don't act like a military robot. It creeps me out."

Bex smiled. "I just want to do this right."

I returned his smile and gave him a hug. "You're doing great," I said before stepping out onto the sidewalk.

Shoving my hands in my pockets to ward off the frosty morning air, I walked toward the front door of our favorite coffee place. The green door swung open and shut with patrons coming and going several times before I reached the handle. Just as I walked in, someone ran into me from behind, nearly sending me to the floor.

A familiar giggle tittered behind me. "Geez, I'm sorry!" Beth said, undoubtedly putting forth every bit of her southern charm. "I was trying to catch you."

My brows turned in. "Okay. Why?"

She shoved a piece of notebook paper at me. "This. Josh got this in the mail yesterday, and he gave it to Chad. It's from Ryan."

I ripped it out of her hand and scanned it. Everything seemed to be fine. He had completed boot camp and was now in specialized training—something about explosives and being a weapons expert.

"Great," I said.

"But he's doing well! He seems okay, right?"

"Yeah," I said, returning the paper.

Kim shoved me from behind. "Hey!"

"What is with you two today?" I said.

"I saw Beth do it. It looked fun. Can I kick you later?" Kim asked, her expression void of humor.

"No, you most certainly cannot." I turned to order, craning my neck once more at Kim to prove I was not in the mood for her antics.

We settled in at our usual table, grumbling about upcoming tests and papers. Beth shared Ryan's letter with Kim and complained about cutting back more hours at work, making their cupboards more bare than usual. As Kim and Beth discussed Chad's foul mood due to his feeling that his man-of-the-house status was at risk, I had an epiphany.

"What are you getting paid now?" I asked.

"Beans," Beth said.

"Well, I *am* the CEO of Titan Mercantile. I need an assistant."

Beth immediately perked up. "What are the hours? My classes are at quirky times, you know."

"I know," I nodded. "If you can swing at least an hour a day, whenever you can get in, I'll match the pay you were making this summer. You had a little breathing room then, right?"

"That's robbery!" Beth squeaked.

"Oh, shut up," Kim snapped. "Nina has money to burn. She doesn't even get paid to work there."

"Yet," I interceded.

Kim continued, "She's your rich friend, Oklahoma; take advantage."

"You have interns for that stuff," Beth said, shaking her head dismissively.

"They're busy."

After a short moment of thought, Beth's mouth spread into a wide smile. "Really?"

"Really."

She threw herself across the table and wrapped her arms around my neck. "I can't wait to tell Chad! I'm sorry. I have to go!" She picked up her things and took a few steps, turning on her heels. "When do I start?"

I smiled patiently. "When can you start?"

"Next week?"

"See you Monday."

Beth's already broad smile stretched to its limit. She pulled the door open, walking with renewed energy in her step.

"Public displays of generosity make me a little queasy," Kim deadpanned.

"Why do you think I did it?" I asked.

"You're sick," she said, winking. "So what do you think about Ryan's note?"

"He wrote Josh and didn't write me; that's what I think." I sniffed.

"Nigh."

"I know," I said, looking out the window.

"You don't know. You thought he'd stick around and pine for you for years until he'd finally move to the mountains, vowing to be a hermit until he died of a broken heart. He was in love with you; he did something drastic. Let it go."

"I do *not* want him to pine for me. I don't want him dying because I hurt him either!"

Kim watched me for a moment, unaffected by my anger. "You don't look as tired today. Did the dreams go away?"

"No," I snapped.

"But you slept last night?"

"Yes. Jared left town, and it's as if I fell into a coma or something."

"Interesting," Kim said. I turned to look at her, but she was staring out the window as if she were searching for something.

"What is it?" I asked.

"Nothing," she said, turning to face me.

"You're acting weird."

"So?" Kim said in her unapologetic way.

"You're right. It's no different than any other day."

We gathered our things, and then Kim offered to drive me to campus. I nodded in Bex's direction as subtly as I could and then yanked on the passenger door of the Sentra. It opened just a crack, and then it was stuck.

"Really?" I complained.

Kim patiently walked around the front of the car, shooing me out of the way. With a light tug, she opened the door without effort and then returned to her side. We both fell into our seats, and I waited for Kim to go through her routine of a fake Catholic prayer before she started the engine.

"How this car still runs is beyond me. How did it survive your summer road trip?"

Kim shrugged. "She stayed behind. I rented a car."

"Oh yeah? That far? That's pretty expensive, Kim. How did you afford it?" I asked.

Kim slowed at a red light and waited before answering. "I told you. I robbed a few liquor stores on the way."

"The truth this time."

"I just told you," Kim said, stoically.

"You robbed a liquor store? Like with a gun?"

"And pantyhose."

The light turned green, and we rode in silence until we reached campus. Kim helped me with the door, and then we walked together, our first class being in the same building. As we walked, I felt a burning question bubble up inside of me. The answer was potentially something I would forever regret knowing. Regardless, I had to know.

"You didn't really rob a liquor store, did you, Kim?" I said, feeling ridiculous for asking.

"No," she said, turning in the direction of her class.

I waited in the hall, watching her walk away. I had been so preoccupied with my dreams I failed to realize Kim's stories hadn't added up, and I didn't catch that she was using her sarcasm to hide something. But hide what? That was all I needed: something new to obsess about.

Bex was waiting for me when I walked out to the parking lot, in the same spot the Escalade usually sat. I was still twenty feet away when Bex relieved me of my backpack and escorted me the remainder of the way to the BMW. He watched me for a moment, with his big blue eyes.

"Yes," I said, opening the passenger door.

A large boyish grin radiated from one side of his mouth to the other, and he enthusiastically commandeered the driver's seat once more. "Jared called, but you were in class."

"Convenient."

"He wanted you to be updated the second you were finished. He hasn't had much luck—a few leads. He's carrying them out today, and he'll be home tomorrow night as promised."

"Why didn't he call me himself?" I asked, unable to clear the venom from my voice. The anger stemmed from the pain of missing him. Ironically, letting an emotion slip now and then made it easier to control them.

Bex sighed. "He misses you. He was afraid hearing your voice would make it worse. He didn't want you to talk him into coming home."

One corner of my mouth turned up, but I quickly subdued it. "I've got to stop by the office for a sec."

"Yep," Bex nodded, turning in the direction of Titan.

~*~

The evening consisted of homework and dinner. Bex proved to be an accomplished cook, no doubt learning from Lillian as Jared did. He whipped up an amazing Pasta Chick Pea Salad followed by Peppered Shrimp Alfredo. I was so full by the time he served dessert that I didn't have enough room to fully appreciate the small slice of cheesecake he placed in front of me.

"You're spoiling me," I said, leaning back in my chair.

"I happened to know Jared cooks for you all the time. I'm just trying to continue the lifestyle to which you've become accustomed."

I raised my eyebrows and smirked. "If you say so."

"And I like to cook," he said, smiling.

"It's a wonder I haven't gained fifty pounds living with Jared," I said, taking my plate to the sink.

"I got these. Go rest," Bex said, pulling the plate from my hands.

"Quit it. It's fifty-fifty around here."

"Yeah, but I can do them faster." He smirked.

"True," I said, yawning.

I trudged up the stairs. Gluttony, in addition to weeks without a proper night's sleep, left me nearly debilitated. My sluggish arms struggled with the pink striped pajamas I'd managed to pull from the drawer, and once my body collapsed to the mattress, I was unable to open my eyes.

And then it was morning—no Jack, no Gabe, no Shax. I had slept an entire night without a single dream, much less a nightmare. I remembered nothing. A full night of sleep was less than a memory, and it was strange to feel rested.

The smell of bacon grease filled the air. I bounced out of bed and trotted to the railing.

"Did you sleep?" I asked Bex, who was bouncing to a tune in his head.

"Yeah," he called. "I was all prepared to tend to your early morning psychotic episodes Jared keeps talkin' about. I'm disappointed."

"Well, I'm not," I said, retreating to the shower.

A night without the dream didn't make sense. We had been by the office; I had even spoken briefly to Kim about the dreams and nothing. Whatever it was, I had to believe the nightmares were over. Sleeping all night in Jared's arms without waking up screaming and soaking the sheets with my own sweat was definitely something to look forward to. I was even more excited for him to come home.

"Did he call?" I asked, tightening my belt as I descended the stairs.

"No, but Cynthia did."

"Oh? Did she say why?"

"I don't know, Nina. Maybe because you haven't spoken to her in three weeks? She starts noticing when she runs out of charity events to keep her busy."

"Okay, okay," I said, picking up my phone.

"Good morning, darling," Cynthia said before the first ring finished.

"How are you?"

"Busy, busy. Why don't you come over for dinner tonight? I haven't seen you in . . . You know I don't remember? How ridiculous. Come to dinner. Six o'clock."

"Yes, Mother."

"See you then, dear."

"That was quick," Bex said, sliding two eggs from the spatula onto my plate.

"Thank you. It always is. She's not one for lengthy phone conversations."

Bex replied with a nod. He was becoming so much like Jared— not one for many words—but it was obvious what he was thinking just by the slightest change in his eyes. Not that a child of Lillian's would be any different, but I was so proud of the man Bex was quickly becoming. He made me feel just as safe as Jared or Claire did, and he was one of the kindest people I knew.

Bex was a constant reminder of the night Shax's henchmen tried to capture me in Lillian's home and the subsequent months I spent without Jared. Every time Bex was around and each time someone mentioned his name, the sound of Harry Crenshaw's vertebrae snapping resonated in my mind. Bex killing anyone seemed so impossible, but I knew better than anyone that *impossible* didn't exist.

The ride to Brown was long. Each passing minute of each class was an eternity. Even lunch seemed to drag on. The clock demanded my attention within minutes of the last time I had looked at it. Normally the irritation surrounding me would be unbearable, but catching up on lost sleep seemed to help.

"Is that a no?" Beth asked, nudging me.

"Huh?" I said, realizing I had missed a large chunk of the table conversation. We sat in our usual spot at the Ratty with one chair remaining empty in honor of Ryan's absence. It was then I noticed a second chair was also empty.

"I said have you heard from Kim? She wasn't in American Public's class. She's not here. I tried her cell but got her voice mail."

"No, I haven't," I said, glancing around the Ratty, "not since this morning."

Beth frowned, leaning against Chad as she always did when she was unsettled. "She never misses class."

Our lunch table was relatively quiet after that, making the minutes pass even more slowly if that was possible.

The afternoon seemed like an eternity, and by the time Bex dropped me off at the front entrance of Titan, I was crawling out of my skin.

Sasha seemed the likely target on which to vent my frustration, but she wasn't in. Annoyed, I rode the elevator to the third floor, settling on Grant as a second choice.

"Afternoon, peanut," Grant called from his office.

"Piss off."

Instantly, I felt better.

"If you didn't own the company, I would fire you for insubordination," he said with an amused grin.

"Insubordination requires disregard of a command. I simply responded to your greeting," I said, stopping abruptly at my office door.

"Is that what you had in mind?" Grant asked, shoving his hands in his pockets, oozing with pride.

"I . . ." I stumbled over the words, reading the letters once more.

NINA GREY
ACTING CEO

JACK GREY
CEO

"It's barely dry," Grant said, teetering back and forth.

I looked out the closest window and anywhere else in the room other than the door to hide my expression.

"It's fine," I said, pushing past him and shutting the door before he could speak again.

Taking a deep breath, I let my body melt into the door. The office still smelled of mahogany, wood polish, and the slightest hint of tobacco. It was as if the room had frozen in time the second he died. I could almost hear him talking loudly and authoritatively on the telephone.

I walked across the room slowly, noting the pictures of him with members of Congress, plaques, a coat of arms, and degrees that adorned the walls. To my disgust, the large painting of my mother and me still hung between the two large windows overlooking Fleet Rink.

"That's going to have to go," I said, collapsing into Jack's large, black leather chair.

The stack of unopened envelopes was my first order of business, and then I read my company emails. Bored as I was, at least it kept my mind from Jared and the time. Just as the sun began to set, my cell phone chirped.

"Hey Bex," I said through a yawn, "almost done."

"Well, that's good news, sweetheart," Jared said.

"Hi!" My voice was far too high to feign anything but elation. In reaction, I leaned over to look out the window to the street. No black Escalade. "You're not coming home tonight, are you?" I said, deflated.

"On the contrary, I will be home at ten. Is that too late for dinner?"

The road noise should have given it away, but I had expected to be disappointed. "Where are you?"

"On the road."

I sighed. "Do I need security clearance for that answer?"

Jared laughed. "I'll tell you all about it when I get home. Bex tells me you had a good night's sleep last night. Is this true?"

"It is. No bad dreams."

"I look forward to watching you sleep the whole night through, then."

"See you soon." I smiled.

My steps were light as I made my way out of the building, and I couldn't contain my smile when I sat in the passenger seat of the BMW.

"You talked to Jared," Bex said with a knowing smile.

"He's coming home."

"We better go move his stuff around and hide his home gym," Bex smiled, pulling away from the curb. "He'll hate that."

I laughed. "You're in charge of the home gym. I'll mix up the forks and spoons."

"I got it covered," Bex said with a mischievous grin. "You have dinner plans."

"Oh, right," I said, sinking into the seat with a huff.

Bex sped to Jared's faster and with more precision than any television car chase I'd ever seen, much less been a part of. He jerked the wheel and let the Beemer slide, counter-clockwise, into the loft's parallel parking spot.

"One of you will get pulled over one of these days, and I'm going to laugh," I said, trying to steady myself once my feet hit the pavement.

"Our boss has plenty of money to bail us out." He smiled.

"I won't bail you out. I'll laugh."

"Even if it was Jared?" Bex said, escorting me up the iron steps.

"Especially if it was Jared."

"I don't believe you. And if Claire found out about it . . ."

"You're right. I'd bail you out." I nodded.

I changed clothes quickly and then followed Bex to the Beemer once again, letting him drive like a controlled maniac to my mom's home.

Arriving within minutes, Bex jumped out of the driver's side to open my door. We traded small talk as he walked with me up the concrete steps, both of us hoping it would be one of our shorter visits. Just as I reached for the handle, Cynthia opened the door, startling me.

"Mother."

"Agatha is ill today. I've barely been able to tend to dinner. Of all days for her to get sick," Cynthia said, looking uncharacteristically disheveled. Her eyes targeted Bex.

"Good evening, Mrs. Grey," Bex said.

She nodded politely. "Will you be joining us, Bex?"

"No, ma'am. I'm simply covering a shift."

Cynthia's cold eyes narrowed at him as she held out her arm to usher me into the house.

"I'll wait here," Bex whispered.

"Probably safer," I mouthed.

She wasted no time. "And where is Jared?"

"Er, resting," I said, cringing at my words. Surely I would be better at lying on the spot by now.

"Hmm," she said, clearly unconvinced. She didn't press the issue; I assumed it was because of the fact that I was safe. Beyond that, she didn't bother to question.

The table had been set, but I helped bring out the soup, salad, and entrée.

"I'm sorry I always have to ask," I said, waiting for her infamous scowl.

"You're predictable," she snapped. Her expression soon smoothed as she scanned the table. "I thought I would try something different: chicken coconut soup and wild mushroom fricassee over polenta."

"Whatever that is," I said, overwhelmed.

"Nina, really. You act as though you were fed take-out your entire life. I have always enjoyed cooking."

"And you never cease to surprise me," I said, smiling.

She didn't ask about Jared's whereabouts again. We stumbled over the small talk and politely discussed the weather. Cynthia hadn't mentioned my father since I returned home from the hospital. I wondered if she ever would. The residual circles under my eyes were a brief topic of conversation, and then I helped her clean the dinner dishes before saying good-bye.

"Dinner was uneventful?" Bex asked, holding the passenger door of the Beemer open.

My eyes narrowed at my former home. "She's up to something. You're sure she hasn't called or talked to Jared?"

"Haven't heard a word." Bex shrugged.

At the loft, I found myself struggling to stay awake to witness Jared's homecoming. Reality television kept my attention for a while, but I finally trudged up the stairs in defeat.

Aw, but they're going to get in the hot tub in a second. The girls get in a cat fight. It's funny!"

"Wake me when he gets home," I said.

"*Aye, aye, El Capitan*," he responded.

"You know you're not supposed to speak foreign languages to me," I grumbled, falling into the bed with my clothes on. My voice wasn't loud enough to travel to the first level, but Bex could hear, regardless.

"I wasn't. Never mind," Bex said, too involved in the hot tub disco party to argue.

Just as I closed my eyes, they popped open again. The alarm clock on Jared's side read nine-thirty.

"You okay, Nina?" Bex called up. "Bad dreams?"

"No," I whispered. Just that minuscule bit of effort was all I could manage. I hadn't realized I was so tired, and it was so much easier to fall asleep without the fear of screaming myself awake.

Ice was beneath me, and my bare toes wiggled against the smooth, shiny whiteness below. That was the only way I was aware it was a dream—my feet were warm and comfortable. My father's office window came into view above me. I was standing alone in the middle of Fleet Rink. Soon my naked feet were adorned with a pair of new ice skates, and Jack stood in the window, smiling down at me. A crowd of people, young and old, circled the space where I stood. Sporting matching red noses, their misty breath puffed out with each word or laugh.

I waved to him and he waved back. Pushing forward, I could hear the blade of my skate scratching the surface of the ice. Looking up again, I noticed Jack was no longer smiling. Instead he bobbed in and out of visibility, pacing back and forth in his office, and then I saw Gabe.

They were arguing.

Oh no, I thought, feeling the tugging feeling again. *No!*

Back in the dusty, stale office, I landed on all fours again. Anger surged through me. My nights had been just returning to normal. I wanted to sleep all night in Jared's arms. I wanted him to see that things were getting better, that *I* was getting better.

"I'm not doing this again!" I yelled, stomping a few steps toward them.

They ignored me, repeating the same scripted dialogue from before.

"Stop!" I said. "I don't want to do this anymore!"

"Are you sure you want to do this, Jack?" Gabe asked.

My mouth formed around each of Jack's words. "Are you sure it's her, Gabe?" He paused for Gabe's reply and then continued, "Then you know the answer." I shook my head from side to side as I spoke along with him, copying him like a toddler, angry and snide.

A ferocious rage overtook me, and I grabbed the book from Jack's hands.

Time stopped. Several times before, I had attempted to physically interrupt and failed. Jack, Gabe, and the book were always very real, but when I tried to interfere, they were the consistency of a hologram. This time the book was in my hands.

Gabe's head turned up in quick motion to face me, his eyes a solid black. "*Ars Notoria*," he whispered in a voice not his own.

The change of events frightened me. I stumbled back, away from my father and his friend. They were frozen in time like everything else in the room. Even the moonlit dust motes were hanging motionless in the air, but I could hear the screeches of the demons as they approached.

The dimensions of the room stretched, and the wood groaned and creaked. As I worked to keep my feet beneath me, I gripped the book tighter in my hands. The possibility of taking it back with me crossed my mind. It was the only reason I would be able to take it from Gabe.

I looked to the large window and closed my eyes. "It's just a dream," I said softly, confident the fall would wake me up. Opening my eyes with the *Naissance de Demoniac* in my hands wouldn't be the most impossible thing that had ever happened to me.

In a full sprint, I bounded for the window, bracing myself to leap through the glass and into the night, but before I could, a searing pain spread throughout my hands. I abruptly stopped and threw the book to the ground. Although the leather no longer touched my skin, the parts of my fingers and palms that had been in direct contact with the binding were charred and smoldering. My hands shook violently as the burns traveled up my arms, and I wailed at the intense heat spreading throughout my body; it was as if I were on fire. The sensation was unlike anything I had experienced before, but I couldn't imagine anything more excruciating.

The sound emanating from my throat didn't sound like my own as I protested the torture consuming me. Any moment the demons would come, and I would beg them for death.

A hole opened up beneath me and I fell. In that instant, the pain was gone, and a soft, cool mattress was beneath me. Jerking to a sitting position, I held my arms in front of me. They were peach and unblemished.

Jared and Bex stood next to the bed with terror in their eyes.

"She was at least four feet above the bed!" Bex said, his eyes wide. "Has that happened before?"

"No," Jared said, his expression exponentially more intense than the agonized look I had been accustomed to waking up to. He was afraid.

"*Above* the bed?" I asked, confused.

Bex sat on the bed and watched me for a moment then took the sheet and wiped the sweat from my hairline. "You were seriously hovering! It was something straight out of the Exorcist!"

I hoped for one moment that Bex was being Bex, trying to make light of the situation. Gauging the storms in Jared's eyes, it was true.

"How is that even possible? What does that mean?" I said, frightened.

Jared looked away.

Bex tugged lightly on my shirt. "Same dream?"

"No," I said, shaking my head. "I was angry, so angry that I took the book from them. It was in my hands."

"You've tried that before, and your hands went right through it." Jared said, his eyes on the floor.

"Not this time. I was so damn mad that I screamed at them and then grabbed the book. And then Gabe . . . He looked at me."

Jared knelt beside me then. I touched his face. He was desperate for guidance from his father. "It wasn't him," I warned. "His eyes were solid black—like Shax's."

Bex shook his head. "How can that be? If it were d— *them,* I would have known. The whole time you were stretched out, suspended, there were none.

"Bex," Jared warned.

"Not a single one," Bex continued, lost in thought. "They crowd Mom's house more than that."

"None?" Jared asked. Bex nodded and Jared stood up again and then began to pace. Finally, he spoke, "Something's wrong."

"But you can feel them too," I said to Jared. His question to Bex puzzled me.

"I can. Bex is more tuned-in to their presence—more so than any hybrid. His sensitivity to them rivals Samuel's."

"Sometimes I can tell when they're even *thinking* about coming around," Bex added.

Bex's frown instantly alarmed me. My mind raced over every second of the dream, trying to think of something that might help. I wasn't sure why they were so disturbed, but for Bex in particular, uncertainty was not something they handled well.

"*Ars Notes* something," I said.

Jared's face transformed from worry to anger. "What?"

I searched my memories again. "Gabe said, '*Ars Notary*' or '*Ars Notes*'—something like that."

Bex looked to his older brother. "*Ars Notoria.*"

"That's it!" I said. "What does it mean?"

Jared sat on the edge of the bed and tenderly touched the sides of my jaw, looking into my eyes. "The *Ars Notoria* is a grimoire. It is the fifth and final part of the *Lesser Key of Solomon*, a collection of prayers given to Solomon by an angel. Those prayers can act as an invocation to God's angels." Jared must have noticed the look of utter ignorance on my face, because he immediately dumbed-down his explanation. "It means we're going to have to get a *Naissance de Demoniac*. My father knew I would know of the *Ars Notoria*. I think it was his way of putting his signature on what's happening to you."

My brows pushed together. "What are you saying?"

"It's not demons doing this to you," Bex said, seeming vexed.

"That leaves one thing," Jared said.

"You think it's Gabe," I said, horrified.

Jared pulled me closer and then leaned his cheek against my hair. "We need that book."

4. EXHAUSTION

The coffee shop meetings stopped. My chair at study group had been filled due to my persistent absences. The only friend from school that I kept in contact with was Beth, and that was only because she was my assistant at Titan.

Fielding her constant questions about my behavior was exasperating, but her help had become indispensable. The dreams were a nightly event, and the sleep deprivation wore on me so much that half of the time I needed Beth to remind me what day it was.

The nightmares were also wearing on Jared, who left me with Bex every day to search for Shax's bible. It didn't take him long to figure out that the second he closed his eyes my nightmares would begin, and minutes later, screams would echo throughout the loft.

A new semester had begun, and still the dreams came. By spring break, Jared grew desperate. Every day he sought Eli and asked Samuel for help. He'd even taunted Gabriel for an answer, and every time, he came home frustrated and empty-handed.

"Coffee?" Jared asked, his voice tired.

"Yes, please."

Once again, our day began at three eleven a.m. I worked on a few papers and studied while the coffee still kept my brain functional. Once the heaviness set in, Jared brewed another pot.

"At some point, this has got to be bad for you," Jared frowned. "I can't get anyone to tell me anything. I don't know how our fathers found where Shax kept the book in the first place. Word gets around. They must know what we're up to. I wouldn't be surprised if I had to travel to Hell to get it."

Weary of the same dialogue, I rubbed my eyes and nodded.

Jared sighed. "I'm sorry. I'm frustrated, and with all the caffeine in your system, it makes me feel a little anxious."

"Ugh! I forgot about that," I said, setting my mug on the table.

The morning sun cast an amber tone against the walls. Summer was just around the corner. My friends at school were discussing tropical vacations and family reunions, and I was too tired to think about the next hour.

My cell phone rang, and I fished in my purse to answer. "Hey Beth." I sighed. "What's up?"

"Kim and I are meeting for coffee. Again. Like we do every morning. And you're invited. Again. Like every morning. Are you going to flake out? Again? Like you do every morning?"

"Sorry. I've already had a pot of coffee this morning. I'll see you in class."

Beth paused. I could hear a muffled, irritated voice in the background. Beth was obviously covering the phone with her hand. "Er, Kim says . . . Kim wants you to come."

"I have a feeling that's not what she said." I frowned.

After the sound of a scuffle, Kim spoke into the phone. "We are going to be at the coffee shop in thirty minutes. And you are going to be there, too, or the Sentra and I will come get you, and you will ride all the way there strapped to the roof like a freakin' Christmas tree. You got me?"

I held the phone away from my ear as she yelled and then cautiously held it within talking distance. "I got you."

"Okay, then," Kim said, satisfied.

"Sorry," Beth whispered before ending the call.

"Sounds as if your friends miss you." Jared grinned.

"They probably just want to yell at me and ask me questions," I said, stuffing books into my bag.

"You should tell them the truth. They'll just think you're crazy and let it go."

I laughed. "You have a point. It's the one time I can be honest with them and not worry about them believing me."

"They wouldn't believe you anyway," Jared said, kissing the top of my head. "I can take you today."

"I know better than to think you've given up."

"No, I'm still working," he said, keys in hand.

Beth and Kim sat with me at our usual table. They both watched me until I began to feel like a zoo animal. An interrogation was imminent. Beth's expression was unsure, nervous. Kim seemed just the opposite. She was ready to pounce.

Beth looked to Kim before she spoke. "How's Ryan?"

Her question took me off guard. I had expected more questions about the circles under my eyes or the gallons of caffeinated drinks I'd consumed during the day.

"He doesn't write much anymore."

"You don't talk about him anymore," Beth said without pause.

"How's Jared?" Kim asked.

"He's . . . fine. Why?"

Kim crossed her arms. "What does he think about the fact that you're a zombie these days?"

I shrugged. "He wants to fix it."

"How's that?" Kim asked.

Too tired for tough questions, my words were more acerbic than I'd intended. "He's a guy, Kim. Guys want to fix everything."

Beth nodded. "If a hammer and nails could solve it all . . ."

"What's he doing to fix it?" Kim prodded.

"Research," I said, blinking away the urge to let my eyes close.

Beth frowned in reaction. "Nina, you fell asleep on your desk yesterday. Grant is grilling me about what's going on with you. I don't even know what the truth *is* so I can keep from telling him."

"You won't accidentally tell him, I promise," I grumbled as I sipped from the plastic lid of my coffee cup.

"The truth is that far-fetched?" Kim asked.

My stomach began to complain from both the amount of hot liquid swirling inside it and the irritating predicament I was in. Being impatient and upset so often due to the lack of sleep took a toll on my appetite, and the overabundance of coffee in my system made me feel ill on a regular basis.

I stood. "We're going to be late."

"Are you sick, Nina?" Beth asked.

"No," I said. My nausea was not what she was referring to.

"Do you have some disease you're not telling us about?"

"No, Beth."

"Could Jared be poisoning you?" she blurted out.

I laughed once, shocked. "Is that why you two brought me here?"

"Are you two into something we don't know about? Voodoo-Witchcraft—Satanist crap?" Kim asked.

"What would even make you say that?" I said, my patience thin.

"Just answer the question," Kim said flatly.

"No. I'm not being haunted by demons if that's what you're getting at, Kim." A part of me wondered if that's what she was asking. She always seemed to be right on the edge of the truth and had the habit of asking all the right questions. Beth being there was just a cover. She knew something.

"I didn't ask if you were," Kim said. For the first time since I'd met her, she was uncomfortable. I watched her for a moment before she pulled on her coat and grabbed her keys from the table. "Class starts in ten."

Beth and Kim watched me with concern as I waved them away and walked to class. It was on the top floor, and I regretted the decision to take the stairs by the second flight. My body felt ten years older. Two or three hours of sleep a night had begun to wear on my muscles, my train of thought, and my patience.

My reflection in a trophy case in the hallway caught my eye, and I stood there amazed. The purplish circles had deepened under my eyes, and my skin was too tired to stay in place. The corners of my mouth hung lazily, and the light in my eyes was gone.

Class was just a few steps away, but my body felt too drained to make the trip. I leaned against the wall. The professor had already begun class, and I listened as intently as I could from the hallway. His words blurred together as he went over the last week's test and then lectured for what seemed like an eternity. The reading assignment was discussed in brief before class let out early.

Even as the other students passed, I let the wall support my weight. The walk to campus from the coffee shop, coupled with the energy I'd exerted taking the stairs, had taken everything out of me. Standing upright was the only thing I was capable of.

After watching the last of my classmates leave for other venues, I focused on the elevator. It was half way down the hall but would take less effort than taking the stairs. I took a deep breath and pushed myself away from the wall. My feet felt as if they had been soaking in cement and towing fifty-pound blocks with each step. My knees began to wobble, and I could feel beads of sweat form on my forehead. Stopping to rest was not an option. If I paused for even a moment, I would have passed out in the hallway.

Finally reaching the elevator, I pushed the button and took a deep, ragged breath. Even breathing took effort. The door opened, and Jared stood before me.

Knowing better than to pretend everything was normal, I reached for his arm and let him support my weight as I took the few steps to stand next to him.

"Nina," he said quietly into my ear, "I think it's time—"

"I know," I said. "We have to find someone."

He walked with me for a while, but once we were in the parking lot, my legs gave way. Jared lifted me into his arms and carried me the remaining distance to the Escalade. My eyes shut and would not open.

I didn't wake when Jared carried me inside the loft, nor did I feel the mattress beneath me when he lowered me into it and covered me with blankets. It wasn't until the sun broke through the blinds that I realized I had been tucked in and slept sixteen hours straight.

"Jared?" I called, my voice raspy.

"Nope, it's just me," Bex said. He sat on the bed, seeming vexed.

"What wrong? And where's Jared?"

"He's been gone since yesterday evening. He caught a break."

"What's with the face?"

"You slept."

"Isn't that a good thing?" I asked, sitting up against the headboard.

"Not for Jared. This makes the third time you've slept solid when he's been gone all night. Can't be a coincidence."

I laughed once. "Are you saying he's causing the dreams?"

"I'm saying it's a possibility the dreams go away when he's not around."

"That's ridiculous," I sneered.

"I'm probably right," Bex said, his teenage confidence overriding his usual politeness. In that moment, he was more Claire than Jared. "And Jared's going to take it hard."

"No, he's not because you're not going to tell him," I said firmly.

"Nina, I have to tell him. You know that."

"My sleep was interrupted by my annoying, incessant screaming at three eleven a.m. just like every other morning. That's the story."

"You don't think he'll know?"

"He's been distracted. It could work."

"It won't."

"Bex! At least try!"

Bex stood up and crossed his arms. "He'll know, and then he won't trust me ever again because I helped you lie to him. Do you know how imperative it is that we trust each other? You really have gone crazy."

He walked down the stairs in a huff, and I blew my bangs from my face, aggravated. Even in his disgust, Bex began making breakfast, and after a shower, I joined him at the table.

"Something came for you yesterday," Bex said, tossing an envelope on the table.

It was from Ryan.

I tore it open and scanned it over for signs of sadness or danger, and then I reread his words more slowly. I went over them again in disbelief.

"What?" Bex asked.

"He's been accepted into the Special Forces."

Bex laughed. "Are you serious? That little butt nugget?"

"It's not funny, Bex! This is . . . Did you know? Has Claire called?"

"No and no," Bex said matter-of-factly.

"Did Jared say anything?" I said, grabbing for my cell.

"Nina," Bex said, holding my wrists gently, "I'm sure it's a miscommunication. Ryan hasn't been in the Army long enough to get into the Special Forces. That's unheard of. I don't see him cutting it anyway. If my sister can incapacitate him, I'm guessing he's a big weenie."

"Claire is a hybrid, Bex! That's an unfair basis for comparison, and you know it."

Bex giggled. The little boy in him was showing. "You're much more fun when you've had some sleep. I can't pass up a chance to give you a hard time when you're coherent."

"Not a good time, Bex," I said, staring at my plate. The one day I could have eaten, Ryan's letter eliminated any appetite I might have had. "You really think it's a mistake?"

"Yeah," Bex said. "No way could that happen. It would take at least three years for someone like him: no education, no connections."

Jared opened the door with an apologetic smile. "Hi, baby."

"Not even a note?" I asked, wadding up the letter in my hand and tossing it in his general direction.

He playfully ducked, as if it were possible that I could have hit him. "Bex was here. What's up? I'm three blocks away, and I'm getting all this irritation from you."

"Did you know about Ryan?" I asked.

"He's still alive. I know that," Jared said, peeling off his coat. He hung it on the rack and then walked to me, kneeling beside me on the floor. "You read the letter?"

"He said he's going into the Special Forces."

Jared thought for a moment and then shook his head. "No, the shortest time for anyone to be accepted is eighteen months in. That can't be right."

"That's what I told her, but she doesn't believe me," Bex said, rolling his eyes. He walked over to the wadded letter and reopened it, scanning the words. "But that's what it says. Maybe he's trying to impress her."

Jared immediately pulled out his phone and dialed Claire's number. Her angry tone carried into the room.

"He's a maniac!" Claire yelled. "He has zero respect for his limited lifespan and tries to throw himself on grenades for his buddies every other day." She huffed.

"Claire, keep your voice down," Jared chuckled nervously. He noticed my horrified expression and turned his head. "You're not serious?"

"I'm exaggerating, but not by much. The grenade part is true, but that was just once."

I wrapped my arms around my waist and walked over to Bex, waiting for more bad news. Bex put his arm around me with a light hug.

"He's saved every man in his company in one way or another. He walks around with explosives on his back while the enemy is shooting at us. You thought your detail was bad. This is impossible!"

"Great," I said, throwing my arms up and letting them slap to my sides.

"It still doesn't explain how he made sergeant in an impossible amount of time," Jared said.

The other end of the phone was silent, and Jared nodded, whispering something so quickly I could barely discern his reply at all. "Okay. Watch your six," Jared said, flipping his phone shut. He watched me for a moment and then sighed. "He still has Claire, Nina. You know her. It's as if he's in military day care."

"How did he make sergeant so quickly?" I asked.

Jared peered at Bex for a moment before speaking. "It appears Colonel Brand pulled some strings. The Special Forces guys are more familiar with how we do things, and it made it easier for Claire to protect him."

"Sending Ryan on more dangerous missions will protect him," I deadpanned.

"Well, since everyone has bad news," Bex said.

"Bex, don't," I said through my teeth, but it was too late.

"What is it?" Jared asked, his eyes bouncing between the two of us.

"Nina slept all night. She didn't budge until seven this morning."

Jared let his words sink in. It was several moments before he moved and then nodded. His hand searched for the closest chair to pull beneath him. He fell into it and stared at the floor. "So that's it."

"Jared, that doesn't mean anything," I said, reaching for him.

He looked to his younger brother. "Now we just have to see how far away I have to be to keep the dreams away."

"This is ridiculous!" I said. "It's happened three times. That isn't a definitive trial by anyone's standards!"

"So we'll test the theory," Jared said, "starting tonight."

"No," I said, shaking my head. "Absolutely not. I didn't move in with you to have to sleep alone every night."

"It's just until we figure this out," Jared said.

"No."

"Yes," Jared said, his tone final.

The air was knocked out of me. I couldn't believe what he was saying, but I was too tired to argue. Tears welled up in my eyes, and I looked away from him.

"Nina."

"I get it. It's okay."

"Let's just try it. See if it works. I'll start out just outside town, and then come a bit closer every half hour. If you have the dream, we'll know."

"This is ridiculous! How are you going to find the damn book if you're experimenting with my dreams?"

"She has a point," Bex said.

Jared frowned. "I have to know."

We tested his theory. The first night, I lay in bed for what seemed like an eternity, waiting to fall asleep. Being alone in our bed felt so cold and depressing. My fingers traced the wrinkles in the sheets, remembering the first time I woke in his bed. That perfect morning, after the night he told me who—and what—he really was seemed like light years away. A tear formed in the corner of my eye and slipped over the bridge of my nose to the white fabric beneath me.

Jared began just on the outskirts of Providence. When he felt I was asleep, he made his way to the loft, a block at a time, every ten minutes or so. He was just over two blocks away when he felt my anxiety. I was in Shax's building. It was apparent the moment Jared backed off, because my surroundings blurred away, forming into the halls of my old high school.

The alarm bleated, and my eyes peeled open. Two full nights of sleep! My body felt a bit closer to normal, but it didn't feel like a fair trade.

Jared walked in the front door, trotted up the stairs, and crawled into bed beside me, wrapping his warm arms snugly around me. We didn't speak; we were just still, letting reality sink in.

"Why would Dad do this? It doesn't seem fair," Bex said from the first floor.

Jared didn't answer. He simply pressed his forehead against my temple and sighed.

Night after night, I slept alone. Jared used that time to harass every connection he had and pursue every lead to learn the location of the book. Seconds after I woke in the mornings, he was at my side.

The days slowly returned to normal. Lectures in class were written down, and my hours at Titan were used for work instead of naps. Beth gladly decreased the number of times she fetched coffee and gave excuses to Grant.

One afternoon she brought me a file and sat in the plump, green leather chair in front of my desk. She had bought new clothes, and her auburn hair had a new shape to it—still short, but different.

Embarrassed that I had no idea how long it had been that way, I took the file from her and sat it to the side.

"I love the shoes," I said.

"Thanks," she said, picking one foot off the floor to bring the yellow stilettos into view. They boasted a big bow on the side, and the heels, soles, and straps were black. "It's a lot easier to dress for work when you have money. Thanks again, Nina. Things at home have been a lot better since you hired me."

I shook my head. "You know I don't mind. You've been a huge help around here."

"Things seem to be better for you too."

"I feel better."

"Have you heard from Ryan? No one's heard from him since he joined that special thing."

My mouth turned to the side. Most of the time I tried not to think of Ryan, the sand, or the bullets flying everywhere while he carried his pipe bomb backpack.

"No," I said.

Beth nodded. The desk phone rang and she stood, pushing line one and answering without hesitation. "Nina Grey's office. . . . No, that file is in the . . . Oh Lord, Sasha, I'll just come find it for you. How long have you worked here?"

Beth hung up the phone and I smiled. "Don't let her take advantage of you. Do you want me to say something?"

"No. I do plenty of that," Beth said, winking.

"I'm heading home. Will you lock up for me?" I asked.

"I always do," she said, waving behind her.

Jared stood beside his SUV with a smile, waiting with arms wide. He had let me fall asleep in his arms the last few weeks and then left sometime after. Jack and Gabe stayed out of my head, and I slept through the night, never realizing Jared was gone. He was getting so good at pinpointing when I would rouse he usually slid next to me just before I awoke. Once again, life was semi-normal.

His hand slid over mine as it rested on the console of the Escalade. "Something came for you today."

"A letter?" I asked, nervous.

Jared let go of my hand, pulling an envelope from his jacket pocket. Ryan had finally written again.

Nigh,

I still think about you every day, sometimes whether I want to or not. Things have been pretty busy. The new company I'm in is a whole new breed of soldiers. I like it, but I miss you. When I get a chance, I sit and watch the sunset and think about our game and the pub and your stupid temper tantrums. I miss it all. Tell everyone I said hi.

Ryan

I folded the paper back to its original shape.

"Do I have to remind you that this isn't your fault?" Jared asked.

Ryan's sudden departure was too much of a coincidence to believe that it wasn't my fault, but Jared, Kim, and Beth all assured me quite regularly that his reasons were purely financial.

He didn't write again after that, and I relied on Jared's intermittent phone calls from Claire to hear of his whereabouts and that he was okay.

Claire still had to pull a multitude of strings to keep a close eye on Ryan. She called home frequently to complain of Ryan's lack of self-preservation, which helped to get him accepted so quickly into the Special Forces in the first place. Claire's phone calls were reason to fear—for Ryan and for her. I chewed my thumbnail each time Jared answered the phone, waiting for him to assure me that Ryan's commando behavior hadn't gotten him killed.

As our small but close group of friends waved good-bye on the last day of our sophomore year at Brown, Ryan came to the forefront of my mind.

"He should be here," I said to Beth.

She held my arm as we walked to the parking lot. "I know."

"He's in the middle of nowhere, prone on a sand dune, trying not to get shot so he didn't have to watch me be with Jared. It's not fair. He should be here with us."

Josh and Tucker were heading to their dorm to pack and head home. Kim walked with them, punching Josh in the arm. The beginning of summer break was bittersweet, and we all knew why.

Beth walked me to the Escalade and, after a warm embrace, left me to find Chad. They would all meet at the pub that night to celebrate, and I would stay at home. It didn't feel right to have fun when Ryan was fighting for his life.

Jared was unhappy with my mood. He didn't ask what it was, but I assumed he knew. I didn't enjoy talking to him about Ryan. It was unfair to him and didn't make me feel any better, so I didn't see the point.

The loft was immaculate, and the summer sun lit the beige walls, making every corner of the room glow. It had been nearly a year since Shax had been in our living room, since Jared threw the book at him that Gabe so desperately wanted us to have. It had been almost a year since I was shot. I rubbed my thigh where the scar still remained.

Jared flipped through the mail at the kitchen table. "What do you want for dinner, sweetheart?"

"It just doesn't seem to get better," I said, shaking my head. "We can redecorate, fill the bullet holes in the walls, and pretend life is normal, but you're gone every night, we aren't any closer to getting the book, and Ryan is gone. It's been a year, and it doesn't feel as if it's gotten better. We're stuck."

Jared raised an eyebrow. "Bad day?"

I sat on the arm of the couch. "He's going to get killed. Every day that he's out there, Claire is in danger. We should bring him home."

"You're suggesting that we go to the Middle East and abscond with a member of the Special Forces?"

I puffed. "It's not right that he's not here."

"You're just letting the guilt eat you alive. You have to let it go, Nina. You have to let him go."

"I know what you're thinking," I said. "This isn't about me having feelings for him. Maybe it is about guilt, but I can't stand it anymore—how Josh and Tucker and everyone else look at me. That's why I don't hang out with them anymore. That's why I don't go to study group. I have been sleeping through the night for months, and I can't go back. The looks on their faces . . . They blame me."

"*You* blame you," Jared said. "I have an idea," he said, pulling his cell phone from his pocket. He dialed numbers and then held the receiver to his ear.

After several moments, a grin touched his mouth. "Claire. How is everything? I see. I have someone here that would like to speak to you. You got a minute?"

Jared handed me the phone. "Hello?" I said, unsure of her reaction.

"It is hot as hell here," Claire snapped. "I have sand in places no woman should experience. It's in my hair, my eyes, and the seat of my Jeep. There's no getting rid of it, even when I get the occasional shower. And my hair looks like crap. So how are things?"

I managed a quiet laugh. "I miss you."

"I miss you too." She sighed. "Don't worry, Nina. I'm taking care of him. He's a cowboy and likes to pretend he's invincible, but despite his best efforts, I'm keeping him alive."

"Thank you."

I could hear the wind whipping against the phone, and she spoke loudly to compensate. I imagined her standing alone in a sea of sand, with big sunglasses and light camouflage clothes blending in with her platinum hair.

"Ryan doesn't want you to feel guilty. He wants you to be happy. He's just trying to get on with his life. He's happy with his choice. Be happy with yours."

"Of course I am. I just . . . Everything feels wrong here. I feel lost."

Claire laughed. "Try driving around with identical sand dunes as your guide. Then you can talk to me about feeling lost. It's a good thing I'm fluent in Farsi, or I wouldn't be able to keep up with him. How's Jared?"

I peeked up at him, his blue-gray eyes comforted that his idea had worked. "He's Jared. He's good."

"I need you to take care of him for me, okay? I'm kicking ass over here, so you can rest easy. Just concentrate on school, and work, and being happy, and I'll get the cowboy home safe. Deal?"

Relief washed over me. "Deal. See you soon?"

"As soon as I can. Gotta go. They're moving," she said. The phone went silent, and I handed it to Jared.

"He's okay," I said.

Jared nodded. "Feel better?"

"A little. Thank you."

Jared took a step toward me and enveloped me in his arms, touching his forehead to mine. "I would do anything, go anywhere, and suffer anything to make you happy. You know that, right? That's all I want."

I lifted my chin to kiss his lips. "I'm sorry. I don't know what's wrong with me."

"You're exhausted. I'm going to run you a bath, and you can soak until your hands get all pruny. I'll have dinner waiting for you when you get out. Then we can turn in early."

I buried my face into his warm chest. "Sounds perfect."

5. LANDSTUHL

The first day of summer break, I took the day off from Titan, and Jared and I went to our oak tree. I lazily traced the details of the carving of our names and let the sweet summer air sweep over my skin. Lunch was served on the blanket he had given me as a graduation gift—before I knew him—and we playfully wrestled and chased each other barefoot in the grass.

Jared was working overtime to prove to me that our lives could be as normal as anyone else's. Even with the bad dreams keeping us apart at night, he had figured out how to get around them and made it seem that nothing was different.

The air smelled of fresh grass and sunshine, and coupled with Jared's scent, it felt a little like Heaven. Summer soaked into my every pore, and I could see that Jared was enjoying my mood. He sat next to me, waiting for me to catch my breath from chasing him.

"Having a better day?" he asked, running his finger lightly across my wrist.

"Exponentially," I said, digging my toes into the grass. "I feel as I did at Little Corn."

"Speaking of that, have you given any more thought to returning to that perfect little chapel we came across there?" Jared said the words casually, but he was fidgeting with the hem of his jeans.

"Wedding date," I said, nodding. I should have seen the topic coming. Jared never broached anything important lightly and always insisted on the perfect back drop. "Does Claire know when she's coming back?"

"No," Jared said, frowning. The hem of his jeans seemed to be irritating him, but I knew it was the direction of our conversation.

"We can't get married without Claire. I'm going to make her wear something hideous."

"Already have your bridesmaids picked out?" he said with a contrived smile.

"Beth, Kim, and Claire. What about your groomsmen? Can't exactly have Samuel and Eli stand in."

"Sure I could. I don't think they would do it, but I could ask." I laughed, and his smile relaxed. "Bex, obviously. Maybe I could ask Ryan. It would help Claire."

"Not funny," I said, ripping out a handful of grass and then throwing it at him.

He shrugged. "Nothing says I have to have as many as you."

I had never considered that the small details of a wedding would be so difficult for him. He had siblings and contacts within the system to make things easier but no friends and hardly any family. His side of the church would be pitifully bare.

"Maybe I'll just have Beth and Claire, and Bex can escort both of them," I said, hoping to relieve him of part of what he perceived as a problem.

I had insisted for so long that our lives be as close to normal as a hybrid and his taleh could get that Jared was bordering on obsession about giving that to me. I knew if something were as important to him I would be equally determined to make it happen, but I didn't want our wedding to be a source of disappointment for either of us.

His eyes turned soft. "You can have as many as you want, sweetheart. I'll figure it out," he said, leaning toward me. His lips touched my cheek bone lightly and then brushed along the edge of my jaw line.

His touch had always had an immediate effect on me, but being alone, shaded from the summer sun by our oak tree, I lost all inhibitions. I pulled his mouth to mine and returned his kiss, letting him know how much I wanted him by the way my tongue eagerly danced with his. I let myself fall slowly against the blanket and held his shoulders, bringing him with me. His lips planted tiny kisses from my ear to my collarbone, and I melted against the ground, feeling wonderfully overwhelmed. His mouth was so warm, and every time his lips lifted away from my skin, little goose bumps formed in reaction to the sudden change in temperature.

My fingers reached inside of his shirt, feeling the lean muscles of his back beneath his soft tan skin. His attraction to me had been a mystery, but I was never ungrateful. There was no doubt that I was lucky. Jared being so close made that fact all too real.

I lifted his shirt over his head and watched as his muscles stretched with each movement. A smile broke out across my face, and his expression mirrored mine, his senses tuning into the emotions that gave me away.

"Have I told you today how incredibly beautiful you are?" he asked, his nose tracing a line from my chin to my nose, where he stopped to kiss me. "If I haven't, I deeply apologize. That's something that should be recognized on a daily basis." He easily unfastened the first button of my blouse, moving to the second.

"You can say it however often you like, as long as you're doing that while you're saying it." I smiled.

His cell phone rang and we both sighed.

"Of course," I said.

He rolled his eyes. "It's Claire."

"Old habits die hard."

He flipped it open. "Ryel."

A stream of words I couldn't understand blurred in different tones. Jared's expression caused me to panic.

"Okay. We're headed to the airport now."

"The airport?" I said, watching Jared dial again.

"I need to charter a jet to Ramstein. No, not Frankfurt-Hahn. Yes, the Air Force Base. It's the closest airport to Landstuhl. I'll take care of it, Frank. Just get it done."

"We're going to Germany?" I said in disbelief. "What's going on?"

Jared ignored me, dialing again. He spoke in German this time. The only thing I understood was Landstuhl. It was the largest military hospital outside the United States, near Ramstein, Germany. The hospital was mentioned in the news frequently because the majority of wounded soldiers from Iraq and Afghanistan were flown there.

In that moment of understanding, I shoved all of our things into the backpack, frantically pulling on my motorcycle helmet. Jared immediately climbed onto his bike, and I jumped on behind him, gripping his jacket as he took off at full speed.

Everything I had feared since the moment I learned of Ryan's decision to join the Army had happened: Ryan had been injured and Claire was alone, waiting to die.

We stopped at the loft long enough to grab money and passports, but we left everything else behind. Jared was quiet, and the way he was rushing to get to the airport made me fear the worst. He led me through the terminal so quickly that I had to jog to keep up with his long strides.

The plane was ready and waiting when we walked onto the tarmac, escorted by only a handful of the airline's employees. Jared spoke quick instructions to the pilot, and then we rushed up the stairs, barely greeting the flight attendant as we passed.

Jared didn't speak during take-off. His fingers were on his lips as his mind processed the situation and the consequences. I left him alone with his thoughts. Just as worried as he was, I wondered about calling Beth or Kim or even Josh. Telling them what I knew would only welcome questions, and explaining how I knew before Ryan's mother or his best friends did would be far beyond my lying capabilities.

Two hours into the flight, I fought with my eyelids to stay open. After the fourth time of jerking myself awake, I finally broke the silence. "This is ridiculous. How could I possibly be sleepy right now?"

"Maybe you should try to sleep," Jared said without looking at me.

I nodded, settling into my seat. My leg jerked, and my eyes popped open again.

"Dreaming?" Jared asked with an amused smile.

"I think I was riding a bike to Germany," I mumbled, leaning against his shoulder.

Sinking back into oblivion, my breaths grew even. It didn't take long to let the airplane noise fade into the background.

The lights were dim in the fuselage. My eyes were blurry, and with the poor light, it was hard to focus. Jared had left his seat. I wondered how long we had been en route and looked behind me to the restrooms.

"Jared?" I called back.

Nothing.

I stumbled to the back of the plane and knocked on the lavatory door. When he didn't answer, I opened it.

Empty.

My eyes strained to see in the darkness, but I could vaguely make out the top of Jared's head. He was back in his seat, patiently waiting for me.

"Thirty-thousand feet in the air with nowhere to hide and you still keep me guessing," I said, falling into my chair.

But it wasn't Jared. Sitting next to me was Gabe Ryel.

I recoiled, the armrest digging into my back as I leaned away from him. "What are you doing here?"

"It's been a while, Nina."

"I'm dreaming, aren't I?" I said, perturbed. Knowing Gabe was behind my sleepless nights and the reason why Jared could no longer be within two blocks while I slept, mustered up suppressed resentment, resulting in a bit more guts than I usually had.

"You must turn back, Nina. It is imperative to make Jared understand that we don't have time for this."

"Time for what? Why do you insist on being so theatrical? Just tell me what we need to do and we'll do it."

Gabe didn't react. "Turn back, Nina."

His eyes were black again. It made me more than just uncomfortable. The ice-blue eyes that I remembered were now replaced by glass balls in his sockets, and it was downright disturbing.

"No. Claire needs us."

Gabe didn't react to my insolence. He simply looked down at his intertwined fingers sitting atop his lap. He wore an expensive suit, the same I remembered when he shadowed my father in the halls of Titan, but his fingers were dirty and worn, as if he'd been digging in soil.

"Find the book."

"How? Jared has talked to Eli and Samuel. No one will tell us anything!"

"This fight is not Jared's. It's yours."

"Great. More riddles," I said, crossing my arms. My muscles relaxed, thinking about the situation at hand. I looked to Gabe. Even with his empty eyes, he was still someone from my childhood that I loved. "Is Claire going to die?"

The plane hit turbulence, and a bit of bouncing evolved into what felt like a several-hundred-foot drop. As I gripped the armrest, Gabe turned to me once again.

"Listen."

"I can't listen if there's nothing to hear!"

"Listen," he repeated.

The plane fell again, causing the overhead storage bins to vomit various items. The already dim lights flickered violently until they surrendered, and the fuselage turned dark.

I jerked awake, and Jared sat where Gabe had been. The lights were on, and the floors were clear of debris.

"It's you," I said, relieved.

"Yes," he said with a confused smile. "Who did you think it would be?"

After a short pause, I shook my head. "No one. Just forgot where I was for a second."

Jared nodded and then rested his hand on my knee. "We'll be there in two hours."

He spent the remainder of our flight on his cell phone. He made arrangements for a car to pick us up at the airport and for a friend, Colonel Jason Brand, to meet us at Landstuhl with visitor identification.

Upon arrival, the pace accelerated. The second the plane came to a stop, Jared had the few things we brought with us in hand, and he held out my jacket.

"It's chilly," he said, helping me twist into the sleeves.

Descending the stairs of the plane, it was clear why Jared had to make so many phone calls. Pilots walked to and from their jets and crew chiefs parked and marshaled jets, while others were busy with flight inspections. Jet engines screamed as they prepared for takeoff.

We had landed at Ramstein Air Base. Jared's connections spanned farther than I had imagined.

We rushed off the tarmac to the waiting car. The driver was a stranger to me. He spoke fluent German to Jared, so I was unsure if he was just a local or someone Jared had met before. He looked about Jared's age. Light blond hair peeked from his dark green ball cap, but his eyes were hidden behind dark sunglasses.

"*Warum gehen Sie nach Landstuhl?*" the driver said.

"*Claire's taleh ist verletzt worden,*" Jared said.

The driver's eyebrows pulled in. He was a friend. Jared mentioning Claire's taleh could even mean that he was a hybrid, and by the features I could see—the light blond hair, the flawless skin, and his lean, fit body—he was.

"*Gutes Glück zu Ihnen, Freund*," he said, shaking his head.

"*Danke*," Jared frowned. He leaned toward me, then. "He was asking why we're here. I told him, and he wished us luck," he whispered against my cheek.

Nodding, I hugged Jared's arm to me. Landstuhl was just three miles from the West Gate of the base. The soldier guarding the gate seemed to know the driver and, after checking out his identification, let us through quickly.

An officer in a blue decorated dress uniform waited at the front entrance of the hospital.

"Colonel," Jared said, shaking his hand. He was definitely not a hybrid with his dark hair and eyes. "Nina, this is Colonel Jason Brand," he said.

I shook his hand. "Thank you," I said.

"Not at all. Claire's pretty famous around here. We've all trained with her at some point," Jason said with a small grin. "Jared, we've got good news coming from the surgeon," he said as we followed him inside. His voice was firm and no-nonsense. It reminded me of the way my father spoke. "Claire is in the waiting room on the third floor. They know you're coming."

Jared nodded. He kept me by his side as we walked to the elevator. The space was quiet, and despite Jason's positive comment earlier, Jared was on edge. He rubbed his thumb compulsively against the top of my hand as he held it a bit too tight in his.

"What can I do," I asked, touching his arm with my free hand.

One corner of Jared's mouth turned up in an appreciative half-smile. "You're here with me. That's all I need."

The door opened to a bustling hallway. The walls were devoid of anything but white paint, and the halls were full of equipment and people. Medical personnel attended to the wounded, wearing either utility attire or green scrubs. Soldiers passed by in wheelchairs, accompanied by their attentive wives or mothers. A few were trying on their new prostheses and learning to walk again.

My stomach instantly felt sick, wondering what was waiting for us in Ryan's room.

Jared pushed through a set of double doors and stopped. Claire, tiny and alone, stood at the end of the hall. She was looking down an adjacent hall, but the second she felt Jared's presence, she slowly turned to face him. His stoic disposition deteriorated as he looked into the eyes of his little sister, and a small sound escaped from his throat.

Claire ran down the hall at full speed and crashed into Jared, wrapping her arms around him. She ran so hard and hit him with such force that it made a clapping sound that echoed through the halls as if a door had slammed. Even with Claire's incredible strength, Jared didn't budge. He lifted her off the floor, enveloped her with his long arms, and squeezed her tightly.

"You didn't have to come, stupid!" she said. Her voice was muffled against Jared's shoulder. When she pulled back to look at him, tears blurred her round ice-blue eyes. "But I'm glad you came."

She reached for me and hooked her arm around my neck, adding me to their embrace. We stood there in silence for a long while, knowing once we let go reality would set in.

Time was not on our side, and too quickly the reunion was over. We walked to the waiting room, dazed and emotionally exhausted. Jared sat beside me on the sofa, and Claire took a chair adjacent to us.

Jared cleared his throat. "I'm going to apologize in advance, Claire. This is hard for me."

"*Déjà vu*?" she said in understanding.

"Something like that," he said, rubbing the bridge of his nose with his forefinger and thumb.

"You mean me," I said softly.

Jared didn't meet my eyes; he simply nodded as he stared at the floor. I had tried to imagine many times what he went through while waiting to hear whether I would live or die after the shootout in the restaurant.

"I remember," Claire said with a far-off look in her eyes. "Mom was there. Bex was stuck in Dubai with Amir." She spoke low and slowly, looking to Jared with weary eyes. "You sat on that horrible fake-leather chair until you couldn't stand it, and then you paced the length of the room until *we* couldn't stand it. It was harder to watch than when Daddy slipped away. Then Samuel came, and Eli . . ."

"They were there?" I asked, surprised.

Jared nodded. "They appeared after I called for Gabriel. I begged him to take me the second . . . I didn't want to know what it would feel like when you were gone."

"Would it be painful?" I asked, touching his arm.

Jared breathed a heavy sigh. "My father described it as weakness, growing so debilitating that eventually every system in our bodies stop." He looked into my eyes. "We literally need our talehs to breathe."

Claire watched us for a moment before speaking. "I had to restrain Jared several times. He couldn't stand the thought of you lying on a table without him, letting strangers—humans—try to save you. He wanted to force his way into the O.R. I'd never seen him so unreasonable." Claire's icy eyes melted when she looked at her brother. "Seeing Jared feel so helpless and desperate—Mom waiting to hear if she would lose you and her son—the collective pain in that room will be burned into my memory forever just as yesterday will."

I grabbed her hand. "And I'm okay just like Ryan will be."

Claire wore what used to be a white tank top, now more of a grey-brown, and khaki utility pants with heavy lace-up boots. A blood-stained hijab sat bunched up in the chair next to her. Her moist eyes and smeared mascara had mixed with the desert sand but only around her eyes.

"Did Ryan recognize you?" I asked.

Claire shook her head. "I should have pulled us out earlier. He looked up at me, but he was pretty out of it. And with the hijab, he could only see my eyes."

Jared placed his hand on ours. "It doesn't matter. What matters is that you're both alive."

"Ryan's company was conducting a raid to extract two contractors who had been missing for a few days. I made a lot of mistakes today, Jared. They were ambushed. I should have seen it coming. I should have heard the snipers get into position, but my mind was full of complaints and resentment." She stared at the floor, deep in thought. "They always raid at night. Everything was off and I missed it."

Jared grabbed Claire's jaw in his hands. "You know better than to beat yourself up about this. What were you telling me in the waiting room in Providence? He's alive, Claire. No one else could have gotten him here with a chance."

She pulled away from him and looked out the window. In her mind, she was still on that street corner, watching the extermination of Ryan's company in real time. "It was like shock and awe out there—one explosion after another." She snapped her eyes shut. The memory replayed in her mind. "I could hear him, but I couldn't see." Her eyebrows pulled in. "I couldn't see."

Her eyes popped open, and she immediately wiped away her tears. "My first glimpse of Ryan didn't surprise me; he was sprinting from the debris cloud with Tommy on his back." She smiled. "Of course it would be Tommy. Ryan's only saved his hide three times already." Her smile faded. "They were close. Ryan felt responsible for him."

Jared stood and walked to the other side of the room. He rubbed the back of his neck; the worry and memories were clearly overwhelming him.

"That was when I decided to move in," Claire explained, "but a sniper clicked on his sights." Claire laughed once. "The jerkface got one off after I severed his brain stem with one bullet, Jared. That shit only happens in the movies."

"So Ryan was hit?" I prodded. My mind raced with where the story would end. I had no idea what injuries Ryan had sustained, and with the vivid detail of bombs and bullets, I needed her to get to the point.

"Twice. A bullet ricocheted off a rock and clipped his right lung; the other blew straight through his shoulder. It was fate. Both injuries are going to send him packing."

Jared glanced at me and then returned to his seat. He leaned forward with his elbows on his knees. "That was when you evac'd?"

Claire sniffed. "He wouldn't let Tommy go. I had to pry all ten of his fingers from the guy's flak jacket."

"Figures," Jared grumbled.

"Ryan's whole unit was wiped out in three seconds. He needed to save *one* of them. It didn't matter that Tommy was dead ten meters from the explosions. Ryan was going to carry him home."

Tears welled up in my eyes and overflowed. "Can we see him?"

Jared hugged me to his side. "He can't know you were ever here. We can't take that chance."

Jared's reasoning made sense. Explaining away Ryan's memories of me at his bedside in Landstuhl would be too difficult.

Claire looked at her dirty hands. "I hauled him to an empty shack off the path and hunkered down. It was a long night. Ryan was going into shock. I used my body to keep him warm. He mumbled a lot, and I talked to him to keep him calm. He was in bad shape." Her eyes glazed over a bit before she snapped back to the present. "We stayed until Morning Prayer and then backtracked east to my Jeep."

Colonel Brand knocked on the door jamb. Jared and Claire immediately stood, and Jared pulled me with him.

"Colonel," Jared and Claire said in unison, both nodding.

"He's out of the woods for now. Doctor Vanhooser is closing, and he'll be in to speak with you shortly. He has been informed that Sergeant Scott is to be kept unaware of your presence."

"Thanks, Jason," Claire said, letting out a big sigh of relief.

"There is something you should know," Colonel Brand said. "Ryan is going to need substantial physical therapy, and after losing his entire unit, his debriefing will be extensive."

"What does that mean for Ryan?" I asked.

"Sergeant Scott's chances to return to active duty are slim," Colonel Brand said without pause.

I was ashamed of the relief the Colonel's words brought me. Ryan would be devastated, and I could only think of myself. Thoughts of Ryan returning to Brown on the military's dime and his empty seat at the Ratty being filled peppered my mind, and I had to cover my smile with my hand.

Jared glanced at me. He knew how Colonel Brand's prediction had made me feel, and his eyes tightened. I sank back into my seat, crimson splashing across my cheeks.

Claire took a walk down the colorless hallway, giving Jared the perfect chance to scold me. Before he got the chance, my cell phone buzzed in my jacket pocket.

"Hello?"

"Grant is out sick, you're gone, and the Japan firm is on line two asking questions I don't know the answers to," Beth barked in her southern accent. "I don't understand half of what he says, Nina. Is there some way to patch you through?"

I smiled. "Just tell him I'm out of town and I will call him tomorrow."

"He said he's been waiting on a return phone call from Grant for a week."

"Then he can wait one more day," I said.

"Where are you? I only have a billion documents for you to sign, and the billing on the Peterman account is messed up."

"Ask an intern. They know the software better than the accountants."

"Nigh," she sighed. "Where are you?"

"Checking on an old friend," I said. "I have to go, Beth. Oh, don't ask Sasha for help. It will give her the mistaken impression that she's needed."

"The friend wouldn't be Kim, would it?"

"No. Why?"

"She's MIA too again," Beth grumbled.

"You can wing it until I get back. I have faith in you," I said, hanging up the phone.

"What?" Jared asked.

"Beth said Kim hasn't been around. She doesn't know where she is. Kim's been doing that a lot lately," I said with a frown.

Jared squirmed in his seat and then looked away.

"Jared?" I asked in an accusatory tone. He didn't look at me. "Do you know anything about that?"

Jared didn't meet my eyes for several moments and then finally turned to face me. After a long puff of air, he took a deep breath and then intertwined his fingers. His expression was exactly as it had been the night he told me the truth.

I looked at him from under my brows. "Is it bad?"

Jared shook his head. "It's dangerous. I won't lie to you, so please let it go."

"We're talking about Kim, right? Lanky, goofy Kim?"

"Let it go, Nina."

My knee bounced up and down as I made the decision, but it had already been made. I was only stalling. Jared looked away again with a sigh, knowing what would happen next.

He closed his eyes, and with one last effort he begged. "Don't."

My knuckles turned white as I gripped the edge of my seat, preparing myself for what he would say. Jared had told me more unbelievable truths in the last two years than even I could believe, and I had seen most of it with my own eyes. Regardless, Kim had been keeping something from me—something Jared knew and I didn't—so I had to ask.

"Jared?" He stiffened the second I uttered his name. Although knowing the truth had never been comforting before, I couldn't stop myself. "What do you know about Kim?"

6. WITCH

"That's not actually his secret to tell," Kim said, strolling into the waiting room.

It took me a moment to process that she was really there and that I hadn't conjured her from my wild imagination.

Kim paused for a moment to acknowledge Jared. When he nodded in her direction, she took a seat next to me. She was in a white t-shirt and jeans, sporting black-and-white checkered Vans, and smelled of cigarettes. Her big brown eyes didn't falter. She didn't seem nervous or out of place at all.

"What on earth are you doing here, Kim?" I asked.

She shrugged. "I could ask you the same question."

"So go ahead. You seem to know all the right questions to ask, anyway," I said, defiantly.

"Kim's just here to help," Jared said.

"Help how? How did she know?" I looked at Kim then. "How did you know to come?"

"How did *you* know?" she asked. She was purposefully goading me, and I wanted to reach out, lace my fingers around her long neck, and shake her with the tightest grip I could muster.

"You're not funny," I snapped.

Kim grinned, clearly enjoying the fact that she had me in such a tizzy. "No, but you are."

I stood up, crossing my arms. If she wouldn't cooperate, I would corner Jared. I pointed at Kim. "How did she know Ryan was hurt, Jared? How did she get here?"

"Plane," Kim answered flatly.

"Shut up!" I growled.

The corners of Jared's mouth turned up slightly, but when he felt my temper rising, he straightened his expression. "Kim is helping us. Finally," he said, shooting an annoyed glance in her direction.

"Bite me," Kim said without emotion, chewing her thumbnail.

His jaws flitted under his skin. "She has been keeping an eye on our situation. What?" he said, frowning.

I stared at him. "I'm just waiting for you to make sense."

Jared returned my expression and Kim laughed once. "Welcome to my world," she said. "He's one big riddle book, isn't he? He just does it to make himself feel important. He wants you to drag it out of him."

Claire walked in and stopped in her tracks. "What is the witch doing here?" she said with venom in her voice.

Kim smiled slightly, but her eyes were devoid of emotion. "Blessed be. Heard about what happened. Good job, G.I. Barbie."

"Move aside, Nina," Claire said in a frightening, low tone. I was too afraid to move, seeing that she was poised to pounce.

Tension in the room had soared to a new level. The waiting room we occupied was in a wing separate from the main hall, so it would be very easy for Claire to let some of her pent-up aggression go in Kim's general direction. Kim didn't seem phased in the slightest.

Jared stood. "Enough."

Claire glanced at her brother. "Does she *have* to be here?"

The longer they spoke as if I knew what was going on, the angrier I became. "What in the hell is going on?" I yelled.

"Sssh!" Claire hissed.

"Are you human?" I asked Kim.

Kim paused in thought. "Some days it doesn't feel like it, but yes."

Jared sat, pulling me to the sofa with him. Claire sat in the seat next to us, fidgeting with her hijab. Kim looked at her watch and then settled into her chair. Suddenly the air felt very easy, the opposite of just a few moments before, but it was forced, unnatural.

"You know those who are aware of demons attract them." Kim said this matter-of-factly, making my reality feel twisted. Jared had told me a few specifics about the creatures from Hell that we called "others" during the talk we had on our first date—the moment we affectionately dubbed "The Conversation That Changed Everything." Kim was from the other side; someone I couldn't tell. I hadn't shared our secrets from that night with anyone, and Kim repeating part of it verbatim disconcerted me.

"Stay calm, Nina," Jared said, quietly and smoothly. He placed his hand on mine. "They feed on aggression and fear."

"So?" I said, shifting nervously in my seat.

Kim's body language was casual but deliberately so. "What we're talking about is going to bring them here, Nigh. The more upset you are, the more access they will have to this situation, so just take it all in. Don't try to analyze it. Just listen and accept."

"What do you mean they'll have access?" I breathed, fighting to keep my fear at bay.

"You're the only one in the room they can attack," Kim said. Her eyes were cold, as if she'd had years of practice working around others. Her demeanor was meant to keep me calm, but it only served to unnerve me further.

"That doesn't help," Jared frowned.

"Just hear me out," Kim said, impatient.

"Listen and accept," I said, taking a deep breath. I looked to Jared, who offered a small comforting grin. I returned my attention to Kim. "Okay. Let's hear it."

Kim's mouth turned up infinitesimally. "When I was sixteen, I was possessed by a demon."

It was hard to concentrate. Months of perfecting the art of keeping my emotions under control was the only advantage I had, and I was determined to keep my cool. "You're kidding."

Kim continued, "I'm going to make this short if you don't mind."

I nodded and Kim rolled her eyes. "The story bores me, so, to get to the point, the Pollocks, my family, descend from Crusade knights. Those Crusade knights used the Holy Sepulchre as an end point of their pilgrimages. You okay?" Kim asked, pausing.

"Yeah," I said casually, "because I don't know what the hell you're talking about!" I yelled.

Jared held my hands in my lap and lowered his chin, looking directly into my eyes. "You need to stay calm. It's important."

I looked back to Kim. "Sorry."

Kim dismissed my apology. "Whatever. You remember learning about the Crusades, Nigh—English knights, Robin Hood, and King Richard?" I nodded. "It has nothing to do with that."

I sighed, and Jared jerked his head to the side in frustration. "You're not helping."

Kim laughed once and looked down. "I'm sorry. I just can't describe to you how much I hate telling this story."

"Try," Jared seethed.

Kim looked to me. "Templar Knights took their crusades to a very holy place in Jerusalem. It's called the Church of the Holy Sepulchre. It was once the temple of Aphrodite. Christians refer to it as Golgotha, the place where Christ was crucified.

"The First Crusade was envisioned as an armed pilgrimage, and no crusader could consider his journey complete unless he had prayed as a pilgrim at the Holy Sepulchre. This is where it gets a little hairy. During my great-great-times-infinity-grandfather's pilgrimage, he came upon something under the basilica of the Holy Sepulchre. It was a book, a bible."

"So you're Bible savers?" I looked at Jared in disbelief. "Cool? I guess?"

"We're not talking about the *Holy Bible* here, Nigh," Kim said. "You've seen it."

"Shax's bible?" I asked.

Kim nodded. "It was kept safely hidden away in the cistern under the basilica, which is where it was rumored that the mother of Hadrian found the true cross and the tomb of Christ."

"Isn't that pretty much sacrilegious? The bible of Hell being kept under what was thought to be the tomb of Jesus Christ?" I said.

Kim rubbed her temples. I had clearly asked a question she'd answered a thousand times. "The Holy Presence there kept Shax and his legions from finding it. My grandfather didn't know that. He removed the book, and after learning of its importance, he vowed to keep it safe. That vow and the book have cursed our family for generations."

"Curses seem to be the popular thing around here," I grumbled.

Kim glanced at Jared.

"I'm sorry," I said, laughing without humor. "This is all a little far-fetched, even for me, and I've seen Shax."

The room grew cold, and Jared and Claire immediately extended their necks, looking to the ceiling. Jared pulled me closer to him, and Claire sat on the other side of me, lightly touching my knee.

The lights flickered, and even with Jared's and Claire's warm bodies on each side of me, I shook from the cold. The dim fluorescent lights created an eerie glow to the air we exhaled, now warmer than the air in the room.

"What's happening?" I whispered.

"For the fiftieth time, Nina, stay calm," Claire said, her voice even. "Nothing will happen to you while we're here. This is just what happens when there's a higher concentration of them than normal."

"Higher concentration?" I asked.

Kim looked above her. "Oh there's probably an army or two around or one really strong one."

I shivered. "Which is worse?"

"One," Claire whispered, her eyes unfocused. She was relying on her senses, creating a thoughtful, confused expression on her face.

Kim returned her attention to me. Her demeanor was baffling. She had always been relaxed and at times aloof, but it was hard to believe she could remain that way with so many others around. Every part of me wanted to run screaming down the hall.

"Anyone who's made the trip to return the book to the Sepulchre never came back. We thought Jack and Gabe stealing the book from my uncle was the best thing that could have happened to our family, until Shax held us personally responsible. That's when I got sick or that's what we thought it was."

Even with the drop in temperature and the knowledge that a million demons might have been hovering over us, I sat hunched over, with my chin resting on my fist, suddenly unimpressed. "You were possessed. As in priests and green pea soup possessed? C'mon, Kim."

"I don't remember most of it. I just know that my father spared no expense to bring in the best of the best, and when Father Gary and Father Carmine were finished, I was different."

Jared squeezed my hand. "When humans are overtaken in that way, they are often left weak for the rest of their lives. Kim kept something with her when Father Carmine finally extracted the demons. They wouldn't have left behind power voluntarily. She took it from them, and because of that, the demons fear her."

"What kind of power?" I asked.

"The all-knowing: understanding dead languages blah, blah, blah. I also know when they move, when they approach, when they leave, and why they're doing it. I think I can take their power at will, but none of them have gotten close enough for me to try."

"So Kim is an asset," Claire said, sullen. "She affects them in ways no one understands."

"I . . . You . . ." A million questions swirled in my head, but the most upsetting revelation was that nothing was separate now. My normal life just had a head-on collision with my life with Jared.

The air around me felt thick and full of static. An end table next to one of the chairs shook for a moment and then slid across the floor a few inches.

"What just happened?" I said.

The table vibrated again and then shot to the wall, the legs squealing as they grated across the tile.

"Sweetheart," Jared warned.

My fingers worked in small circles against my temple. "Okay," I whispered. I worked to release any negativity that the demons could use to fuel their power. "What now?"

"I can help you," Kim said, uncharacteristically sympathetic. "I can help you find the book, Nigh. They'll tell me. They have to."

All expression fell from my face. "So you're like . . . You're like the demon whisperer. My wacky friend Kim. That's just great."

Kim nodded, unaffected by my jab.

"You never said why you're here," I said.

"I wanted to check on Ryan. I also have news."

News was usually the job of Samuel, and I wondered why Kim had been sent instead. The more I knew, the less any of it made sense, which was annoyingly typical.

Claire crossed her legs, settling in her chair. "Well? Tell us already."

"Jared and his covert operation tipped them off. He's asked too many questions, and they know what he's after. The book has been moved six times in as many days. We've got some work to do when we get home."

Jared glared at Kim, annoyed. "I have to look it over before we take it back. There are things within those pages that could help Nina."

"That was the deal, wasn't it?" Kim replied.

Jared nodded and then looked to his sister. "Now that Ryan's stable, we should head back. Did the Colonel say how long you'd be here?"

Claire shrugged. "At least until he's stable enough to ship stateside, and then we'll probably be at a VA rehab until he's functional. I'll keep you updated."

I stared at the small table that had slid across the floor. Two hundred or so demons had been swirling about, and they were already onto the next subject. The air had returned to its normal temperature, but watching an inanimate object glide across the room left me uneasy—not that I had felt anything close to composed since Gabe had infiltrated my dream on the plane. Life was spinning out of control again, but this time there was no normal life to escape to.

One third of my anchor to normal was lying in a hospital bed and another sitting beside me, talking about things so opposite of the realm of ordinary that it was difficult to remember she was part of my other life at all.

Anger consumed me. I felt I'd been lied to. "What deal are you two talking about?" I asked.

"Your man is going to help me return the book to the Sepulchre if I help him get it from Shax," Kim said.

"Were you going to tell me about any of this?" I said to Jared.

Jared took my hands in his. "We talked about this."

"Yes, that you would omit things that didn't directly involve me, but first Ryan and now Kim? They were my friends, Jared!"

"We still are," Kim said.

I ignored Kim. "Are you sure I can't see Ryan?" I asked Claire. She shook her head with an apologetic expression. "It was good to see you again," I said to Claire, hugging her. "Kim . . ." I trailed off, unable to find anything nice to say.

Kim had betrayed me, sneaking her mystical bullshit in the back door and sucker-punching me with her possession-crusades-basilica sob story. Now she was supposed to help us find the book because of her oh-so-spooky-to-the-demons powers. I didn't care! She was supposed to be my normal, and she had ripped it right out from under me.

Gabe had wanted us to turn back, and I couldn't help but wonder if I wasn't supposed to know about Kim. Could Gabe's appearance be mundane as a paternal need to protect me again, or was it something different? Maybe Kim wasn't supposed to help us. Maybe she was working for the other side.

I had almost reached the elevator when Jared called my name. Soon, his hand was in mine. He stopped mid-step, causing me to jerk backward.

"We have to go," I said, tugging him down the hall.

Jared stopped me again. "Would you please tell me what's going on?"

"No," I snapped, smacking the button to the elevator. "That would require me telling you the *whole* truth, and that's not really how our relationship works."

The door opened, and I pulled Jared inside. We were alone, and for the first time, I felt I could breathe. I leaned against the wall and sighed. "This isn't happening."

"What isn't happening? Nina, talk to me," Jared said, putting his hands on the wall at each side of my head.

"She's my friend, Jared! She was on the other side, the side that kept me grounded and sometimes kept me sane, but now it's gone! It's all gone!"

Jared cupped my face. "She's still your friend. Your life at Brown is no different."

"It's not different? It's disappeared!"

He frowned. "Let's think of this as a positive thing. You have someone to talk to about this now, someone on the other side who understands."

I crossed my arms. "I needed them, Jared, so I wouldn't get lost in all of the Heaven/Hell fiasco."

"She's human, Nina. She may handle it differently, but she knows how you feel. She knows what it's like to know things and be different because of it. Embrace it."

"Embrace it," I grumbled. "You don't understand."

Jared took my hand and kissed my fingers. "This is a good thing. With her help, we can find the book."

"Great!" I said as the doors opened to the main floor. "Let's find the damn thing and get rid of it! Take it back to the church, I'll stop having the dreams, Kim can be Kim again, and I can get my life back!"

Colonel Brand waited next to the car that would take us to the base. Jared and I had remained silent during the trip, but once the plane took off from the runway, he began again.

"Nina, we can't just take the book back. We have to read it and find out why Jack stole it from Kim's uncle in the first place."

"Because Jack was crazy, that's why," I snapped.

Jared sighed with frustration. "They've been telling us why in your dreams."

I thought for a moment, recalling Jack's words on the roof. *He had to save her.* I could think of only two women in the world my father would risk his life for. The inscription on my ring leading to a deposit box only Jared and I could access . . . He had stolen the book to save me.

But from what?

I narrowed my eyes. "Are you insinuating that I'm keeping something from you? Because that would be just totally and completely hypocritical."

Jared frowned. "No. But we need to find someone who can interpret what your dreams mean."

"Who would know, Jared? Besides Eli or Samuel. They wouldn't tell us, anyway, right? Who would know?"

"Asking them again wouldn't be a good idea. Kim said they're already onto us. It's impossible to keep a secret in that realm. We need a human."

"A human isn't going to be able to make sense of my dreams, Jared, unless it's someone who already knows. One of Graham's men, maybe?"

Jared shook his head, deep in thought. "Claire didn't leave any of them alive. Anyone who might have known anything about it is long gone."

An idea popped into my head, instantly creating a sinking feeling in my stomach.

"What is it?" Jared asked, concerned.

My mind instantly searched for other options. I was desperate to make the name stuck in my throat a last resort, but she was our only choice. "My mother," I whispered. "Cynthia would know."

Jared's brows pulled in for a moment. "Jack left her in the dark."

"You don't really believe that, do you?" I asked, incredulously.

He peeked over at me and then relaxed. "You're right. How to get her to tell us anything is the question."

"She'll tell us," I said, determined.

7. THE PERFECT STORM

"Isn't this a surprise," Cynthia said, fussing with her hair. "I'm on my way to the Komen fundraiser, Nina dear. We'll have lunch tomorrow."

I sidestepped, guarding the front door. "This is important."

Cynthia laughed once, not amused. "Not more important than breast cancer, I assure you." When I didn't move, she cocked her head. The expression she used for immediate intimidation lit her face. "You will let me pass this instant, young lady."

Instinctively, I obeyed. Seeing that she was in no mood for antics, I decided to try the blindside approach.

"Daddy stole a book from someone a few years ago. Do you remember?"

She blinked a few times, my words clearly unsettling to her. "Your father was in shipping, Nina. What interest would he have in a book?"

"He did it, Mother. I've seen the book myself. Jared's held it in his hands."

Cynthia's cold eyes darted to Jared and then narrowed. "I must ask at this point, Jared. Are you *trying* to get Nina killed?"

"No," Jared said emphatically, taking a step toward her. "No, that's why we're here. We need to know why Jack took the book. What was inside that he was hoping to find?"

Cynthia relaxed, lifting her chin. "Nina, you'll find that if you ignore things they tend to go away. Now, I really must be going."

Jared's jaw twitched, and then he took an obstinate step in front of the door.

"I'm sorry, Mrs. Grey, but I can't allow you to leave until you tell us what you know."

Cynthia stood unaffected, as if she could brush past Jared if she chose, but she was simply too much of a lady to shove her way through.

"What makes you think I know anything?" she asked, a tiny smirk on her face.

I crossed my arms. "Because you know everything, Mother."

A small grin of satisfaction crept across Cynthia's face. "Your father underestimated that particular talent of mine for years. It's nice that someone noticed."

"We need your help, Cynthia," Jared said. "Why did Jack think Shax's book could save Nina?"

"The truth will only hurt you, dear," Cynthia said. Her words were meant to be empathetic, but her eyes were devoid of emotion.

I pressed my lips together in hard line, taking her warning very seriously. Before I could make a decision, Jared spoke.

"I'm only going to ask you one more time, Cynthia. What do you know about Jack's reasons for taking the book?"

Cynthia chuckled. "Empty threats rarely compel me to comply."

Jared leaned against the door. "I have all night, Cynthia. How important is this fundraiser to you?"

"Very well, then," Cynthia said. She shifted her weight, clearly irritated. "Your father never wanted children. I wasn't exactly maternal, so I never questioned him. But when you came along, Nina, it changed him. He seemed to watch you as if he were waiting for something. I asked him, once, why he stared at you that way. His expression held both disgust and shame, but he didn't answer. He simply walked away."

Her words cut so deeply that I felt physical pain in my chest, as if a thousand needles were boring their way to the center.

Jared took my hand. "Jack adored Nina. He died trying to save her life."

Cynthia laughed without humor. "You misunderstand. The first time Jack held Nina in his arms, nothing else mattered. There was nothing more precious in his eyes," she paused, "but he was afraid."

I struggled to swallow the lump that had developed in my throat. "Of what?"

"You, I suppose," Cynthia shrugged. Her eyes switched to Jared then, resentful and accusing. "When your father recognized that you were in love with Nina, he shared a story with Jack. It was a story within the last passages of the book you're so desperate to acquire about a human woman giving birth to a son of God and that child would disturb The Balance."

My face twisted. "You mean the story of the Virgin Mary and Jesus? What could that possibly have to do with Jared and me?"

Cynthia sighed. "No, dear. Sons of God are angels. Hell believes a human woman will give birth to an angel, a powerful angel who will threaten their power here."

Jared frowned. "That doesn't make any sense. Why Nina, then? Human women have been giving birth to half-breeds for centuries. And even if Nina and I had a child, the baby would have just a quarter of divine blood in its veins, nothing for Hell to be concerned about."

"A human woman gave birth to Jesus Christ, Jared," Cynthia retorted.

"He was human," I said.

Cynthia raised an eyebrow. "A mortal man who performs miracles and rises from the dead? That's some human. Now if you'll excuse me . . ."

Jared didn't budge, still unsatisfied. "Gabe and Jack believed Nina to be the woman in the prophecy, and they stole the book to try to figure out a way to stop it?"

"They stole it twice," Cynthia corrected, "first, from a family, the Pollocks. They had spent lifetimes protecting it. Shax and his men alerted the Pollocks somehow, and your fathers were detected. While they and the Pollock men were distracted with one another, Shax absconded with his book. It was several months before Gabe located the book again and was able to successfully retrieve it. That's when it all began."

"Mother," I said, impatiently, "when *what* began?"

Her eyes widened a bit, and she raised her hands, her fingers flared. "This, Nina! This! When protecting you and your father became difficult for the Ryel's—when dark things began surrounding our home on a daily basis—his *death*. Honestly, Nina! What else could I mean?" she said, exasperated.

"Okay. Okay, I'm sorry," I said to calm her.

She relaxed and then smoothed her expression. "Now, if you don't mind, I really must be going," she said, brushing past Jared.

Jared's features tightened, instantly metamorphosing to anger. "I'm trying to save Nina's life, and you're worried about being on time for a party?"

Cynthia looked back at me with a sad expression. "It's a mother's duty to protect her child, but sometimes, we must let them save themselves."

Her words stung me. Our relationship was never what one may call close, but when the occasion called for it, she extended some emotion. She had never been cruel or unkind, but at that moment, I felt like an orphan.

My mother walked to the waiting car quickly, disappearing when Robert closed the door behind her.

Jared pulled me into his arms, and I let my cheek burn against his chest.

"I can't imagine how you must feel right now," Jared whispered against the top of my hair, "but I want you to remember two things: Cynthia feels helpless, and that's not a feeling she deals with appropriately, and I want to remind you that I love you, and that love is unlike anything I've ever felt before. If she makes you feel unworthy or unwanted in any way, know that every breath you take is precious to me."

I nodded, unable to thank him for the words I didn't even know that I needed to hear.

We walked to the large staircase, and I slumped to the first step. "I don't want to . . . I can't think about her anymore."

Jared nodded once. "So let's think about what she said."

A small laugh escaped my throat. "That I'm the woman in Hell's prophecy? I've been told several things in the last twenty-four hours that are, quite frankly, ridiculous, and Cynthia's story gets the prize."

Jared didn't smile. "What if it's true? It's not as if Cynthia is the most creative person on the planet. Why would she lie?"

I craned my neck, looking at him in disbelief. "Jared? I can't *believe* you're falling for her nonsense! My father never wanted children? That's absurd! Jack was the best father anyone could ever hope for. You've said it yourself. He worshiped me."

"Cynthia didn't say he didn't like children. I took it as he hoped to prevent something. We need to do a little digging in your ancestry."

I rolled my eyes. "Wild goose chase. You're wasting time even discussing this."

"What do you know about your family?" he asked.

"What do you know about *your* family?" I retorted.

Jared's brows moved in. "I have an uncle in South Dakota. My grandparents are gone, you know that."

"So are mine. My parents were only children, Jared. I have no family to speak of."

"So we start with the grandparents on Jack's side," he said, standing. "Where does Cynthia keep stuff like that?"

"Stuff like what?"

"Family albums? Newspaper clippings? A family tree?"

"I've never seen anything like that." I shrugged.

Jared sighed. "Jack has a coat of arms in his office. You can't tell me family wasn't important to him."

I cupped my chin in my hand and thought for a moment. Cynthia's words replayed in my head. Kim's story and Cynthia's were now meshed together—intertwined because of the prophecy and the book it came from. Somehow life was even less normal than when a demon stood in my apartment. I felt like a freak.

"My father's office . . ."

"You thought of something?" Jared said, pulling me to my feet.

My eyes widened. "Last year, when I was in Jack's office for the Port of Providence file, one of his cabinets was locked. I never found the keys to it. When I found the file I was looking for, I sort of forgot about it."

Jared pulled me to my feet, quickly climbing the stairs. I tugged on the drawers of the row of file cabinets until I found one that wouldn't budge. "That's it," I said. "The keys in the desk don't work. I've tried them."

Jared looked around the room and then casually yanked the drawer. It made a loud popping noise, but it opened easily enough—for Jared.

"Well, that's one way to do it," I grinned.

Jared fingered through each of the papers. "You start with the bottom drawer. We'll meet in the middle."

I sat on my knees, pulling open my designated drawer. There were old pictures, overseas bank accounts, but nothing about family. The familiar frustration from the last time I had spent rummaging through his office for clues clouded my brain.

Jared powered through three drawers before I finished one, but when he reached the fourth, he stopped. He held a paper in front of his face and then looked beyond it to the adjacent wall.

"What is it?" I asked. Before he could answer, I noted that it was a drawing of a coat of arms, similar to the one hanging on the wall.

"Does the name "Franks" mean anything to you, Nina?" he asked.

I shook my head, pushing myself to my feet. "No. Should it?"

"You're Irish, aren't you?"

"Yeah? So?" Some days I had patience for his step-by-step approach of getting to the truth. This was not one of those days.

"It's a common misconception. Surely Jack wouldn't display something that didn't specifically belong to him."

"You lost me," I said, hoping he would get to the point.

"Coats of arms were designed to designate a knight whose face would've been covered during battle. They are inherited from father to son, so it wouldn't make sense to have a 'Grey' coat of arms for an entire family or last name. Jack wasn't the type to buy into that nonsense, so this must be the original, passed down."

"Okay."

Jared scanned the drawing. "This is similar, but it's not the same, and it's unlike any crest or coat of arms I've ever seen."

Jared handed the paper to me, and I recoiled at the misshapen beast. It had the body of a large cat, perhaps a panther or leopard, and large paws, which I guessed to be the paws of a bear. Seven heads ascended from its body with horns and crowns sitting atop those horns. It was grotesque.

"This is our family's coat of arms? Sick," I said, handing the drawing back to Jared. "No wonder Jack changed it. He couldn't hang something that monstrous on the wall."

"This is very similar to the creature in Revelations," Jared said, staring at the twisted black lines on the paper: "the heads, the horns, the crowns. . . ."

"What *creature*?" I said, warily.

Jared made a face and then pored over the other files in the drawer. He stopped for a moment and then leaned in closer to the document that made him pause. His shoulders slumped. "*Agh!* No," he whispered, his head falling forward.

"What is it?" I said, afraid of what he might say.

He nervously rubbed the back of his neck, pulling the paper from the drawer. He looked once more and then shut his eyes tightly.

I fidgeted. "It's bad, isn't it?"

His eyes slowly opened, and the twin storms of his irises sent panic throughout my body. He glanced at the coat of arms on the wall. "I promise you, Nina. You don't want to know."

"I think I have to know at this point," I said, pulling the paper from his hand.

Jared shook his head. "I can still figure out how to save you without you knowing everything. We've talked about that before. Trust me when I say that you don't want to know this."

I lowered my eyes to the paper. It was a list of names, similar to a family tree, but it only followed one line. My name was at the bottom. Higher on the list were names such as Dagobert the third and Clovis the first. The name at the top, Merovius, had two fathers: King Clodian and another name that caused my legs to disappear. I dropped the paper to the floor.

Jared supported my weight. "Sweetheart?" he said, pulling my chin up so that he could see into my eyes. He lifted me into his arms and carried me to Jack's desk chair, kneeling before me.

"What . . . What does that mean? What the hell is a Beast of the Sea?" I wailed.

Jared shook his head. "It's just a story, Nina, nothing more."

"Tell me," I whispered.

Jared's jaws fluttered. "I don't want to."

"What am I?"

A small smile touched Jared's mouth. "You're human. You just have some pretty potent blood running through your veins."

"I need to know," I said, touching his cheek with my fingertips.

Jared seemed just as horrified as I was. In the beginning, he had tortured himself over bringing me into his world, stealing away my mundane life forever. Now it was I who regretted involving him in my life—we were both spiraling into a nightmare that didn't seem to end.

Jared sighed. "Merovingians. You're a Merovingian, Nina. A very long time ago, your family ruled with divine power, under the belief that they were direct descendants of Jesus Christ."

"Jesus didn't have children," I scoffed.

"The myth is that Jesus and Mary Magdalene were married and their children are the ancestors of the Merovingian blood line. It's known in less-human circles that the story was perpetuated to keep the Merovingians in power. There are people even today who believe it."

"So you're saying it's not true? That's a relief. I'm at least somewhat less of a freak."

"I'm saying the Merovingians perpetuated the myth to survive. They *are* descendants of immortals, but the truth would have made them pariahs in their time. They would have all been hunted down and put to death."

"I am no longer relieved," I said, blowing my bangs from my face.

Jared looked away, cautiously choosing his next words. "Have you heard of the Nephilim, Nina?"

I shook my head, dreading where his story would go.

"Okay," he said. "Have you heard of the story of David and Goliath?"

"Yeah," I sniffed. "The skinny kid that threw a rock at a giant's head and killed him."

"Goliath was not one of a kind. He had family, people—Antediluvian Giants. Some called them Anakim. Others referred to them as Nephilim. They had many tribes, and their remains have been found measuring anywhere from nine-and-a-half feet to fourteen feet. Some have two full rows of teeth. They were different, not completely human. The *Holy Bible* acknowledges their origin in Genesis 6:2,4: '*That the sons of God saw the daughters of men were fair, and they took them wives of all which they chose. The Nephilim were on the earth in those days, and also after, when the sons of God came in unto the daughters of men, and they bore children unto them.*'"

"Sons of God? Like the ones Cynthia talked about?" I asked.

"Yes. Angels."

"Do you know the whole Bible by heart?" I asked, attempting to detour the frightening thought swirling in my mind.

"Most of it," he said. A corner of his mouth turned up slightly. It vanished as quickly as it appeared. "God wiped out the Nephilim with the great flood because their blood was contaminated, so to speak. He needed a direct and pure line from Adam to Abraham because they were prophesied as the forebears of the Messiah. Noah was his way to cleanse the blood line and ensure the prophecy would occur."

"My brain hurts," I complained, rubbing my head.

Jared kissed my hair, wrapping his arms around me. "Do you understand what I'm telling you?" he whispered softly. "Jack didn't want children because he knew he carried Nephilim blood and the Merovingians are part of the prophecy in the *Naissance de Demoniac*. He knew when I fell in love with you that you and I would meet all of the requirements."

"What requirements?" My voice was muffled from pushing my face into his chest.

"A prophecy requires certain elements to come together in order to come to fruition, Nina. A descendant of the Nephilim procreating with a hybrid . . . It's the perfect storm. Remember when Eli told us that only seven other human/hybrid cases had happened since the dawn of time? How many of those humans do you think were Merovingian? Jack knew you were the woman in the book because he knew what he was and what I was. Once he knew I was in love with you, he made the decision to steal Shax's book to try to find a way to protect you."

"From what?" I cringed. I kept asking questions I didn't want the answers to.

He lifted my chin to face him. "That's why we need the book. I need to find out what interest they might have in a child we might have. I don't know if they want it to happen or they will fight to prevent it. It depends on what that scenario means for Hell."

"Wait," I said, my mind finally focusing enough to form coherent thoughts. "You said the Nephilim were wiped out in the big flood. So how can I be related to them?"

Jared raised his eyebrows once, sighing. "That was a tactic used to keep Jesus' blood line pure. That doesn't mean fallen angels taking human women didn't happen after that."

"Oh," I said, deflated. "I'm five foot four, Jared. How is it even possible I could have even an ounce of giant blood in me?"

Jared chuckled. "You're Irish too. Makes me wonder how you're Merovingian. They were leaders of the Franks, early German and French."

"Well, now I know Jack was wrong. I couldn't be French. The language is lost on me."

Jared's face turned grave. "We should take this seriously, Nina. We're in the middle of a war. If I could leave you, that would be one thing, but I can't."

My mouth flew open. "Why would you even say that?"

"Because it's the right thing to do—disappear from your life to keep you safe. As long as we're together, you're in danger."

"I won't let you," I said, grabbing his shirt. The thought of being without him terrified me. "If I can't be with you, I don't care what happens to me."

Jared grabbed my hands. "I know. That's why I won't leave you. And now that we know what you are, we need to find out who is threatened by it. And as frightening as it is, threatening Hell is the better option."

8. VALEDICTION

An unexpected knock on the door revealed Bex standing on the landing, holding a half-eaten apple. A backpack hung from his shoulder, signaling that he would be staying the night.

"You called him, didn't you?" I accused Jared, crossing my arms.

Jared slipped on his jacket, preparing to leave. "You've had a long forty-eight hours. You need sleep." He hugged me then, squeezing a bit too tightly.

Bex shifted his weight nervously, holding the door open with one hand, holding his apple with the other.

"Come on, Nina. You're going to give me a complex," Bex said. "I brought doves to put in the oven." A sweet, hopeful smile lit his face, and I relaxed.

"Okay," I said with a half-grin.

Jared patted Bex's arm as he passed, but just as he stepped out onto the landing, I grabbed his jacket. "Wait. What if it's different? What if he needs to tell me something?"

"Who?" Jared asked. His attention focused on me once again.

"Gabe or Jack. We've learned a lot today. Maybe the dream will change."

Jared and Bex traded glances, and then Jared sighed. "Tomorrow."

"I didn't think we have time to spare," I countered.

"We don't, but . . ."

"I'm right. You know I'm right. So stay," I said, pulling him into the loft.

Jared pointed at his brother. "Don't go anywhere."

Bex shook his head and then shut the door behind us. "No way, I wanna see this."

"Great, now I'm a circus freak," I said, making my way to the table. Jared pulled out my chair and I sat, taking his hand and kissing his palm in appreciation. We had spent the last two days together, yet I felt I hadn't seen him at all.

Jared sat across from me with a smile. "You are far from a circus freak. You're amazing. Big difference."

"Watching me float and scream is not amazing," I grumbled.

"You only floated once," Bex pointed out, unwrapping the dove and seasoning it before shoving the baking dish into the oven.

We discussed the possibilities for over an hour. How I could do things in my sleep that I couldn't do in a conscious state?

"It doesn't matter how. What is important is why," Jared said.

"It matters to me," Bex said.

"You're going to overcook your birds," Jared said, nodding to the oven.

Bex jumped up, tending to dinner. He placed our plates of tender, steaming dove and mixed vegetables in front of us and then returned quickly with his own. "I've got to figure out how to do that. If she can do it, we have to be able to do it, right?" he said to Jared, shoveling meat into his mouth.

"She's not doing it, Bex," Jared said. His eyes darted from me to Bex in warning. It was clear he didn't want to dwell on the subject during dinner.

"Oh, right," Bex said, chewing.

After I finished the dinner dishes, I retreated to the downstairs tub, lingering long enough to let my fingers transform to dried raisins, and then I wrapped myself in my favorite terry cloth robe, making my way to the bed. Jared was waiting for me, his hair still wet from the shower. I crawled under the sheet next to him, relaxing my cheek against his bare chest.

I breathed him in, focusing on the moment, bathing in the gift of peace and stillness. No one spoke of others or giants. It was just us in our quiet space in time. In those moments, I found Heaven, and he was there with me, I could tell, as he pulled me in closer.

"I'm right here," he whispered. "Nothing bad will happen to you. I swear it."

"Don't swear." I grinned, my eyes growing heavy. That heaviness rested over my entire body, warm and inviting. Jared's skin felt like a silky electric blanket against mine, and I let myself sink into it. Any light that seeped through my eyelids extinguished, letting the darkness take me deeper into oblivion.

"Nina," a voice said somewhere in the shadows.

"I'm here," I said sleepily.

"You've really done it this time."

"Daddy?" I said, sitting up. I was in my old bedroom. Jack sat at the foot of my bed. He was as I remembered him, his salt-and-pepper hair perfectly in place, his dark no-nonsense eyes looking softly upon me, clean-shaven, and in his favorite grey suit.

He smiled, but his eyes were sad. "I'm sorry I failed you. You'll have to save yourself now."

My lower lip quivered. "Why didn't you tell me?"

Jack placed his thick hand on my ankle, his expression pained. "I tried many times. I couldn't bear to see those sweet eyes turn sad. I wanted you to have everything, Nina, most of all a normal life."

I smiled. "I hope it's nice where you are," I said, my eyes burning from the salty tears lining my lower lashes.

"The only thing missing is you."

I laughed once and looked down at my hands. "I wish you were really here. I need you."

"Find the book, Nina," Jack said. The change of his voice made me look up. His chin was lowered, and he looked at me from under his brow—the way he always had when he wanted me to listen.

"Daddy?" I said, seeing movement behind him, slowly approaching us from the darkness.

Shax strolled into the light. His black eyes hadn't changed.

"It's time to wake up, Nina," Jack said with an apologetic expression.

I glowered at Shax. "No," I said, anger bursting from every pore in my skin.

Shax's head cocked to the side like an animal. "What is she to us, Jack? Why do you protect her so?"

"Because she's my daughter," Jack said firmly, standing. He walked to the bedroom door and then turned to face Shax, his hand on the knob. "You've underestimated my family many times, beast. This time may be your last."

Shax waved him away, and a loud noise forced me to cover my ears. Misshapen arms exploded through the door, throwing splintered wood onto the floor and my covers. Before I could recover from the noise, Jack was pulled through the door. Only traces of his blood on the door jamb and carpet had been left behind.

"No!" I screamed, reaching out from my bed.

Shax took a step closer and I recoiled.

"Stay away from me," I said, looking around the room for something to use to defend myself.

Shax lurched forward, his wild black eyes and sharp features inches from my face. I scampered back, first against the head of my bead. Panicked, I continued to crawl backward away from him and found myself halfway up the wall.

Shax stood, looking up at me. He smiled with his crooked mouth and perfectly white teeth. "Running will get you nowhere, precious. We know what you are."

He jumped, landing on all fours on the wall. My arms and legs couldn't move fast enough as I climbed backward up the remainder of the wall. Shax's arms and legs made quick jerking movements as he moved slowly toward me. His body looked twisted and unnatural.

When I realized I was on the ceiling, looking down at my bed, I closed my eyes.

"Wake me up, Jared! Wake me *up*!"

I opened my eyes, and I was back at the loft. Jared, Bex, and the bed were all twelve feet below me.

"*Agh*!" I screamed as I fell face-down onto the bed.

"I've gotta learn how to do that!" Bex said, jumping once with excitement.

Jared immediately turned me onto my back. "Nina?" he said, brushing my hair from my face.

"I'm fine," I said, angrily.

"That was creepy," Jared said, scanning me with his dark blue eyes.

"She was like Spiderman! That was freakin' incredible!" Bex said. "I bet I can do that. I'm going to try."

"We can't float or climb walls," Jared said through his teeth. The skin around his eyes was tight with worry.

"But she's human! Even if she's influenced, if she can do it, we must be able to!"

Jared's brows pulled in. "What happened?"

I took a breath. "Jack was there."

"And Gabe?"

"No, but Shax came. He said he knew what I was. Jack said that Shax had underestimated our family before. He said to get the book."

Jared nodded. "That's the plan."

"I think he meant now," I said, feeling a sense of urgency.

Jared looked to Bex, who was looking around the loft, listening.

"Bex?" Jared said.

Bex nodded.

"We all need to pack a few things," Jared said. "We're going to be gone for a couple of days. I want to be in the car and ready to go in five minutes."

Jared's and Bex's forms turned obscure as they raced around the room at impossible speed, and I immediately pulled on a hooded sweatshirt and jeans then shoved my bare feet into sneakers. Jared held the door open for me as I pulled my hair back into a ponytail. The iron steps knocked and echoed with my footsteps alone, although Bex was in front of me, with Jared following behind.

Bex threw our bags into the back of the Escalade then froze. He looked into the air, waiting for something.

"Are they coming?" I whispered.

Jared paused then took a step toward the loft. "No," he whispered.

Bex shook his head. "They're here."

Jared left me then. My eyes barely kept up with his blurry form sprinting into the loft.

"What?" I said. Bex moved in front of me in a protective stance then gasped.

The building exploded. Multiple balls of fire rolled into the sky. Debris shot toward Bex and me, and he turned his back to the explosion, shielding my body from the blast. I crawled out from under him, seeing the bright orange glow of heat and smoke that used to be our home.

"No!" I wailed, reaching over Bex. I knew trying to escape from him grip was futile, but the explosion had happened less than a second after Jared had reached the stairs, and I was desperate to get to him.

I looked up to Jared's little brother. His eyes were wide. He clearly didn't know what to think. We waited there, and even though the fire roared before us, everything was silent.

I waited for Jared to emerge from the rubble. Every second that passed seemed like an eternity, and panic began to overwhelm any rational thought I tried to have.

"Come on, Jared," Bex said, his grip on my arms a bit tighter.

"Go get him," I demanded, my voice broken and shaking.

"I have to stay here with you," Bex said. He seemed confused and in shock.

I pushed at Bex. "He's in there somewhere! Go *get* him!" I screamed.

Bex grabbed each side of my face, looking deep into my eyes. "They are *here*, Nina. They're all around us. I can't leave you."

"Good kid," Jared said from behind us. His hair and clothes were singed, his face covered in soot, and the skin on his cheek bone was scraped and bleeding, but he was alive.

He held up two dusty picture frames: one with the black-and-white picture of me he took the day he fell in love with me and the other of us playing at the beach in Little Corn.

"Don't do that to me ever again!" I yelled, balling up my fists and landing them straight onto Jared's chest.

He wrapped his arms around me tightly. "I'm sorry. I realized what was about to happen, and I had to go. These pictures were the only things in the loft I couldn't lose."

We turned to watch at our home fall in defeat to the fire. The beams creaked as they gave way, and glowing ash was thrown into the sky, floating all around us. My eyes poured out rivers of tears. I'd never realized how much I loved the loft until I witnessed it dying in front of me. Memories of our first date, listening to our song for the first time, cooking together, laughing, watching Claire and Bex grow a little more each time they entered the front door—it was all gone, reduced to cinders.

Sirens sounded in the distance.

"We have to go," Jared said, gently escorting me to the passenger side of the Escalade.

As he pulled away, I watched the flames and glowing smoke until I couldn't see them anymore and then turned to face forward. Jared placed his hand over mine, and then Bex put his hand over ours.

"It had to be Donovan," Bex said.

I shook my head. "No. Claire took care of all the humans who might be a threat to us."

"Except Donovan," Jared said. His knuckles turned white against the steering wheel.

Bex leaned back in the seat. "He's the closest human to Shax. Claire left him alive because he's the taleh of a half-breed."

"What?" I said, looking to Jared for confirmation.

He nodded. "Isaac. Very fast, very strong, but emotional. He's been known to make mistakes, but he's still dangerous."

I blinked, processing what Jared had said. "So to kill Donovan we'd have to kill a hybrid."

"Not just any hybrid," Bex said, "the son of Michael, a deadly angel in the Holy Army, a warrior of God. At His word, they would exterminate entire blood lines, entire kingdoms."

I laughed once. "*The* Michael? You're joking."

"Not *the* Michael, but he was very respected in that family of angels until he fell in love with Isaac's mother," Jared said, pulling the Escalade down a road leading us out of town. "Michael belongs to a family of angels that embodies God's wrath, and if harm came to his son, that would be an act of war against Heaven. That is the only reason Donovan is still alive."

The Escalade bounced over the uneven gravel road, and Jared came to a stop just outside a familiar chain-link fence. We walked hand in hand to the warehouse where I met Eli. Jared pushed the button and we waited. Nothing.

"I thought you said he wouldn't speak to you?" I asked.

Jared stood—silent, patient, and calm. Twenty long minutes passed, and then we were finally buzzed in. The breath Jared had silently held, he released. "Thank you," he whispered.

Bex led the way through the dusty cement hall. My footsteps echoed throughout the capacious room the hall opened up to, encased by a hundred dirty windows.

As before, we waited in the center.

Jared's and Bex's faces were marked by soot from the fire. Their expressions were composed, waiting for Eli to decide to show himself.

An hour passed and still we waited. Jared slid his arms from his jacket and hung it on my shoulders. I hadn't even noticed the cold, but once the added heat was around me, I shivered.

"Patience," Jared said. His words could have been directed at me or at Bex. I wasn't sure.

After another hour, the columns of glass were ignited by the rising sun. Rays of white pierced through, illuminating the elegantly floating dust motes in its path. Glowing yellow squares infringed upon the shadows, and soon the entire floor glowed and warmed with the glorious grace of morning light.

"Nina," a voice called from across the room. Eli walked toward us, his eyes focused only on me. He was dressed in the same attire he wore the last time we met: the crisp white shirt, the jeans, and sandals. His hair was spiky and blond. He made a clicking noise with his tongue. "You aren't getting enough rest."

"But you knew that," I smiled sleepily.

One corner of his mouth turned up, but it wasn't quite a smile. "I'm sorry, cupcake. I haven't been much help."

"Can you help us now?" Jared asked.

"We would love to, Jared. We've been instructed not to," Eli said. Compassion was in his eyes but not apology.

"But why?" Bex asked, genuinely confused.

Jared watched Eli for a moment and then frowned. "They won't intervene unless The Balance is disturbed."

Eli reached his hand to me, and I took it. He pulled me into him gently. He towered over me, and I felt like a child wrapped in his arms. Emotion overwhelmed me, and I let myself tremble and weep unreservedly in the quiet sanctuary of his embrace. Jared's hand touched my shoulder; Bex's smaller hand touched my back. A sob that had been hiding somewhere deep within me found its way to the surface.

It felt good to cry. I had just seen my father for the first time since his death. With the pressure and horror of being the center of a story Hell took very seriously and now hearing that Heaven was unwilling to help, hope was dwindling. Crying was a sweet release, and in Eli's arms, it was natural, much like a tearful moment in my father's lap when I was hurt or frightened.

Eli released me and tenderly grasped a lock of my hair. "You have grieved for your former life, Nina Grey. It is time to rise up as the woman you are: strong, determined," he smiled, "and stubborn." He walked away from us, looking at the sky through the windows. "Humans see life as so precious when it's fleeting. Add in the defensive instincts of a mother, and you're nearly unstoppable, even in your fragile shell. It's more inspiring each time I see it."

"You know she's not pregnant," Jared said.

"Yet," Eli said, turning with a knowing smile. "Let us visit again when the time is right, at the time when you have no more questions to ask but one."

"What question is that?" I asked, but he was gone. "Damn it."

"We need to get Nina back," Jared said.

"Back to where, Jared? Did you forget your house is toast?" Bex said.

I shook my head, still in disbelief. Jared enveloped me in his arms, warmer and even more inviting than Eli's.

"You have three choices, Nina: Cynthia's, Lillian's, or Kim's."

"Kim's?" I sneered. "Even if I did still consider her my friend, I have no desire to live in the dorms again."

Jared grimaced. "She's the safest, option, Nina, and, yes, she's still your friend."

"Why is she the safest?" I asked.

Bex grinned. "They don't mess with her. She's like bug spray."

I smiled. "She would hate that if she heard you."

Bex pulled a gun from the back of his jeans and scratched his head with the barrel. "Okay. Where to, then?"

"I still have things at Cynthia's. We'll go there," I said, taking in a deep breath. Luckily, Cynthia was consistently busy with charities, so she would be out and about more often than not.

"*You'll* go there," Jared said.

My mouth fell open. "I'm not going anywhere without you. You told me once you couldn't go back to that again. What happened to that?"

"It's not my first choice, I assure you," he said, an uncomfortable grin twisting his mouth.

"It's my house, Jared. You're coming," I said. I looked at Bex, then. "And there's a room for you too."

"I have a room. Thanks," Bex said.

"Nina," Jared began.

I held up my hand. "If you make me go to that house alone, I will spend all of my time in Jack's office. I'll move my bed in there. I swear to God."

Jared had once told me that Jack's office was the only room in my parents' home that wasn't wired with microphones or cameras. Jared could still hear me, of course, but having to guess what I was doing drove him crazy.

Jared smiled. "Don't swear at Him. We need Him on our side."

I frowned. "You know what I mean."

He sighed. "Cynthia's it is, then."

9. KILLING THE MESSENGER

Nothing goes as planned. People say good-bye, buildings burn, and the impossibility of moving back in with Cynthia Grey after the age of eighteen can actually happen.

As I stood before the colossal home my father left to me after his death, I felt a bit nauseated at the prospect of walking its halls everyday again. Some of my best and worst memories happened within those walls: Jack chasing me down the halls, cooking my first meal, my father dying before my eyes, and everything I thought he was slipping away as I read a hidden file on the second floor.

But it was still home.

The gravel crunched beneath my feet as Jared walked me up the steps to the front door. The sun had hidden behind the thick clouds that were quickly moving in, and the air smelled like a mixture of winter and spring.

I took a deep breath and let it out as the wind blew the blond strands of my hair against my cheek. "I'm going to get unpacked and organized. I have to go into Titan before they think I've defected."

Jared tossed the keys to Bex. "Update Mom and Claire. I need you back here at six thirty."

Bex nodded once. "You got it."

The smell of freshly brewed coffee filled the air as we walked in, and Cynthia's heels signaled her approach. She stopped suddenly in the foyer.

"Oh! You startled me. Really, Nina, you could at least call if you're going to visit so early."

"We're not visiting. We're moving in," I said, making my way up the stairs.

Cynthia rushed to the first step, looking up at us. "What on earth are you talking about?"

Jared turned to face her. "Donovan set explosives in the loft. Everything except what's in our bags is gone."

Cynthia paused for a moment, a common tactic of hers to calm her voice before she spoke when she was angry or taken off-guard. "Well, I'm glad Nina's safe. How long will you be staying?"

"Indefinitely," I said.

I had reached the top before she spoke again.

"You're filthy," she snapped, her heels clicking to the kitchen.

I smiled. She was always snippy when she didn't want to show emotion—the soft sort.

Trying to find a professional ensemble from my high school wardrobe was nothing short of frustrating. It was then that it hit me that all of my belongings were gone: everything Jared and I had purchased together, the bed we shared, the downstairs tub. Different items in the loft flickered through my mind. It was strange how each of them, however insignificant they used to seem, were attached to a memory.

Tears pooled in my eyes and escaped down my cheek. I wiped them away and groaned. "I have nothing to wear! What was I thinking buying this crap?" I yelled. "Not a single pair of pumps matches anything in my closet!"

Jared sat on the end of bed, letting me express my anger and frustration with an understanding expression. After the rage-fueled tirade to find the right pair of shoes, I rode with Jared to Titan Mercantile.

We didn't speak for most of the trip. Jared kept his eyes on the road, no doubt formulating a plan for the next step in finding the book. I was too tired to initiate conversation, or to try to find out piece by piece what plan of action he was considering.

"See you soon," Jared smiled.

I kissed his cheek then stepped out onto the curb, looking back once more before pushing through the entrance doors.

Beth waited for me in my office, already organizing my call list in order of importance.

"And don't forget the conference with the Japanese firm at nine," she said, her head down.

"I've told you a million times, Beth. Yawatahama. It's not that hard if you practice."

Beth raised her hands in frustration and then dropped them, letting the papers in her hands slap her thighs. "I sound ridiculous," she said. "Sasha laughs at me every time I try."

"Oh, to hell with Sasha. Ask her to say something German. She sounds like a bloated mule."

Beth laughed out loud, surprised at my mood. "You're not sleeping again, are you?"

There were two quick knocks, and then Grant opened my office door wide, keeping his hand on the knob. "The prodigal daughter returns! How was your trip?"

"Great, Grant. I'm busy, what do you need?" I said, putting the phone to my ear.

His expression screwed, his nose wrinkling in disgust. "The Bainbridge group will be here in twenty minutes, Nina. Why didn't you just wear pajamas?"

From collarbone to scalp, the burn of infuriation ignited my face in what I was sure was a beautiful shade of tomato red. My outstretched arm, with a rigid, pointed finger at the end, silently warned Grant to leave.

"Back away slowly, Mr. Bristol. No sudden movements," Beth said.

Grant nodded, stepping backward until he was out of sight.

Beth placed a small bag on my desk. "Foundation, blush, mascara, and gloss. Get it on. I'll meet you downstairs in fifteen."

She closed the door softly behind her, and I took a deep breath. *Just get through the day.*

My cell phone rang once. "Not now, Jared," I said aloud, knowing he could hear. The second ring cut short. "Thank you," I whispered. I opened the compact from Beth's bag and looked at myself in the mirror. "Holy Banshee, Nina! Get yourself together!" I said to myself.

Sasha stood next to the coffeemaker in the meeting room. "Miss Grey," she said, handing me a fresh, steaming mug.

"Thanks," I said, frowning with confusion at her bi-polar disposition. Wondering what she was up to was not on my agenda for the morning, not to mention I didn't have the time or patience for it. That wouldn't stop me from finding out, however.

The meeting went smoothly, and then I returned to my office, opening the door long enough for Beth to follow me through. I turned to see Grant and Sasha just behind her, but I shut the door. "Not now," I said flatly.

"Okay, Nina. Totally unprofessional," Sasha said, half laughing half surprised.

Beth watched the door for a moment in shock and then turned to me. "What the heck's going on with you?" she asked. "And what's that smell? Have you been camping?" she said, sniffing once.

I puffed, blowing my bangs from my face. "No. The loft is gone. Burned to the ground."

"What?" Beth yelped.

"Keep it down. I don't need a bunch of sympathetic well-wishers in and out of my office all day. Do me a favor?"

"Sure, honey, anything."

I pulled a black credit card from my purse and handed it to her. "Go shopping for me. I need work clothes mainly and undergarments and a new briefcase. Makeup. You know what I use. And," I looked down, "I want a pair of those," I said, nodding to her pink satin pumps. Even in my foul mood, I couldn't stop admiring the black lace collar and bow at the toe.

Beth smiled. "Yes, ma'am. You need a place to stay?"

"I'm back at home."

"Yikes," Beth said, her mouth pulling to one side.

"Tell me about it. And, Beth? If you can find anything to get the smoke out of my hair, get it. I don't care how much it costs."

"Lemon juice," she said. "Then wash it out with shampoo. That's what I do after I visit my uncle."

I nodded. "Thanks."

Beth shut the door, and then I heard a scuffle.

"I said *no*!" Beth said, stumbling back against the door.

Sasha pushed her way through and then smiled, smoothing her blazer and hair. "Nina. I need to talk to you."

Beth stared at Sasha as if she'd gone insane.

"Nina," Sasha said with a smile, breathing hard from her scuffle with Beth. "It will just take a minute."

"It's okay, Beth," I said, motioning for Sasha to sit.

Beth narrowed her eyes. "Maybe for you, but if I wasn't at work I would have kicked her bony little ass," she said through her teeth, slamming the door.

"Well," Sasha said, settling in the seat, "so much for southerners having manners.

"Keep in mind Beth holds grudges," I said, thumbing through papers on my desk.

"What do you mean? She's *Southern*." She said the word with disdain. I could see in her eyes that at least five generations of Eastern audacity had blinded her to how tacky she sounded.

I looked up. "Yes, well, they're polite. That doesn't mean you can't make an enemy out of them."

"Oh," Sasha said, looking back to the door nervously. "I, er, Grant wanted me to ask you about the Christmas party."

I raised an eyebrow. "I have faxes coming out of my ears, and you're shoving your way into my office to talk about finger foods? Don't waste my time."

"No, no." she fidgeted. "I wanted your permission to chair it this year. I was hoping we could make it into more of a ball."

"A ball," I deadpanned.

Sasha smiled widely. "Yes."

I waved her away. "Check with Jessica on the second floor about the budget. Stay within parameters, and personally, Sasha, I couldn't care less."

Sasha's strained smile barely lasted until she reached the hall.

The rest of the day passed without event, or maybe it was because no one dared to approach me with anything less urgent than my office being on fire. The consequential spunk the insufficient sleep had graced me with was working. I hadn't enjoyed Titan that much since I moved into Jack's office.

By the time five o'clock rolled around, I trudged to the elevator and welcomed Jared's arm when he offered it. The sluggish, heavy feeling over my body was familiar. I was reverting back to my former zombie days.

"No, you're getting sleep tonight. Bex will be there at seven."

I wondered if I'd said anything aloud, but didn't have enough energy to ask. Just sitting in the passenger seat, watching trees and pedestrians move past my window, was exhausting. If I'd been coherent, I would have felt ridiculous for the permanently shocked expression on my face as I tried to keep both upper lids away from the lowers by pushing my eyebrows as high as they would go.

Jared wrapped his arm around my waist, leading me into the house. When the old, heavy door closed behind us, Jared stopped.

"Nina," Cynthia called, appearing from the hallway. "You have a guest waiting for you in the great room."

I puffed.

"Let me take your things, love," Agatha said, pulling my makeshift briefcase from my hand.

"Thank you," I mumbled. I walked down the main hall into the great room, blinking to focus once I recognized that it was Kim sitting alone on our large green sofa. She sat on the edge of her seat, her hands balled tightly together atop her knees. I sat across from her in my mother's favorite Italian occasional chair.

It was then that I noticed Jared hadn't joined us but had gone upstairs to prepare for a night away.

"Kim," I said, blinking slowly.

"Looks like you need a nap," she said.

"Nightmares."

Kim looked to the floor, nodding. "Nigh, you don't get to hate me. I would understand if the demonic voodoo stuff gave you the heebie-jeebies, but you're just mad because you think I lied to you."

The rankling produced a second wind. "You did lie to me. I don't even know you."

Her head popped up. "And I know you? Jared's half-angel, and you're not exactly your run-of-the-mill Brown co-ed yourself, Miss Merovingian. Have they told you what that means?"

"They told me," I grumbled.

"So I just came to tell you that we're still friends. And you can like it and let me piss you off as I used to without worrying if you're really pissed. Got it?"

"Whatever, I'm pooped," I said, pushing myself from the chair.

"Really? We're good?" she asked.

I turned and, seeing her expectant eyes, I smiled. "Yeah, Kim, we're good."

Kim stood and then held out both of her arms, jutting her lip out. "Hugs?"

"Quit it."

She let her hands fall to her thighs with a slap. "Well, thought I'd try."

I walked her to the door, and she leaned close to my ear. "I'm going with Jared tonight. I'll try not to make out with him while we're hunting down your book."

"You're a good friend," I said.

"Kiss noise," Kim said, jogging down the drive to her Sentra. How had I missed that horrid thing? I was more tired than I thought.

Jared met me at the bottom of the staircase. He held my arm for a few steps and then gave up, lifting me in his arms and carrying me up the stairs.

"Shower," I said.

Jared lowered me to the overstuffed mattress in my room. "In the morning. Bex is here. Sleep."

I'm not sure when I fell asleep or how long Jared stayed, because I was unconscious the moment my head hit the pillow. The nightmares stayed away, even after my previous nightmare of Shax being in that very room. I was so tired and slept so hard that I didn't dream at all.

~*~

I peeled my eyes open to see Bex standing at the end of the bed.

"Just so you know, that's creepy," I said, rubbing the sleep from my eyes.

"Not as scary as your hair." He frowned.

"Wow, you're grumpy this morning."

"Cynthia won't let me near the kitchen."

After three knocks on the door, Cynthia backed into my room, a tray in her hands. "Good morning. I thought I would bring you breakfast."

"Does Agatha have the day off?" I asked.

"No, she's downstairs. Why?" Cynthia asked.

I watched my mother for a moment in disbelief and then shook my head. "Nothing. Thank you."

Cynthia left as quickly as she came in. "Mind the coffee, dear. It's hot," she called back as her heels clicked down the hall.

Bex's eyebrows were nearly touching as his frown deepened. He had never been to my parents' home, to my knowledge, and he wasn't enjoying it at all.

"She warms up," I said.

"That's not what I've heard," he grumbled.

"I'm going to hop in the shower. Has Jared called?"

"No," he said, picking up the remote control. He switched on the television. "But he's on his way."

I thought about that for a moment and decided I already knew the answer. They could sense each other, and Bex was the most in tune out of the three hybrid siblings.

My morning routine finished without event, including Jared's return home. "I thought you said he was coming," I said, tightening my robe.

"He is," Bex said, his eyes stationary on the screen.

"Nina, love?" Agatha called from the hall.

"Yes?" I said, opening the door. Agatha was holding several bags, and Beth stood behind her, her arms full of bags as well.

"You said you lost everything," Beth said, brushing past me to the closet. She disappeared into my walk in, hanging the plastic-covered clothing on the nearly-empty iron rods.

I opened the door, watching her pull shoes boxes from one of the large sacks. Once she was finished, she looked at her watch. "Crap! I gotta go."

"Beth."

"Yes?" she said, whipping around.

"Thank you."

She smiled. "Don't thank me. That was so fun. I think I went a little overboard."

She waved and then rushed back the way she came, her legs moving a thousand miles per hour. I shut the closet door behind me and pulled the first outfit I touched off its hanger. When I walked out into the bedroom, I froze in my tracks.

Jared stood in the center of my room, covered in dirt and blood, and his was face scraped and blotchy.

"Oh my . . . Oh my God!" I yelled, rushing over to him. "What happened?"

Kim walked in behind Jared, untouched. "I told him not to go without me, but he's faster than I am."

I touched Jared's face. "What did you do?"

He grimaced. "The book was in my hand. I had it."

"Where were you?" I said, helping him pull off his jacket. He was stiff and cringed with pain.

Kim's usually stoic expression twisted as she watched me pull his t-shirt up and over his head. "Warwick," she said. "We got the book, but Donovan was there."

Six raw, bloody, and swollen bullet holes dotted different areas of Jared's torso, accompanied by a large gash along his shoulder blade.

"Jared!" I screamed.

Bex left without a word.

"Where are you going?" I called after him.

"He's going to find something to pull the fragments out."

I helped him to the bed and then took a deep breath. It didn't help. Tears welled up in my eyes. "You're going to be okay, right?"

Jared managed a smile. "Yes. I'll be good as new this time tomorrow."

Bex returned with a towel full of different items. "Isaac was too much for you, huh?"

"Isaac," Jared scoffed, rolling his eyes. Donovan and his Glock. And I plowed through approximately eighty demons before I got to them."

"If you had waited for me to catch up with you, you wouldn't have had to waste your time with them," Kim snapped. She looked to me. "The second he learned the location of the book, he took off. I was twenty minutes behind him."

I glared at Jared. "That's not like you to be so impulsive and reckless. What were you thinking?"

Jared sighed. "That I wanted this to end."

Plink. Jared cringed, and then Bex dropped bullet remnants into a bowl.

"I can't watch," I said, covering my eyes.

"You can't go anywhere until we're finished here. Then I'll take you to work," Bex said, pulling out another bullet.

"Watch the blood. Don't get any on her sheets," Jared said, cringing again.

"I'll get new sheets," I moaned. I took Jared's hand in both of mine.

"It's okay," he said. "We'll try again."

"And hopefully not be so stupid about it this time," Kim said from the door way.

"Do you think I care about that? I don't want you near that book ever again!" I said, my voice higher with each word.

"Okay. Okay," Jared said. "Don't get upset."

"Why would I be upset? My boyfriend comes home looking as if he just escaped from a horror movie." I took one of the wet cloths Bex had brought upstairs and used it to wipe a deep cut above his eye. "Tell me everything."

"The details aren't important," Kim said.

"The bottom line is I failed," Jared said, his teeth clinched.

Kim shrugged. "We know who's guarding it, what they're capable of, and every angle of their defense, Jared. I wouldn't call that failure."

"So what's Isaac like?" Bex said, dropping more fragments into the plate.

"He's highly trained," Jared answered.

"And psychotic," Kim said. "You should have seen them. It was like a scene from Rambo. Neither of them would quit, and they're both hybrids, so it was like a never-ending fight scene. One punch here, knife wound there, elbow, face punch, and then one of them goes flying across the room. Lather. Rinse. Repeat."

"That's enough," Jared said.

My stomach wrenched at her words. "Please don't go back. Not until Bex or Claire can go with you."

Jared looked away. "It's not that I couldn't handle it on my own, Nina."

"That's not what I meant," I whispered.

He frowned, apology in his eyes. "I know. I'm sorry," he said with a sigh. "Kim's right. We did learn a lot last night. The problem is Claire's not here and Bex has to stay with you."

"What about someone else? Another hybrid?" I asked.

Bex laughed once. "If it comes down to it, we'll have to take Donovan down. No one is going to help us down another hybrid without good reason."

I looked down at Jared's bloodied hands and then back to his stormy blue-gray eyes. "And saving me isn't good enough for them."

Jared nodded. "We have to persuade them that something big is coming, and to do that, we need the book."

Kim knocked on the door jamb. "Now that's irony. Come on, Nigh. I'll take you to work."

"Is that okay?" I asked Jared.

"I'd rather you wait," he said.

"Don't be ridiculous," Kim said. She pulled up her shirt, revealing a handgun stuffed halfway into her jeans. "I'm packin', demons run when they see me coming, and as Donovan learned last night, my right hook is wicked accurate."

The glance Jared and I traded turned into involuntary smiles.

"Bex will be right behind you," Jared said.

I kissed his cheek. "Maybe I should stay home today."

"This is nothing. You should see the other guys," Jared said with a wink. "Go on."

Kim lifted my briefcase off the floor and held it out. I rushed to the bathroom, washed the blood from my hands, and then followed her down the stairs.

"Let's take my car," I said.

Kim shrugged. "Whatever."

As promised, the ride to work was safe and uneventful. Bex pulled into the parking lot on his new barely-street-legal Ducati Streetfighter just as I stepped out of the car. The bike was a humming soprano, pushed to its limit until Bex slid in to park.

Kim stayed behind as I rushed into Titan, thankful that being the CEO sort-of-in-training granted me a spot on the elevator.

"Good morning," I said to my co-workers as the doors slid closed.

Riding in close proximity to so many proved not so lucky after all. The thought of everyone breathing in such a confined space made me a bit claustrophobic.

When the elevator doors opened, I pushed my way out, taking a deep breath when my heels hit the carpet. "Oh, thank God."

Grant's door was open, his ankles were crossed on top of his desk, and he was lazily leaning back in his chair. My momentary relief from the elevator was short-lived, and my face screwed in disgust.

I made a bee-line for my office, hoping Grant would be too comfortable to get out of his chair.

"Hey, peanut," Grant said just as I sat down.

"Nina," Beth said, walking in with her head down. She was biting on the end of her pencil, concentrating on a notebook planner. "The meeting with Yawa . . . Yaw . . . the Japanese is on Thursday, but the Wellingtons will be in town and hoped to squeeze in some time."

"Make time. I'd love to steal them away from Donaldson," I said, tapping a pen against my desk.

"Sounds as though it's a better day," Grant said, nodding. He bowed out without another word.

"Now it is," I said, noting Beth's smile as she stifled a giggle.

"So," she said, forcing her smile to fade. "Chad's been asking. Have you heard from Ryan lately? Or at all?"

I no longer had to fight a smile; my face immediately fell. "No, nothing."

Beth nodded. "I hope he's okay."

"If he weren't, we would find out, right?" I said to reassure her.

She took a deep breath and nodded. "Right. I've gotta make some copies. You want coffee?"

"No, thanks."

Once Beth was off doing other things, Grant returned.

"I actually had a point to coming in here. I need to talk to you about Beth."

"Oh?"

Grant flashed his million-dollar smile, and I had to physically restrain myself from recoiling.

"Peanut, I realize she's your friend, but it's not exactly cost-efficient to keep her on-board during the school year."

"Are you suggesting I fire her?" I said, raising an eyebrow.

Grant sighed. "You're not looking at this objectively. You're in the office, yes, but technically you're still an intern until you graduate. Why would I pay someone to assist an intern?"

"Because I told you to."

After a short pause, Grant smiled, wider than before. "You're going to do just fine here."

"Thank you, Grant. That will be all."

He shook his head, chuckling to himself as he left the way he came.

~*~

I was buried under a few stacks of documents when Beth brought me back to reality with her chirpy voice. "Time to go home, Nigh."

"Oh." I looked at my watch and then smiled. "Home."

I haphazardly stuffed a few files into my briefcase before rushing down the hall and then pressed the button. As soon as the doors opened, I hopped inside, fidgeting the entire trip to the first floor. The doors slid open, revealing the brilliant late-afternoon sun gleaming through the lobby glass. Jared was waiting by the Escalade, a contrived smile on his face.

"What is it?" I asked, after greeting him with a quick kiss. My excitement to see him was infiltrated by a sense of dread. The two didn't settle well, and I instantly felt nauseated.

He raised a pair of my sneakers. "I thought we could check out what's left of the loft. See if anything's left."

I could only nod, dreading the sight of our home reduced to a heap of ash.

"Put these on," he said. "It'll be hard enough sifting through everything, let alone in heels."

I took the shoes in my hand and then sat on the curb. Jared handed me a pair of socks, and I tugged those on followed by the sneakers. He watched me in silence, a residual, forced grin on his face. He wasn't looking forward to the aftermath any more than I.

The drive seemed to take an eternity, yet it still wasn't long enough for me to prepare. When Jared pulled to the curb, I stumbled from the Escalade, each side of my hair bunched in my fists. "Oh my God," I whispered.

Jared milled about the charred remnants, bending down once in a while to inspect something not quite destroyed.

"There are a few boxes in the back," Jared said. "Would you grab one?"

I took wide steps and hopped until I was clear of the debris then went to the Escalade and opened the hatch. I brought back a large cardboard box. There were two more, but it was overly optimistic to bother with them; the few belongings that were still intact couldn't fill the first box. Silverware, a few brittle-edged pictures, the monitor of my laptop, and a set of throwing knives were among the salvaged. Yellow tape surrounded most of the carnage, highlighting the place that was once our home.

My hands turned black as I dug carefully through the black mess under our feet.

"What are you looking so ambitiously for?" Jared asked.

"I was hoping we'd find at least pieces of your journal, but I haven't even seen the binding. Have you come across it?"

He smiled. "I keep it in the Escalade. It's safe and sound."

"Good," I said, overwhelmed at the mountain of rubble.

"We should go. The fire marshal has already interviewed me twice. If anyone sees us poking around, it's going to attract attention."

"I guess." I stood up from my squatted position, dropping a charred piece of the frame that contained the last picture of my father.

"I'm sorry about that," Jared said. "I should have tried to get that out too."

"It's not your fault. They did this to get a reaction, to see if we'd retaliate or if it would cause dissension between us. The last thing I'm going to do is give them what they want. It's just stuff."

Jared walked over to me, tenderly wiping my face. "You're covered in soot. Let's go home."

"That's not home, Jared. This was home and it's gone." I was surprised at the tears that welled up in my eyes. Crying hadn't crossed my mind until that very moment.

"Maybe we should start looking for a place?" he smiled.

"So they can torch it too? No, thank you."

Jared's expression was pained. "It won't happen again."

"You don't know that," I said, tugging on his hand, leading him to the Escalade. "We have no idea what they'll do next."

10. NEW

Summer wound down, and Beth and I undertook the process of delegation. Our schedule at Brown would make it impossible to maintain the hours we'd been keeping at Titan.

Jared made frequent calls to Claire to check on Ryan's progress, which steadily improved, at times faster than Claire would have liked. To our surprise, Ryan wasn't fighting the decision to decommission him. He was focused on getting well and getting back to the States—something none of us had anticipated.

As promised, Jared didn't try another ambush on Shax or Donovan and Isaac. Instead, he became obsessed with constructing a fail-safe plan, one that included a Plan B and additional help. He refused to let the book get away from him a second time.

Bex had grown two more inches, which was a good thing. His inflated ego needed all the room he could give it.

Jared and I spent my last day of summer break at our oak tree. We stretched out across a blanket that Jared had spread over the grass just inside the shade of the tree. I kept my eyes closed, quiet and lazy, listening to the bugs buzzing and the grass dancing in the wind.

"You're officially a college junior tomorrow," he said with a proud smile, brushing the petals of a wildflower down the line of my jaw.

"I am," I said. "Another summer gone. Just one more left before I graduate."

Jared squeezed my hand, turning his attention to the carving above us. "Hmmm. Where do you see yourself this time next year?"

I breathed out a laugh. "I have no idea. Why don't we make this an annual event? We spend the day at our oak tree the last day of summer break next year too." Jared grimaced, and my expression mimicked his. "What?"

He worked to smooth out the deepening line between his brows. "Nothing."

"Jared," I warned. I became impatient very quickly when he kept things from me, and he seemed to be taking that risk more frequently.

He sighed. "I was hoping your answer would be different; that's all."

"Different how?" I asked.

"I was hoping you would say you saw yourself *married* this time next year," he said quietly.

"Oh," I said, sheepishly.

"I'm trying very hard to be patient about this," he said, his voice suddenly strained. "I don't understand why you're putting it off." He chuckled nervously. "I thought we'd be married by now." His eyes were still bright, but I could hear the edge of worry in his voice.

"We've discussed this, Jared, a lot. I don't have time to plan a wedding right now. It's not that I'm putting it off. I've just got a lot on my plate is all," I said, twisting my ring around my finger.

Jared rested his hand on mine. "I know you do. But it doesn't have to be an elaborate event. We're engaged. We're living together. Is there a problem I should be aware of?"

"Of course not." I smiled. "I just need a little more time."

Jared's contrived smile didn't hide the heavy disappointment in his eyes, but I pretended not to notice. I wanted to marry him more than anything, but I wanted to do it right. I certainly didn't want to feel rushed to get home from our honeymoon because of chapters to study, papers to write, or learning how to run another department of Jack's company.

"A year is a reasonable engagement." He clenched his teeth and frowned. "Two years is . . ." He was clearly vexed by the idea of waiting another year.

I touched him on the arm. "We won't have a two-year engagement, Jared."

"So you're going to settle on a date sometime this year?" he asked, hopeful. The look in his eyes made it impossible to say anything but yes.

"I will. I just have to find time to plan a wedding between twenty hours of school and Titan." I felt my expression compress as I thought about the ramifications of my statement.

Jared looked ahead, his eyes tightening with focus. "I will find time. I will *create* time if I have to."

"Well, you do have Divine connections. I'm sure you could make that happen," I teased. I peered up at the giant tree, squinting from the sunshine poking through the leaves. The branches swayed with the breeze, and I smiled. "I love it here."

"Good. I do too."

"It's so amazing that Gabe brought Lillian to this exact spot." My eyes lingered on the rudimentary heart and initials of Jared's parents and then followed the elegant details of the vines and leaves inside the heart with our initials inside. I looked back to Jared's glowing blue-gray eyes. "Is there anything you can't do?"

"Just get my fiancée to actually marry me," he said, winking.

I pressed my lips together into a tight line. "I said I'd set a date."

"I'll believe it when I see it." Jared said, raising an eyebrow.

"Is that a challenge?"

"Whatever works." Jared grinned.

"I promise. I'll set a date."

"Within the next ten years?" he asked playfully.

"I'll set a date for this year," I said, raising my chin.

"This year. Really?"

"Did you think I was kidding when I said yes?"

"No. I just didn't realize when you said yes that you meant *someday.*" His tone was lighthearted, but I felt a twinge of guilt in my chest. Jared immediately reacted. "I'm kidding, sweetheart," he said, tucking my hair behind my ear. Instead of the ends of my hair wrapping around the bottom of my ear as it used to, it brushed against my shoulder.

I looked down, picking at my fingernails. "I know, but it's true. You didn't expect a long engagement."

"Well, I assumed maybe a year with everything happening so fast. But when the year came and went and you never so much as mentioned it . . ."

"Oh. You think it's not important to me," I said, my face feeling hot.

"I didn't say that," he quickly backpedaled.

I looked up at him under my lashes. "But that's what you're thinking."

"Well," he hesitated, "you do tend to insinuate that there are other things you'd rather focus on. I understand, but I can't help but be a little disappointed. It was my idea after all." He grinned, kissing my forehead.

I slowly crawled into his lap. "I love you, Jared Ryel. There is nothing I want more than to be your wife. I promise to get right to work on that date, okay?"

Jared beamed. "*Thank* you." His lips traveled to mine but quickly pulled away. "You'd better keep this to yourself. I think Mom has finally accepted that no amount of encouragement on her part is going to produce a wedding. It's probably best to let her think you have other things on your mind."

"Good plan," I said, pushing him back against the blanket.

He smiled. "Speaking of Lillian, she invited us to dinner. Apparently, she has a surprise."

"A surprise . . . Do you know what it is?"

Jared shook his head. "Not a clue."

I looked at my watch. "We'd better get going if we're going to wash up and make dinner."

Jared stood up and brought me with him. We rolled the blanket, and I fastened it to the back of Jared's motorcycle. Then we made a quick stop at the loft, trading the bike for the Escalade.

After a quick stop at Cynthia's, Jared drove us to his mother's. We had been to Lillian's more than enough times for me to get past the night of the invasion, but no matter how many times we made a visit, an overwhelming sick feeling still came over me as we pulled into the drive.

"No need to be nervous," Jared said.

"I'm not. I'm starting to wonder if it's post-traumatic stress," I said with a half-smile.

Jared didn't share my humor over the subject. "It's a possibility," he said as he opened the passenger door.

We walked to the house, and Jared stopped abruptly.

"What?" I asked, scanning his face.

He was working far too hard to mask an emotion. "Nothing. Everything is fine."

"Jared," I said as we walked. "Something's wrong."

"No. No, everything's fine."

The closer we got to the door, the harder my heart throbbed against my chest. Jared reached out with one finger to press the doorbell.

The door swung open and I gasped. "I don't believe it."

"Well, that's a hell of a reception. I missed you too."

"Claire!" I squealed, wrapping my arms around her neck.

She didn't hug me back but stood with her hands on her hips. "You confuse me."

"I'm sorry!" I said, breathlessly. "I just . . . I wasn't expecting you."

Lillian walked to Claire's side, casually crossing her arms. "Surprise," she said with her warm, sweet smile.

"Wait," I said, my eyes darting to everyone. "Does this mean that Ryan is . . . ?"

Claire nodded. "He's at the Providence VA Hospital to finish his rehabilitation."

My hands flew up to my mouth, and then I hugged her again. "I'm so glad you're home," I whispered into her ear.

"Me too." Claire smiled.

We sat at the table for dinner. The symphony of our laughter filled every inch of the house. I cleared the dessert dishes and listened to them talk and giggle. I waited in the kitchen, smiling to myself as I soaked in the sound of love Bex, Claire, Lillian, and Jared exchanged, even in their teasing.

"Nina?" Jared called.

"Coming," I said, starting the dishwasher.

"I'm sure Nina wants to hear more about her friend," Lillian said.

Jared's expression changed so slightly that I was sure no one at the table noticed but me. The skin around his eyes tightened as the corners of his mouth turned up—something he always did when he tried too hard to cover how he was feeling. I took his hand in mine and squeezed. He seemed to relax an infinitesimal amount, and I shook my head.

"Tonight is about Claire," I said.

Claire touched the napkin to her mouth and rolled her eyes. "He's a machine. He's been working like crazy trying to get well. His psych analysis wasn't exactly . . . He told them about me."

"He saw you?" Jared said.

An awkward pause sent tension into the air. "He thinks he did," Claire said. "My face was covered with the hijab, so he only remembers my eyes, but they're questioning how a woman with the small frame he described could have carried him out."

Bex chuckled. "What a pinhead. Did he really think they would believe him?"

Claire stared at the table. "He told them I was American. He told Colonel Brand he thinks he knows who it was."

"Not good," Jared said.

Claire looked up. "But he only told the Colonel, no one else. After they gave him the results of his psych eval, he insisted he be placed in Providence."

"Way to go, Claire. You blew your cover." Bex smiled.

Jared leaned his elbows on the table. "This is serious. You need to stay out of sight, Claire. Lay low."

"I know," Claire grumbled, her eyes returning to one spot on the tablecloth. "I could say the same thing to you, you know. No one's torching my house."

"What?" Lillian said, her eyes darting to Jared.

He glared at Claire for a moment and then looked to Lillian. "There was a small fire. Everyone is fine."

"A fire?" Bex said. "They set explosives at the loft. Everything's gone."

"Who's *they*?" Lillian asked. She was concerned, but not in the way a typical mother might be. She didn't seem overly worried about Jared's well-being. It was clear she was years ahead of me as far as experience with hybrids. She knew exactly what her children were capable of, and I wondered if I would ever have that same peace of mind.

"Donovan," Jared said.

"Interesting," Lillian said, thoughtfully. "How do you plan to resolve that, son?"

"We're going to need help that won't come," Jared replied, clearly frustrated with his own words.

Claire's eyes narrowed. "You talked to Samuel?" Jared nodded and she continued, "Eli?" When Jared nodded again, she shook her head in disgust. "It's that bad?"

"Eli talked about a balance," I said. "They won't get involved."

"You know," Claire said, leaning forward in her seat, "if it gets to that point, we could force them."

"That better be one frightening, desperate point," Bex said. "That would mean war."

Lillian held up her hand. "That would be a last resort." She stood, making her way to me. "Nina, what I'm about to ask you will be very difficult, but I need the truth."

"Okay," I stuttered, worried what she was going to ask.

Lillian lowered her chin. "What did Gabe say to you on the plane?"

Jared frowned. "What are you talking about? He didn't come to her on the plane."

I bit my lip. "Actually . . ."

"Why didn't you tell me?" he said, noticeably angry. Before I could answer, he began again, "Don't you know that everything is important now?"

"Jared," I said, embarrassed, "he said to go home. He said not to see Claire. I knew you wouldn't leave her there alone until you knew she was all right."

Jared looked to Claire and then to Lillian. "Does he talk to you?"

His mother smiled. "At night. Only if it's important. She knows about Kim now?"

"Yes," Jared answered.

Lillian's mouth pulled to the side, disappointed. "That was a mistake. Your main focus should be the book. It's vitally important that you have it in hand."

"Kim and I made a deal," Jared explained. "She'll help us obtain the book if we help her return it to Jerusalem under the Sepulchre where her ancestor found it. She wants to free her family of it."

Lillian's eyes flitted about as she thought. "If she's helping you, why would your father try to keep Nina away from her?"

"Away from Kim?" I asked. "She's harmless."

"Is she?" Claire snipped.

"Dad is wrong this time. We need her," Jared said, clearly uncomfortable. Gabe was the foundation of their family, a fallen angel from Heaven, pure-blooded. The thought of him making a mistake was a hard pill to swallow, and even Jared wasn't convinced of his own words.

Everyone at the table sat silently, processing the situation. Finally, Bex spoke. "We're all here. Let's go get it."

"We need a plan," Jared said. "And we can't leave Nina unprotected."

"So Bex watches Ryan and Nina, and you and I go," Claire said.

Jared rubbed the back of his neck. "I've already tried. I'm telling you we need a plan."

"You went there and didn't leave with the book?" Claire said, raising an eyebrow.

"He had it in his hands," Bex said, chuckling. Jared shot Bex a sharp look, and the boy's smug expression immediately vanished. "Sorry," he said, clearing his throat.

"I was a little outnumbered," Jared explained. "By eighty or so."

"So?" Claire said, unimpressed.

Jared huffed. "We'll talk about this later."

The ride home was long, and the air in the cab of the Escalade was thick with tension. I didn't dare talk first. Jared's jaw was tight, and his knuckles were white as he gripped the steering wheel. He drove closer to Bex's typical speed, impatient with the stop lights and traffic.

Jared parked in the drive and then appeared at the passenger door. Without a word, he helped me to the ground. I wrapped my arm around his, and we walked in quiet understanding.

After a long shower, I set out clothes for fall classes the next day. Jared waited for me, sitting on the end of the bed.

"You're not staying," I said, more of a statement than a question.

He stood. "Bex will be outside. I won't be far." He tightened the belt of my robe and then encompassed me in his arms, leaning down just inches from my face. "I'll see you in the morning," he said, pressing his warm lips softly against mine.

He intended the kiss good-bye to be quick, but his lips lingered on mine. I ran my hands over the perfection of his chest and stomach and then made my way to the bottom of his shirt, reaching underneath the fabric to touch his soft feverish skin.

"You could stay," I whispered, smiling against his mouth.

"I want to," he said, his voice strained.

"Just for a little while? I won't keep you long," I began to raise his shirt, but he gently restrained me by the wrists.

"Bex is downstairs."

"Crap," I said with a grimace. My hands fell to my sides, and I blew my bangs from my face in a huff.

Jared left me alone, and I ambled to the bed. Once my head hit the pillow, I was surprised that the yearning for his warm body beside me or thoughts of Ryan or Jack or the upcoming day of tedious bombardment of syllabi and introductions never crossed my mind. Heaviness came upon me, and I gladly succumbed.

~*~

"Nina!" Beth shouted from the end of the hall. She rushed to catch up and then threw her arms around my neck. "Can you believe we're back already?" She looked around, scanning faces of passing students.

"No," I said, grinning at her endearing over-enthusiasm for everything.

I didn't bother bringing my laptop; every class would be the same. Beth filled me in on the last few details she'd taken care of at Titan, and we discussed the monstrosity that was Sasha and the fact that she would be staying on.

"How far does she think she'll go in that company, now that she's made an enemy of you?" she asked, rolling her eyes.

"You make the mistake of believing she thinks. She did take on the Christmas party. It makes me wonder what she has up her sleeve."

"Hopefully breath spray," Beth said, covering her mouth. "I can't believe I just said that." Beth giggled and I shook my head.

My attention was diverted to a group of boys that walked through the door. Josh led the group. As Ryan's best friend, he wasn't a fan of mine and made it quite clear that he'd rather not be around me. Chad admitted that Josh accused me of being the reason Ryan left. Beth came to my defense, of course, but that didn't make him wrong.

Once Josh caught a glimpse of me, his eyes became unfocused. He looked right through me before pretending to be deeply engrossed in whatever his friends were saying.

Beth glared at him as he found his seat. "He really needs to get over himself."

"He's just being the same kind of friend to Ryan that you are to me," I mumbled, fiddling with my pen.

"Guess I can't fault him for that."

I found myself fighting the urge to tell her that Ryan was not only back, but just a few minutes away. Not being able to see him when he was so close was bad enough; even though I had thought of several different scenarios where I could happen across that information, I couldn't tell Beth until Claire gave me the green light.

"Good morning," the professor said, passing out the intro packet for the class.

I sighed when Beth handed me a stack of papers, and I took my own, passing on the rest. I didn't bother thumbing through the pages like the other students, but settled into my seat, making a valid effort to pay attention. The mundane pieces of my life used to be what I was so desperate to hold on to. In the last month, it was all I could do to make an active effort to be a participant. College seemed trivial compared to the other part of my life.

After classes, I smiled at the sight of Jared's Escalade waiting in its usual spot. He had warned me that morning that I wouldn't see him at lunch. He said it was to give me time to catch up with the girls, something about "holding on to a shred of normal." I was too busy being offended to hear.

He quickly opened my door for me, and I wrapped my arms around his middle.

"Well, hello," he said, amused at my eager affection.

"Oh, like you didn't miss me too," I said, smiling up at him.

He raised one eyebrow. "Do you even have to ask?" He watched me settle into my seat and then sighed. "I thought I should tell you Claire called. Ryan should be released soon."

"Can I see him yet?" I said, a bit more enthusiastic than was appropriate.

Jared tried to hide his disappointment at my words. "He hasn't told anyone he's here. How would you explain your visit?"

The tightness around his eyes gave him away. He was still worried. Now that Ryan had been wounded and was home after such a long time away, I imagined his concern was at a new level.

"Ryan and I are different people now. Everything has changed," I said, touching Jared's cheek with my fingertips.

"As long as Ryan is in love with you, I will always have reason to worry."

I leaned in to kiss him. "How can I convince you?"

Jared pulled away from me, shifting uncomfortably.

"What is it?" I said, frowning.

"Don't get mad," he began.

I crossed my arms. "A disclaimer? This should be good."

He took a deep breath. "Until we find the book and figure out a way to keep you one-hundred-percent safe, I think the intimacy should be kept to a minimum."

"Oh, for the love of God, not this again," I said, rolling my eyes.

"It happens all the time, Nina. We can't risk it," he said, covering my hand with his.

I smirked. "You can't use your abracadabra to figure it out?" I leaned in to kiss his neck. "Haven't you heard of the rhythm method? We'll put our own spin on it."

"I would consider myself an intelligent person, but no, can't say I've heard of it."

"You just figure out when I'm ovulating, and we abstain for those few days. Voilà! Birth control. We have the hybrid edge."

Jared's nose wrinkled in disdain. "That doesn't seem like a solution to me." He leaned away from my kisses, and I crossed my arms in a pout.

"It's better than your proposal." I frowned. "Are you saying you can't do it?"

"What makes you think I can?"

My eyes narrowed. "Eli said once we were intimate your senses would change. You've never once mentioned how or even if they have."

"That discussion is better left alone," he said, maneuvering out of my embrace. He faced forward, clearly unwilling to elaborate.

"Tell me I'm wrong," I said, lifting my chin in defiance.

Jared quickly commandeered the driver's seat, shoved the gear shift into drive, and pulled into the street. "Nina, I shouldn't have to tell you this, but I will. I love you more than anything on this earth, more than anything in the universe. I love you more than life, more than my family, and I love you more than I love being with you in that way. Your safety is, and will always be, my first priority. This isn't the kind of risk I took sitting beside you on that bench the night we met or telling you what I am. Making a mistake concerning an accidental pregnancy will mean an all-out war, because that is exactly what will have to happen to keep you alive."

The smile or wink I was hoping for never came. He had always been careful to protect me from the truth without telling a lie, but the seriousness of the situation warranted a bluntness Jared usually avoided.

It took a long time for me to reply. My initial reaction was to complain, but Eli's words echoed in my mind. He had told me it was time to break away from being the victim. He was very clear that my time to feel sorry for myself was over.

That gave me an idea.

I attempted a small smile. "I understand you know better than I do what will happen. You know exactly what consequences to expect when a choice is made—especially if it's the wrong one. I'm human, Jared, but that doesn't make me frail. You have to give me more credit than that. It's time you teach me some of what you know."

Jared's forehead wrinkled. "Like what?"

"How to shoot a gun, for instance, and basic self-defense wouldn't hurt."

Jared pinched the bridge of his nose. "A gun isn't going to help you in this particular situation, sweetheart, much less a solid knee to the groin."

"You don't think I can do it."

"Why would you need to when you have me?"

"What if you're busy?"

He raised an eyebrow. "You mean too busy to do my job? The one that includes protecting the love of my life from certain death?"

He was trying to scare me, but I stood my ground, determined to prove my case. "Do I have to remind you of the night at the restaurant? Claire stayed behind while you took care of business?"

"That's different. I would've never left you if Claire hadn't been there."

"If I had known how to shoot a gun, I could have helped. That's all I'm saying."

"Teaching you just enough to make you dangerous is not helping. It gives you the impression that you're capable of more than you actually are."

My mouth fell open. "Now that's just insulting. Do you really see me as helpless?"

Jared laughed once, amused. "No. Definitely not, but we're not dealing with Graham anymore, Nina. Others are an enemy you don't want to piss off by shooting at."

"Fine," I said, a fake smile tightening my face. "I'll have Bex or Claire teach me. She's offered before."

Jared clenched his teeth. "Neither of them will do it without my explicit permission, and if they do, you're going to start something you can't take back."

"That's not *fair*!" I said, fully recognizing the whine in my tone. I waited until my voice could sound calmer and then spoke again, "I happen to know there's a gun club in Cranston."

"You're not going to let this go, are you?" Jared said, slowing as he pulled into the drive.

"Probably not, no," I said. Jared huffed in frustration. "It's just that I . . . It's suffocating being in your shadow. According to you, my life is constantly in danger and I have to wait for you to save me. It would be nice to know if for whatever reason I'm alone that I can do something to protect myself."

Jared's eyes met mine and then he nodded once. "Okay. We'll start Saturday."

11. FAVOR

Jared's lessons were not easy. When I caught a break from him, Bex pushed me further. When I wasn't at school or Titan, the three of us were in the field by the oak tree, aiming, punching, blocking, ducking, attacking, and subduing. It was mentioned more than once that I was a fast learner, and Bex said that I was a natural with any gun they put in my hand.

Jared didn't agree. He thought I was clumsy, slow, and impatient.

Sleep came more easily than ever. Every night, I fell into bed, my muscles screaming for rest. Dreams of Jack were replaced with calculated moves and steps I would take to get the upper hand in hand-to-hand combat. Jared would tend to my sore spots. Regardless of his efforts, the area would inevitably be a series of purple splotches in the morning.

The weeks passed, and once the trees shed their leaves, winter wasted no time covering the debris of fall with a blanket of white. Ignoring Cynthia's protests, the boys moved the furniture in the great room to transform it to a sparring ring.

The target practice, weight training, and sparring were nearly a daily ritual. Jared and Bex were always present. Once Claire caught wind of our new hobby, she came when she could. I always looked forward to the days she would join us.

Claire was more than capable of doing everything her brothers could, but I related to her with the knowledge that she had to work that much harder to prove herself. I would never be as fast or as strong as the hybrids, but I earned their respect with my stubborn refusal to quit or rest. Claire understood my resolve, and when she looked at me, she assumed strength when the boys assumed weakness.

The mirror was proof of not only my mistakes from the bruises but my hard work. My arms weren't nearly as tight as Claire's, but they were taking on a toned look that I was proud of.

The day before Thanksgiving, Jared finally offered his first word of encouragement.

"Better," he said with an emotionless nod.

That single word gave me the determination to continue. I was only human, but if I could keep up with Jared, Claire, and Bex, I could hold my own with Donovan or Shax's other human minions. At least I could try.

Thanksgiving Day arrived. Cynthia attended the Macy's Day parade in New York with some of her charity chums, and I helped Claire and Lillian in the kitchen while the boys set the table and kept the dishes washed.

Every one of my favorite spices and herbs permeated the air. Laughter was the background music to the busy atmosphere. Lillian noticed a difference in me right away and wanted to discuss my training. She took a keen interest in it, wishing she had thought of it as well.

Bex set the turkey on the table and sat beside his mother. Claire grabbed one of my hands. Jared took the other.

"Our Lord in Heaven," Lillian began, "thank you for our many blessings: the wonderful food on the table, the health and safety of our family, and that we are all sitting together on this day of thanks."

"Amen," Jared said, nodding.

"Aye Men!" Bex said, digging into the various dishes on the table.

Partway through dinner, I noticed Claire was quiet, thoughtfully chewing and smiling at the appropriate times in conversation. Jared of course noticed when I did, and he watched his sister.

"Claire?"

She met his eyes but didn't speak.

Lillian smiled. "She's fine. Let her be."

"This is good, ladies," Bex said, his mouth full of food.

"Thank you, son," Lillian said. "Jared? Would it be a good time to ask how much longer you'll be engaged?"

"No," Jared said, shaking his head with a smile. "I just got her to agree to set a date, Mom. Don't ruin my hard work."

I laughed. "She has a point."

"She does?" Jared said, surprised.

I patted his knee. "My parents' anniversary is on a Saturday this year."

Lillian's eyes brightened. "Oh, it is! How wonderful! June first, then?"

Jared turned to me, cautious. "June first?"

"It's an easy date to remember," I shrugged.

"Of this year?" Jared asked, cautiously hopeful.

Lillian and I shared the same boisterous laugh. "Yes, honey. Seven months from now."

The smile that crept across Jared's face was slow, but it spanned from one side to the other. "June first."

The conversation was monopolized by wedding plans after that, and the afternoon was filled with excitement and anticipation.

We said our good-byes with kisses and hugs to Bex, Claire, and Lillian, and then Jared led me to the Escalade by the hand. Once inside, he leaned over the console, took my face gingerly in his hands, and pressed his lips against mine.

When he finally pulled away, I felt a bit dizzy. A small twinge of guilt settled in. It was so easy to make him happy, and I had grossly procrastinated something so simple.

Jared drove slowly to the house, brushing my hand with his thumb as he held it. A storm had rolled in, and it fed into the new energy that almost crackled in the air between us, as if he couldn't wait to get home. He intertwined his fingers in mine, kissing each of my fingers. "I feel as if you said yes all over again."

"I told you I would set a date."

"You did," he said. His mouth widened to a broad grin. "Man! I feel like I want to stand on a rooftop and scream! This is one of the best days of my life!"

I giggled, nearly manic from Jared's mood. Just as the moment peaked, it fizzled.

"What are you doing?" I said. He slowed the Escalade to a stop. "You're not really going climb onto a rooftop, are you?"

"No," he said, his smile fading fast. "I spoke too soon."

It was then that I noticed the blue and red lights dancing all around us. "We're being pulled over? But you weren't speeding."

"That's not what he wants."

I grabbed Jared's hand, seeing the dark silhouette of the police officer. The windshield wipers knocked back and forth as we waited for his approach. He knocked on Jared's window with the butt of his flashlight.

"Officer," Jared said, pressing the button for the window. The dark glass buzzed as it lowered and then disappeared, revealing a face I had longed to see again.

"Ryan!" I yelped. My mouth fell open in utter shock.

"Good evening, Nina. I'm afraid I'm gonna have to ask you to step out of the vehicle."

"Don't be an ass. It's raining," Jared said.

Ryan nodded. "Just accompany me to the cruiser, ma'am," he said, sounding very professional and detached.

I nodded, looking to Jared. "It's okay. I'll be right back." I kissed him and then scrambled to open the door. I tried to be calm to preserve Jared's feelings, but Ryan was just a few feet away. I had been so desperate to see him and had waited so long any false composure at that moment was impossible.

"Nina," Jared called after me, but the tires sloshing through the wet pavement as cars passed by drowned out the following words.

It was wrong, but in my haste to speak to Ryan again, I ignored Jared and ran to the cruiser at full speed, paying no attention to the rain.

The air was biting, and the rain instantly dampened my clothes. I yanked open the passenger-side door, assuming it would be as cozy as the Escalade.

It wasn't.

"Cheese and rice!" I said, crossing my arms and bending at the waist. "You could hang meat in here!"

"Sorry," Ryan said, turning up the heat. "I keep it cool so I can wear my coat. Can't really waste time putting it on before I make a stop."

I laughed once. "A cop?"

"Yeah." He smiled and looked down. "Yeah."

"I guess this means you're not coming back to Brown."

"Looks that way," he said without humor.

He was thicker than I remembered, but his face was thin. Lean was probably a better word. A hardened expression replaced his sweet smile. He appeared older; a long, weary line of disappointment and horrendous experiences no man should ever have to encounter reflected in his once-bright green eyes.

By his hesitation alone, I could tell the effort to pull me over wasn't due to the anticipation of a happy reunion.

"You stopped writing."

"I did," he admitted. "I used to sit on a dune and watch the sun set, thinking about you, writing half of what I wanted. That was my nightly routine for a long time."

"My postman has some explaining to do."

"I only sent a few of them. I was in love with you for a long time, Nina."

"I'm sorry," I said, trying to swallow the lump that had formed in my throat. It was pointless to apologize after what I had done to him, but the words fell out of my mouth.

"Why? I'm not the first guy to go to war after my heart got broken. Half of my buddies wrote home to girls who didn't love them back. Some of them had girls who quit waiting. I was one of the lucky ones, even though your smile haunted me for a long time."

"Is that supposed to make me feel better?" I said, wrinkling my nose.

"No," he said, matter-of-factly. "After leaving, going halfway across the world, I still missed you. I didn't think it would ever go away, but something changed, Nina."

"Oh?"

Ryan smiled. "I quit loving you."

I nodded, my feelings conflicted. A small part of me was hurt and maybe a bit jealous that he had finally gotten over me. The rest of me was overjoyed. "That's good, I guess?"

"No, that's wrong. I still love you. I will always love you as my friend, but I'm in love with someone else."

A grin streaked across my face for a fleeting moment. "That's exciting. Do I know her?"

"Actually, I think you do. And I need your help."

"Anything. I sort of owe you, don't I?"

Ryan sighed, nodding. "That's where I was going with this." He paused for a moment. "You ever get the feeling you're never alone, I mean, even when you are?"

His words spoke to every moment of my life, but I remained quiet.

Ryan ignored my silence. "Do you remember the night Jared came into the bar? And the last night we were together?"

My heart began to pound. I didn't know what direction the conversation had taken, but I felt instantly uncomfortable. "What about it?"

"I remember three things about both of those nights: Jared's sister, how strong she was, and those crazy blue eyes. Everyone else says I'm crazy, Nina, but, you, I know you'll understand."

"Don't be so sure," I said, feigning bewilderment.

Ryan huffed, frustrated. "The night in your father's office, you said I couldn't tell anyone about our plan because Jared would find out. I thought he was in the FBI or something, but it's bigger than that, isn't it?"

I touched his arm. "You're seeing someone professional, right? About what happened to you over there?" The words had to be said to protect those I loved, but the guilt was overwhelming. Ryan didn't deserve that from me—he had come to me because he trusted me to believe him. If the consequences were different, I would have been the friend he'd always been to me, but my choice was clear.

He paused. Anger made the skin around his eye twitch. "What makes you think anything happened to me over there?"

"I uh . . ." I swallowed. "I really should be going," I said, reaching for the door handle.

Ryan grabbed my arm. "I saw her eyes. The day she saved my life, I saw her. No one has eyes like she does, and no woman that size could have carried me out of there. Tell me where Claire is, Nina."

My door flew open, and Jared pulled me to my feet. Ryan scrambled out of his cruiser, desperate. "I just want to talk to her," he yelled over the rain. "I don't need to know how she did it. I just need to see her again."

Jared glanced at me and then back to Ryan. "Unless you're charging us with something, we're leaving. Good to see you again, Ryan."

"I'm not crazy!" Ryan said, desperately. The rain was more of a downpour, but he was unfazed.

My steps were small and quick, trying to keep up with Jared as he led me by the arm to the Escalade. Once inside, I turned around, holding the seat with both hands as I watched the standoff between the two men I loved in such opposite ways. Ryan, in his puffy, standard-issue policeman's coat simply watched Jared glower at him. It was a new side of him, and I half-expected a nasty exchange of words.

Jared slammed the car door behind him before shoving the shifter into gear. The speedometer passed the point of speeding before we were out of Ryan's radar range, as if Jared dared him to stop us again.

"Okay. Jared? Jared!" I said, fumbling with my seat belt.

"He knows."

"It certainly seems that way," I said, bracing myself as Jared weaved through the traffic. "Claire will lay low for a while as you said to. It will be fine."

"You heard him, Nina. He's been holding onto this for months. He's not going to let it go."

"Okay, so we figure it out. It's not the worst thing that could happen right now. You told me, and the world didn't come to an end."

"Yours did."

I winced. Jared feeling that way had never occurred to me. "That's not true," I said, shaking my head. I rested my hand on his. "Everything before that night was make-believe. This is what's real."

Jared pulled into the drive of my parents' home and then waited for the garage door to open. "You don't work for the police department, Nina, the same one that Claire meticulously picked off a year ago."

"He just wants to know why he saw her in the desert, Jared. It has nothing to do with Graham."

Jared closed his eyes, exasperated. "Maybe not to Ryan, but for someone who can't pass his psych evaluation and is still in physical therapy, he was accepted into the Providence PD without a hitch. It wouldn't be hard for someone to connect Ryan to you, and anyone who could pose a problem knows you are a direct connection to me, Claire, and Graham. This is not an innocent oops, Nina. This is a potential threat."

"Everything is a potential threat to you people," I grumbled.

"You people? Since when are we not on the same side?" Jared said, taken aback. He shook his head and then headed to the house without waiting.

I followed in silence, cursing myself. An hour before, we had set the date of our wedding. Now I was getting the cold shoulder.

Bex sat the top of the stairs, cleaning his fingernails with a large knife, nodding to us as we passed. He was less of the boy I knew and more like his older sister. Even Lillian's unparalleled goodness couldn't prevent Bex from losing his innocence.

Jared rubbed the back of his neck. "I'll, er, I'll see you in the morning. I've got some things to do."

"You're going to find Claire?"

"We need to talk."

"Okay," I nodded, wrapping my arms around him. He shifted, uncomfortable in my arms. "I didn't mean it. I suppose I'm just surprised at your reaction. He's not in love with me anymore. I thought you'd be relieved."

I gripped his t-shirt in my fists, bracing for him to pull away. Instead, he paused in thought, considering my words. "That means Ryan being Claire's taleh means something else, and we don't know what that is."

I sighed, irritated at his negativity. "Maybe it just means that they are supposed to be together. Like us."

Several emotions scrolled across Jared's face, finally settling on a mixture of relief and delight. He tightened his arms around my back. "You think so?"

"What other explanation is there?"

A wide grin spread across Jared's face. "It doesn't matter. I like that one."

12. THE ONE

"No way."

"Way."

"A cop?" Beth said, her voice an octave higher.

"One of Providence's finest," I replied.

She took a sip of coffee and then shook her head. "I don't believe it. Chad hasn't said a word."

"Ryan hasn't told anyone."

"He told you."

My eyebrows shot up. An explanation consisting of Claire, explosions, and the ice blue eyes in Ryan's memory would take the conversation to an unfavorable end, so I kept it simple. "*Touché.*"

The bell above the coffee ship door chimed, and we both looked up, waiting for Kim.

"Where is she?" Beth asked, disappointed.

"Late." I knew she was with Jared, but I couldn't exactly share that with Beth. She was the last bit of normal I had left, and I wasn't going to share her with the crazy part of my life—even if that meant lying.

"Was Jared just pissed beyond belief?"

"Um, kind of, I guess, but not about that."

"What about, then?"

"That he pulled us over for no reason, I suppose." I lied again. For a moment, I silently counted how many non-truths I had told her in the span of just a few minutes and wondered how many more I would have to tell. Beth was my best friend, but it was for her own good. If there was a lesson to be learned in the chaos of my life, ignorance *was* bliss.

Beth and I chatted about upcoming papers to write, meetings at work, the upcoming Christmas party that Sasha had been obsessing over, and, of course, Ryan.

"We'd better get going," Beth said, glancing at her watch.

"The wind is terrible today," I said, pulling on my coat, hat, and scarf. The snow was falling in large chunks, and the street had already turned into a grey, slushy mess.

"I know it sucks," Beth said. "Fall is non-existent here."

"Oh. Right. You don't get much snow in Oklahoma, do you?"

Beth laughed once in disbelief. "Yes, we get snow, sometimes a foot or so. It's just on top of an inch of ice."

"But . . . it's a southern state."

"So?" Beth said, waiting for more crazy to come out of my mouth.

"Never mind."

We walked to the Beemer together, trying to navigate the patches of snow that hadn't been cleared.

"Hi," a deep voice said, greeting us.

"Ryan!" Beth said, throwing her arms around our friend.

He was in plain clothes, leaning against my car nonchalantly. He didn't seem nervous or out of place at all, until Beth smacked him, hard, on the back of the head.

"Hey!" Ryan said, defending his head with his hands from another blow.

"What is wrong with you? Taking off on all of us like that, going off to *war*, and not letting us know you're okay or that you're back in town? We've all been worried sick! Chad is gonna be *pissed*!"

"Okay, okay!" Ryan said, bracing for another assault. "I'm sorry."

Beth relaxed. "If you haven't called him by the time I get home tonight, I'm telling him. And you are *so* going to get it."

"I'll call him. I'll call everyone. I've just been kinda . . . I don't know what to say."

"Say, 'I'm home.'" Beth crossed her arms, unimpressed with his wounded expression.

"Take it easy, Beth," I said. "He just needed to come back on his own terms."

"Exactly." Ryan nodded, thankful for my explanation. "I came to ask you to dinner. We have some talking to do."

"O-Okay," I said, surprised.

"Jared's not going to like that," Beth lilted.

"Where do I pick you up? Jared's place?"

"It sort of burned down," I said, shifting.

Ryan didn't flinch. "Okay, so where, then?"

"We're at Cynthia's for now."

Ryan's eyes were always the windows to his thoughts. That was one thing that his experiences hadn't taken away from him. He was planning something.

"Seven o'clock?" he asked.

"How about I meet you there?"

"Where?"

"I don't know. Wherever you want to eat."

"I haven't decided yet. I'll just pick you up."

I sighed in frustration. "See you at seven, then."

Ryan walked away like a robot accepting a command. He offered no smile or any other expression, too preoccupied with his next move.

"That was weird," Beth said, pulling on the handle. "Open up, already, it's freaking freezing!"

"Oh, it's not that bad," I said, rolling my eyes and clicking the keyless entry.

Throughout the day, I waited for Jared's call. He hadn't come home that morning, passing on the message via Bex that he and Kim were in Woonsocket, just south of the Massachusetts' line. Bex assured me that it was to speak with the priests of St. Anne's and that he wouldn't be engaging the enemy.

At lunch, I called Bex. "Why hasn't he called?"

"He'll call," Bex said, bored.

"Why did Kim go if they're just going to a church?"

"It's just a guess, but maybe she knows the contact their questioning."

I blew my bangs from my face, frustrated. "You two are being very secretive these days."

Bex sighed. "Go be a co-ed, Nina. I'll talk to you later when you call to ask if Jared's called again."

I looked to Beth. "That little . . . He hung up on me."

"He's a teenager. You remember being a teenager?"

"Vaguely."

"He's got all these feelings and emotions, and didn't you say he was home-schooled?"

"Yeah, but he's only thirteen. He's barely a teenager."

Beth stared at me. "You're joking, right?"

"No, why?"

"There is no way that kid is thirteen! He's a mammoth! He looks at least sixteen!"

"Nope. It runs in the family."

"You're going to give birth to a toddler. Think about that," Beth said, giggling to herself.

"We're not . . ." I waited, hoping Beth wouldn't take it further. Any such hopes were lost when her eyes widened.

"You're not what? Going to have kids?"

I shrugged, trying to play it off. "We haven't really talked about it, but it's not something either of us would die to experience. I'm an only child. Babies—kids—really aren't my thing."

"Well, there's nothing wrong with that. I just didn't know you felt that way. I bet Jared would be an amazing father."

"He would be." I nodded. Her words stung me, something I hadn't expected.

The afternoon was long. Bex hadn't called with news of Jared, and the wait was making me grumpy. Jared always called, unless he was in trouble, and because he knew that I knew that, he should call, a lot.

After my last class, my feet couldn't move fast enough to the Beemer. I pulled out my cell phone and dialed, the same time searching my purse for keys.

"He hasn't called," Bex answered.

"Something's wrong. Have you talked to Claire?"

"Yes. Nothing's wrong; he's just busy."

"Then he would have called!" I said. Just as I slammed the phone shut, the Beemer and Bex came into view.

"Get in. We're going to Woonsocket."

Bex laughed without humor. "No, we're not. Jared said to take you to Titan and then home. We're to wait for him there."

"Well, I don't work for Jared, nor am I trying to earn the big-brother approval, so get in the car or move."

Bex did neither. "I have orders, Nina."

He wasn't as easy to persuade as Jared, because he wasn't worried about making me angry. I had to try a different approach. He might look like a man, but he was still a thirteen-year-old boy.

"Bex Gabriel Ryel, if you move a finger to keep me here, so help me, I will call your mother and tell her you used your hybridness to restrain me against my will!"

His stoic expression wavered as he considered the consequences. "Fine," he said, his entire body relaxing. "Get in the car. I'll drive."

I pushed up on the balls of my feet to kiss his cheek. "Thanks, Bexster!"

His face screwed into disgust as he wiped the place where my lips touched his cheek. "Yuck!"

With Bex driving his typical speed, the trip took less than twenty minutes. He sat in silence, pouting and no doubt planning the excuses he would offer Jared.

When we arrived, I gasped at my surroundings. St. Anne's was a work of art, looming with both authority and elegance over the quiet town. As beautiful as the outside was, the interior was breathtaking.

Meticulously detailed murals of angels and saints adorned the walls and ceilings, with a larger one as the focal point. The painting was of Jesus, his arms outstretched, surrounded in light, and rows of angels, who basked in his glory. The entire room was inspirational, and a strange feeling came over me as I walked down the center aisle.

Row after row of wooden pews bordered our way to the altar anchored at front of the church, where Jared and Kim stood with a priest.

Jared's expression wasn't surprised or confused. He glanced once in my direction and then continued his conversation. Jared's clear disregard only served to exacerbate my growing impatience with him.

"Excuse me, Father," I said, interrupting him. I pulled Jared a few steps away, purposefully glaring at Kim as I did so.

"I can't do this right now, Nina. I'm working."

"I thought *I* was your job? You know it worries me to death when you don't call. Do you do it on purpose?"

"Nina, calm down."

"I couldn't concentrate in my classes and checked my phone every five seconds, hoping you would at least send a one word text—something! It would take just a moment of your time to set my mind at ease. You spend half of your life incessantly protecting me from everything and the other making me *crazy!*"

"Child—" the priest began. His words had a hidden accent behind them, possibly British, diluted by years of service in America. His plea was cut short when the hundreds of candles glowing around us were extinguished in succession, from one side of the stage to the other.

The priest watched me warily. "What is she?" he said, taking a step back.

Jared took my hand. "This is she, Father Francis. She is the one."

The priest held his trembling hands to his mouth and then reached out to me. He grabbed my free hand with both of his and held it tightly. "The Mother," he whispered, his eyes scanning my face with adoration.

Bex lifted his chin. His eyes closed, but not before his lashes flickered as his eyes rolled back into his head. He took a deep breath, as if he were feeling the air around us, reaching with invisible tentacles to a different plane. "Jared," he whispered.

A loud repetitious banging echoed throughout the cathedral, and Father Francis dropped my hand, rushing to the large doors of the entrance.

"You should stop him," Kim said to Jared.

"Father, wait," Jared called. He grabbed my hand, following quickly behind the priest.

The banging persisted, so loudly that I released Jared's hand to cover my ears. The large doors vibrated with each blow.

"Make it stop," I said, closing my eyes.

Kim and Bex were at my side, and Kim touched my shoulder before taking a few steps forward.

The banging grew louder, and the door threatened to give way to the hammering from outside.

"Make it stop!" I yelled over the noise.

"Father," Kim said, gently moving him to the side. She reached out with both hands, laying her palms flat against each door.

I grabbed Jared's arm, and then a quiet settled upon us, seeming more ominous than the banging.

Father Francis pushed open the doors, and we all stood in horror at the sight before us.

"Lord in Heaven," Father Francis said, making a quick sign of the cross.

"They . . ." I began, unable to finish.

"Crows. Nice touch," Kim said.

Hundreds of lifeless, black birds littered the steps and sidewalk. The doors were covered in bloody splotches, dotting every place the crows had crashed into head first.

"Mommy!" A small girl screamed. She pointed as her mother rushed her by the hand to their parked car across the street.

Pedestrians stopped and stared at the unbelievable sight, pointing to the church and to the small horrified group hovering in the doorway.

"Let us get inside," Father Francis said, shooing us backward into the church. He pulled the doors shut, shaking his head. "This was a warning. They know what she is, and they are not happy she's here."

"Merovingian?" I said, a sudden feeling of desperation evident in my voice.

The priest's face twisted in disgust. "Merovingian. *Bah*," he grunted, shaking his head. "Nephilim," he said, his voice returning to its soft tone. He touched each side of my face gently. His skin was tired and wilted, making it nearly impossible to see the kindness in his eyes, but it was there.

"Tell me," I said, a weak smile grazing my lips.

"You are the woman clothed with the sun," Father Francis said, in awe.

I looked to Jared. His expression was pained, but he offered no explanation.

"What?" I shook my head. "Pardon me, Father, but what the hell does that mean?"

He took my hand and gestured for me to sit in the nearest pew. He sat with me, my hand in both of his. Kim, Bex, and Jared all took a seat as well, scattered around us.

"In Revelations, the Bible speaks of a woman clothed in the sun, with the moon at her feet, and she is with child in arduous times. She brings forth a man child who is to rule all nations. It speaks of the Holy Mother."

"Okay, but what does that have to do with me?" I said, frustrated and confused.

"A woman of the same description is also the center of a prophecy of the *Naissance de Demoniac*. The main prophecy speaks of a woman clothed in the sun with the moon at her feet and the crown of ten stars on her head—a daughter of the Nephilim. She brings forth a son of God."

"I know. The child disturbs the balance, blah, blah, blah." I looked to Jared. "You had to come to Woonsocket to hear something we already know?"

Jared leaned his elbows onto the ridge of the pew, touching my hair with his thumb. "Father Francis is a scholar. He has studied the writings of the *Naissance de Demoniac*. I came here to ask for help."

"If he knows what it says, we don't need the book," I said, excited. "Can't you just tell us what we need to know?"

Father Francis squeezed my hand. "These prophecies are not in the stars or in the dreams of old men. Our world is a story that has already been written. The human-born angel will disturb the delicate balance of Heaven and Hell. It will be a new angel, not created in the dawn of time as all the others." He smiled, but it didn't give me peace the way he had surely meant for it to. "Demons fear the unknown as humans do—possibly even more so because of the limited truth they do not know."

"So we can't stop it," I said.

"But that won't stop Hell from trying," the priest said, his voice grave.

"I can't stay here. I have to go," I said, jumping to my feet. I ran out the front door, stopping when I felt the carcasses of birds under my feet. My hands flew to my eyes, overwhelmed.

"It's okay," Jared whispered in my ear, sweeping me into his arms. He carried me across the street and then carefully set me in the passenger seat of the Beemer. His warm hand brushed the bangs from my face. "Get her home, Bex."

Bex nodded, turned the ignition, and slammed the shifter into gear. It took us half the drive time to reach Cynthia's than it took to get to St. Anne's.

Bex parked in the garage and helped me up the stairs to my room. His normally playful, innocent eyes offered sympathy and concern well beyond his years.

"We'll figure this out, Nina. We're not going to let anything happen to you. You know that."

"I don't want anything to happen to *you*," I said softly. I patted his shoulder and then walked into the bathroom, removing my clothes slowly and feeling numb.

The steam floated up from behind the shower curtain and spilled over, filling the room with thick hazy warmth in minutes. I stood under the water, as hot as I could stand it, and tried to remember what Eli had said about being strong. Crying for my normal life was futile. Frivolous emotion would help nothing. Still, a heavy, portentous feeling settled over my entire body, weighing me down so much that the tile below my feet seemed to dig into my skin.

The more we learned, the worse it was. Preventing the prophecy was useless, and even if we succeeded, Hell wouldn't allow the possibility.

The shower knobs complained when I turned them off, strangling the pipes. I towel-dried my hair and then wrapped my robe around me. When I pushed the door open, a ghostly cloud of steam followed me as I walked across my bedroom floor.

I sat at my vanity, raking a comb through my damp, messy hair. The sea of black birds at the church haunted my thoughts, and the crunching sound their bodies made as Jared carried me across the street replayed over and over in my mind.

"Don't forget about dinner with Ryan tonight," Bex said.

"He won't be here until seven," I said, glancing at the clock. I still had an hour left.

The main entrance door slammed in the lower level, and I heard not one but two pairs of light footsteps ascending the stairs.

Jared stopped in the doorway of my bedroom. "Hey."

"Hey," I said. I kept my back to him, but met his eyes in the mirror.

Claire appeared beside him. "I heard."

The overly ceremonious doorbell chimed throughout the house. Moments later, Agatha joined Jared and Claire in the doorway of my room. "It's a gentleman, love. A Mr. Scott to see you."

I rolled my eyes. "He's early." I stood, tightening the belt of my robe and then stormed through the path Claire and Jared made for me as they pressed their backs to the wall.

My bare feet tapped against the stairs as I quickly made my way to the spot where Ryan stood.

"You're early," I said, crossing my arms.

Ryan smiled, his eyes scanning every corner of the room. "I'm sorry. I'll wait."

"Agatha?" I called. When she didn't answer, I gestured for Ryan to follow me. "I'll show you to the great room." Too late I remembered we had rearranged the furniture for our sparring matches.

"Redecorating?" Ryan asked, shoving his hands in his pockets.

"Something like that," I said. "I'll just be a minute."

Ryan nodded, and I jogged up the stairs. Jared and his siblings stood in the center of my room when I returned, seeming nervous and out of place.

"It's just Ryan," I said. Once the words came out of my mouth, Claire's eyes widened, and she shoved me aside, pushing my bedroom door shut.

Her finger touched her lips, and she waited, keeping her hand against the door.

"Nina?" Ryan called, knocking twice.

"Yes?" I said, shrugging to Claire.

"I couldn't help but notice the Lotus Exige you have parked out front. New car?"

Claire's eyes squeezed shut, and then she looked at me again, shaking her head.

"Er, no, I believe my mother has company this evening. I'll meet you downstairs, okay?"

It was silent for a few moments, but then Ryan knocked on the door again.

"Yes?" I said, unable to hide the irritation in my voice. I glanced back at Jared, hoping he would give a sign as to what I should do.

"Isn't that the same car Claire drove the night we first saw her at the pub?"

When Jared held out his arms and shrugged, I sighed. "I can't remember, Ryan. Do you want me to get ready or not?"

"The thing is," he said, his voice just on the other side of the door, "I ran the plates, and it's registered to Claire Ryel."

For the first time, Claire looked nervous. She rubbed the back of her neck the way her brother rubbed his when things between us were tense. It struck me as funny, and a smile forced its way to the surface.

"It's not funny!" Claire mouthed silently. When I covered my mouth with my hand, a smile crept across her face as well.

"Uh," I said, turning once again to Jared. He rolled his eyes, gesturing for us to somehow fix the mess we'd made. "She was here. She was here earlier helping me, er, pick out a dress."

"So she walked home?" Ryan said from the hall.

"No. No, she didn't," I said, stalling.

Claire desperately pointed at Jared.

"Jared took her home!" I said.

Ryan puffed. "Okay, but the Escalade is parked behind the Lotus."

"Shit!" I whispered, interlocking my fingers on top of my head. "He . . . took her home on his motorcycle."

Claire gave me a thumb's up, and I relaxed a bit, hoping Ryan would accept my story.

"Nina," Ryan said. "Could I talk to Claire for a minute? Just . . . Just for one minute." The door handle moved, and Claire's hand instantly gripped around it, refusing to let it budge a millimeter more.

"She's not here, Ryan. I told you."

"Then open the door."

"I'm not dressed."

"I've seen you that way before."

Jared frowned and I laughed once. "It's different now."

"Claire?" Ryan said. "Can I talk to you? Please? I won't take up much of your time, I swear. I just need to, uh . . . Wow," he chuckled, "I feel really stupid right now."

I cringed, knowing I would have to be mean to him. "You should, since she's not here," I said.

"Claire, please?" he asked.

Claire leaned her forehead silently against the door. She bit her lip and sighed. "Go away, Ryan."

"Claire?" Ryan said, his voice excited. "Please open the door."

"Nina told me what you said. It's sweet, but," she cringed, "you're crazy."

"I know what I saw," Ryan said, his tone notably less enthusiastic than before. "I know you were there."

"Right. I was in Afghanistan or wherever, sniping Al Qaeda and carrying you over my back for miles. Sounds like me," she snapped.

"I just want to see you," Ryan said. "I need to see you to be sure."

Jared shook his head, and Claire's expression grew impatient. "Beat it, Ryan," she said.

After a short pause, Ryan hit the door with the side of his fist. "I'm not leaving until I see you!"

"What are you going to do?" Claire yelled, taking a step away from the door. "Wave your shiny badge around and impress us to death?"

"Open the door!" Ryan demanded.

"No!" Claire said.

"Fine!" he replied. "But I'm not giving up on you."

He stomped down the stairs and slammed the door.

13. LESSON

"I need the keys to your bike," Claire said, holding out her hand to Bex.

He frowned. "Why?"

"Because I have to follow him, and he knows my freaking car! Give me your keys!" she said, jerking her hand toward Bex, impatiently.

In one swift movement, Bex handed his motorcycle keys to his big little sister. She wheeled around, sprinting down the stairs.

"Don't forget the helmet," he called after her.

"Shove it!" she yelled before slamming the door.

I walked to my vanity, sitting hard onto the delicate pink cushion of the bench. "This is bad."

Jared took slow steps to stand beside me. "Ryan is the least of our worries."

"That makes me feel much better," I said.

Bex left us alone to sit on the stairs, and Jared pulled me from the bench to sit beside him on the bed. He didn't speak for a long time, lightly brushing the skin of my arm from wrist to elbow with his fingertips.

"Do you understand what could happen?" he said softly, his eyes still focused on my arm.

After a short pause, I took a breath. "Yes."

He meant my death. Dying at the hands of the most inhumane, cruel beings on three planes wasn't peaceful—I'd planned to die in my sleep—but it was an end. I wondered what would take place in that moment and what ways Jared would suffer in the days following my death.

His eyes were dark, the skin around them tight but tired. The helpless feeling surrounding us was suffocating.

"I know what Father Francis said," Jared said, his voice breaking, "but I can't believe that. I have to see the book for myself to be sure. There has to be a reason our fathers wanted it so badly. Gabe must have known there was a way to stop it.

"Stay with me," I said.

"I can't."

"Just for a while. Just until I fall asleep?"

Jared met my eyes, and I could see that he would let me win.

We lay together above the sheets, silent and thoughtful. I imagined Jared was carefully plotting a way around Donovan and Isaac in his mind, praying for a conclusion. Shax had stayed one step ahead of Jared—even Kim, his secret weapon—and he was frustrated.

Jared's arms tensed. Bex's light footsteps rushed down the stairs and the front door opened. After a few moments, another set, heavier than the first, returned with him. Kim appeared in the doorway, out of breath and wide-eyed.

Jared sprung from the bed, pulling on his jacket. "Stay with her, Bex."

"I should go," Bex said.

Knowing they were going to try to capture the book, I jumped from the bed, pulling on a pair of sneakers. "He should go. I'll go too, and if anything happens, Bex can help."

Jared frowned while he made his decision. "Nina . . ."

"We don't have time for a lecture," I said. "You know you have a better chance if Bex is there."

He nodded, clearly conflicted. "Let's go."

The streets were filthy, lined with mounds of dirty snow. The Escalade flew at three times the speed limit, racing against the moment Shax realized we'd found him.

Jared slammed on the brakes in front of an old apartment building on the outskirts of town, and he and Kim rushed in. Bex was stoic, waiting patiently for a signal. My knees bounced nervously as I bit at my thumbnail.

"Here," Bex said, pulling a handgun from the back of his pants. "If I go in, keep this with you. The safety's on, so—"

"Take it off before I fire, I know."

Bex smiled. "You'll be fine. Just don't go in."

The waiting was excruciating. The night was too quiet, the building too dark. I had expected immediate flashes of gunfire and for Jared and Kim to run out, with snarling, misshapen beasts in pursuit.

Bex picked at his nails, seeming bored but patient. I checked my handgun again, making sure it was loaded and ready.

"We really need Claire here. We have to figure out how to get the three of us in the same room with Shax and keep you protected at the same time."

"You're just itching to get one in on him, aren't you?" I smirked.

"On Shax?" Bex said. "Jared's fought a hundred of 'em. They react to me the same way they do Kim. They won't come near me. It's irritating."

"Why?"

"I don't know, but it better not be because of my age or anything like that. I'm ready," he sniffed.

"You are," I said, my voice absent of sarcasm.

Bex turned to me with a small smile, reminding me of his innocence. "Yeah?"

"Absolutely. How much time have we spent together, with Jared nowhere in sight? I'm the hardest taleh case there is—dirty cops and demons after me day and night—and I don't have a scratch. Maybe they stay away because they're scared?"

Bex nodded, satisfied. "Yeah. Probably so."

Suddenly, Jared and Kim appeared, walking slowly from the back of the building.

"No go?" Bex asked as Jared slammed his body into the driver's seat.

"They were already gone," he seethed, his jaw muscles fluttering under his skin.

"Shax is playing games with us," Kim said. "Otherwise, he'd move it out of town or out of the country. He wants you to doubt your judgment, and he's using me to bait you, to wear you out."

"There has to be another way," Jared said, slamming the shifter into gear. "We're making the same mistakes."

"Are they all the same?" I asked.

Jared, Kim, and Bex turned in my direction.

"The books. Are they all the same? You said there were others. Is there another one we can get to? One that belongs to a demon that doesn't know we're coming?"

Jared and Kim traded glances.

"It's not a bad idea," Kim said.

"Waste of time," Bex replied.

"Nigh, Shax's book is the only one that we know of that has been brought to this plane. The others . . . We'd have to go to Hell to get," Kim explained.

"So that's out," I said.

"Unless," Bex began.

"No," Jared said, cutting him off.

"Unless what?" I said, touching Bex's arm.

"We could talk someone with access into getting one."

Jared sighed. "No one is going to do that, Bex. It would start a war."

"Samuel would." A small amused smile touched Bex's face.

"Enough," Jared said, pulling into Cynthia's driveway.

We all stood in the driveway, tired and looking a little lost.

Kim stretched and then patted my backside. "See you in class tomorrow."

I shook my head in disbelief. She was so unaffected by it all. Kim ducked into her Sentra and slowly pulled away, more than likely heading to her dorm room at Brown.

The headlight of Bex's motorcycle shuttered as Claire pulled into the drive. She was noticeably upset.

"What is it?" I asked, watching her place the bike on its kickstand.

She fidgeted and then put her hands on her hips, looking down to her boots. Her long bangs fell into her eyes as she procrastinated. "I missed one."

"Who?" Jared said.

"Kit Anderson."

"That will be a problem," Jared replied.

I frowned. "Who's Kit Anderson?"

"Ryan's partner," Claire said, combing her hair back with her fingers, frustrated.

"You sure?" Bex asked, surprised.

"Ryan went to his house tonight," Claire said. "Donovan called while he was there. Anderson was only on the phone for a moment, but it was Donovan."

"What are you going to do?" I asked.

They all craned their necks at me.

Claire made a face. "What do you think, Nina? I've got to get rid of him."

My mouth fell open. "But it's Ryan's partner. He just lost his whole unit. You're going to kill his partner?"

"Better than you," Bex said, climbing onto his bike.

"Where are you going?" Jared said.

"Home. I need to check on Mom and make some calls."

Jared nodded and then looked at me. "Let's get you inside. You're cold."

I looked down at my ensemble: a coat over my robe and tennis shoes. I'd been in such a hurry to ride along I'd barely dressed. "Okay," I said, following him inside. Jared had told me over a year ago that he could sense my feelings, but I would never get used to him noticing them before I did.

In my bedroom, I kicked off my sneakers and peeled off my coat, falling into the bed. Jared crawled into bed beside me, outlining my body with his. Jared's warmth was like being submerged in light; being so close to him was unlike any calm I'd ever felt in my life— even as a girl, when Jack was alive. Jared's presence causing the nightmares was the worst punishment of all.

Jared sensed my unease, and he pulled me closer. "Stop thinking," he whispered in my ear. His soft lips grazed the gentle fold of my ear as he spoke, and I nuzzled closer to him, hoping Gabe would let him stay just one night.

Sleep came quickly, despite the excitement of chasing after Shax and my discontent.

It felt as if the moment I closed my eyes I was awake, covered in sweat and screaming for my father. Jared held me, this time silently. There was nothing left to say that hadn't been said already. Reassuring me that it was just a bad dream was pointless.

"Coffee?" he said.

"No," I said, pulling on his shirt. "Don't leave me. Just stay," I said between breaths.

He kissed my forehead, whispering sweet comfort in French in my ear. I didn't know what the words meant, but it was so soft and soothing, I was relaxed against his chest in moments.

I took in a deep breath, inhaling his incredible scent. A tingling traveled the length of my body, and I extended my neck to kiss the lobe of his ear.

"Nina," he warned.

"I miss you," I said, kissing tiny sections of his skin until I reached his lips.

"It's not a good time for us to—" he began, but I kissed him, cutting off yet another lecture.

"I don't care," I said, tears filling my eyes. "I need to forget, just for a little while. Help me forget."

Jared looked deep into my eyes, weighing a decision, no doubt. I leaned against his mouth once more, and this time he returned my kiss, cautiously giving in. His soft full lips worked against mine, but not in the way I wanted. I could still feel a wall between us.

I pulled his t-shirt over his head, but when I tugged at the belt of my robe, he gently held my wrist. "Sweetheart . . ."

The frustration and fear finally boiled over, and I fell into his chest. Tears pooled between his chest and my cheeks.

Jared gently cupped my shoulders and held me away, looking into my eyes. "Don't cry," he said with a frown. "Please don't . . ." He trailed off, sighing at the messy sight of me.

"I can't stand this." I shook my head. "I can't stand this, anymore. If I can't be with the man I love . . . What is the point in being alive if I can't live?"

Jared made a hush sound and kissed my forehead. His lips made a trail down the bridge of my nose, and when his lips met mine, he leaned me back, tenderly against the bed. I shamelessly took advantage of his moment of weakness before it passed.

My fingers dug into his shoulders, and I kissed him in the way I reserved only for our most intimate moments. Jared reacted exactly the way I wished he would, pushing away from me just enough for me to untie my robe. Jared lowered his body, letting his skin warm mine.

My heart raced as Jared's mouth made a wet line down my neck. My knees arced on each side of him, every part of me waiting eagerly for Jared to ignore the voice in his head warning him against such unreasonable human desire. As loud as those voices might have been, he could sense my need to be with him in that way. I knew that would drown out any noble protesting.

For the first time in months, we lost ourselves in each other. Not a single moment did I worry or regret, and neither did Jared—until it was over.

Peacefully against his skin, my head rose and fell with his deep breath. "Don't say it," I said with a smile.

"It's a little late to say anything," Jared said, kissing my hair.

I frowned, unhappy with his response. Instead of insisting that he show just an ounce of happiness about what had just happened, I decided changing the subject would be more effective. "You know the Christmas party is next weekend."

"I know," he smiled, beginning to relax.

I stretched. "I assume you've bought a suit."

"I did."

"I need a dress," I said, my brows pulling together.

Jared laughed, momentarily forgetting about anything but the mundane details of our normal life.

We giggled and snuggled until the sun filtered through the curtains, and then Jared walked across the room to dress. I turned on my side to watch him, propping my head with my hand. Knowing how many bullets and wounds he'd sustained in the last few years, I was amazed that his skin was flawless. Every inch of it.

"What are you plotting over there?" Jared asked, smiling.

"Absolutely nothing, I'm simply appreciating your form."

He pulled a pair of light blue boxer briefs up his legs and over his bare backside. "Is that so?"

I pulled the sheet across the room with me, hunting for something casual to wear to Brown.

"That's not fair at all. I should be allowed to appreciate as well." He smiled, but that smile quickly faded as he pulled me behind him.

Bex knocked twice before walking in. "Geez! Really?" he yelled, closing the door.

"Knocking doesn't count if you just walk in!" Jared growled.

I backed into the closet, mortified.

The door opened again and Jared sighed. "We *are* allowed privacy," he said, his voice low and angry.

"I've seen it all before," Claire said. "Hey," she smiled, poking her head into the closet. "You wanna hang out today?"

"Don't even think about it," Jared warned.

"She's learning, isn't she?" Claire snapped. "She's got to see it sometime!"

"She's not learning that," Jared said.

"You've got business today anyway," Bex said.

Kim walked in, confused by the number of people in the room, coupled with our lack of clothing. "I'll just wait outside."

"I'll go too," Bex said.

Jared glared at Bex and then at Claire. "She's not ready."

"I need her for a distraction in case Ryan shows up," Claire said, irritated that she had to explain.

"Use her as bait?" Jared seethed. "No."

"Why don't you tell me what's going on and let me make the decision?" I said. Being spoken about as if I weren't in the room was quickly becoming my least favorite thing.

"Claire's going to take out Anderson," Jared said, frowning.

"You're going to kill him?" I asked. Claire nodded. "Right now?"

She watched me, annoyed.

"But I have class," I said, completely aware of how absurd the words sounded.

Jared pushed Claire and Bex backward. "That settles it. Out."

Claire ducked under her brother's arm with little effort. "If Ryan shows up, you could help," she said, appealing to my better nature. "Otherwise, it could get ugly. He might try to protect Anderson."

"Wait," I said. "Just let me think about this for a minute."

Jared froze and then turned to face me. "This is a bad idea. We can take him out to lunch or something to distract him. I'm not letting you get in the middle of one of Claire's hits, so—,"

"Kim has class too," Claire said, her voice smooth and persuading. "Jared needs *her* help today."

"She doesn't go to class half the time anyway and still has a four-point-oh," I grumbled. "Watch you take a man's life?" I said, unsure.

"Yes," Claire said, "and help if Ryan shows."

"What about the lunch idea?" I asked, looking to Jared.

"Ryan's on duty," Claire said. "I can't wait around for him to take a lunch break. It doesn't work that way and Jared knows that." Claire snarled her lip at Jared.

I nodded. "Okay."

I walked into the closet with a purpose, shutting the door behind me. It was finally quiet, but only for a fraction of a second before Claire was banging with her fist. "Let's go, princess. I don't have all day."

"I'm coming!" I growled. Black jeans and a black turtleneck seemed like appropriate assassination attire, completed by tying my hair into a tight, low bun. When I emerged, Claire's face lit up.

"I have boots that would look amazing with that."

"I can't wear stilettos on a hit," I said, annoyed with her sudden cheerful demeanor.

Claire wrinkled her nose. "Why not? I do it all the time."

With that, we all made our way down the stairs and out to the drive.

Jared tugged on my arm before I ducked into Claire's Lotus. "Claire will keep you safe. Just keep your head down, okay? Do everything you're told."

"I promise," I said. Jared was still nervous, despite trusting his sister's capabilities, and although I sympathized with his feelings, it was nice not to be the one worrying for a change.

Jared kissed my cheek before disappearing behind the black windows of the Escalade. Kim hopped into the passenger seat, but not before waving to me like a child leaving for the zoo. I shook my head and waved back.

"Today!" Claire snapped, revving the engine.

Bex and I piled into the passenger seat beside Claire. She drove us to North Providence and turned on Mineral Spring Avenue, parking in a McDonald's parking lot not a block from the red brick walls of Ryan's police station.

"You're kidding. It's seven in the morning! You're going to gun down a cop in broad daylight?" I said in disbelief.

"Will you pretend I know what I'm doing for two seconds?" Claire snapped. She slipped on her large glasses and nodded to an officer walking out to a cruiser.

"Anderson?" I said.

"Yep," Claire said, waiting a beat after Anderson pulled out onto the road before she turned the wheel and pressed on the gas to follow.

She stayed so far behind the black and white that I thought a few times we'd lost him. Claire's eyes were focused, however, and what I couldn't see, she saw as if it were right in front of her.

"Okay," she said, slowing by the curb. "Let's set up shop," she said to her brother.

Bex nodded once, pulling a hot pink duffel bag from the back seat.

I eyed the bag and then smiled at Bex.

He rolled his eyes. "I've tried to get her to bring black ones. Or even brown or green. She won't."

"I may be a ruthless assassin, but I'm still a girl," she said, popping a stick of gum in her mouth.

We kept a low profile: climbing over fences, dodging dogs on chains and play equipment, and finally sneaking into a two-story building. The stairs were unusable, the bottom half lay on the floor, and the top half hung by only a few dilapidated boards.

"What now?" I whispered.

Bex threw me over his shoulder and then hopped from the wall to a beam to the next floor. Even from my angle, he looked like Spiderman. I couldn't imagine why he thought he needed to float. He could climb walls easily enough.

Claire took a single leap, grabbing the landing where the stairs met the second floor, and then swung to our position.

"You can put me down, now, Bex," I said.

"Not yet," he said, taking a running jump to the half-exposed rafters. "Okay," he said, helping me balance. We were sitting on a few beams lined together that formed what used to be the attic floor.

Claire lay on her stomach beside me, clicking the pieces of her rifle together. "They're going to meet here," she whispered. "Don't make a sound. Anderson is *very* paranoid. That's how he's made it this far. If you tip him off, it will be a while before we get a chance like this again."

I nodded, watching Bex pull his own rifle from the bag. He didn't set it on its stand in front of him; instead, he set it in front of me.

"Just look through the sights. Don't take the shot, even if you have one. It's just for practice," he said in a low voice.

I began to whisper affirmation, but voices below startled me. Claire slowly put her hand on the barrel of my rifle and then let go, situating herself to aim.

"Look through your sights," she whispered. I did so, and three men in suits came into view, along with a man in uniform. "Count them. How many do you see?"

"Four," I said.

Bex leaned in beside my ear. "Look by the entrance."

I slowly moved my rifle in the direction he referred to and spotted two more. To my surprise, the men were not in uniform but in suits. Their broad shoulders and extra-large frames reminded me of old movies about the mob.

"Bodyguards," Bex said. "Look closer at their jackets. You see the slight bulging on each side?"

"They're armed," I breathed.

With one finger, Claire turned the adjustment on her rifle. The tiny click sound it made seemed as loud as a jet engine to me, but the noise was so insignificant it was inaudible to the men below.

Bex touched my elbow with the back of his finger. "She's going to account for crosswind and range-to-target, but this is an easy shot. Once the gun goes off, try to relax. I'll get you down and out of here, and by the time you blink twice, we'll be on our way home in the Lotus." His low even tone reminded me of an emcee for a televised golf tournament or the narrator for an African Lion documentary—minus the accent.

Claire held her breath, peering into the scope. She bit her lip and began to squeeze the trigger.

"Damn it," she whispered. "Ryan just pulled up. He's a block north. You and Nina intercept him; I'll meet you in twenty."

"Wait—" Before I could protest, Bex lifted me off the wooden beams and climbed out the broken slats of an old vent, dropping more than thirty feet below. He landed smoothly and tugged on my hand. "Come on," he said, keeping his voice to a whisper.

We ran down the alley as fast as my legs could move, slowing only when we reached the next street down.

"This way," Bex said, leading me by the hand across the street, this time at a reasonable pace.

"Nina?" a voice called.

I turned to see Ryan walking toward us, confused, but happy to see me.

"Hey," I forced my best smile, trying to control my breathing. "Clocked-in already?"

"Yeah," he smiled, flicking his badge. "What are you doing this far north?"

"Uh."

"I made her drive me to my girlfriend's house," Bex said.

Ryan blinked and then scanned Bex from top to bottom. "Oh, I thought you were Jared."

"Bex," he said, offering his hand to Ryan. "Jared's little brother."

"Amazing, isn't it?" I grinned.

"Well, I'm supposed to meet my partner. I'll call you tonight, Nina."

"Meet your partner?" I said, surprised.

"Yeah. Work stuff."

Bex and I traded glances, and then Bex tugged on my coat. "Well, don't want to keep Mandy waiting."

Ryan smiled. "No, man, you probably don't. See you guys around."

We walked at a forced pace until Ryan was out of sight, and then Bex pulled on me again. He was barely at a jog, while I was sprinting full speed until we reached the next block over, where Claire waited in the Lotus.

"It was a trap," I said, breathlessly. "They were waiting for Ryan."

"I know," Claire said, her eyes focused and menacing.

She raced down the street, weaving in and out of traffic until we reached Brown University. "What about Ryan?" I said.

"I'll take care of it. Bex will wait here until Jared's finished. I have some things to wrap up."

I nodded and then watched from the curb as she sped away.

"Tell me," I said, turning to Bex.

"I only heard a little as we were leaving to cut off Ryan, but Donovan sent those men to collect him. They were going to use him for bait."

"So now Ryan's a target."

"We're all targets."

14. IT'S YOUR FUNERAL

"I was right," I said, letting Jared take my coat. "It looks like Christmas threw up on the conference room."

"You were right. And how ridiculous, when you're decoration enough," Jared said, kissing my cheek.

Loud, obnoxious music made it necessary to practically yell at each other. Red, green, and gold tinsel draped every surface in the room, and the employees, with their dates, loitered in a perfect half-moon around the DJ, careful not to cross the boundary of the dance floor.

"I'm going to tell the DJ to turn it down a notch or ten," I said.

Jared nodded, watching with amusement as I walked with purpose across the wooden floor.

"Excuse me," I said. The DJ bobbed his head, concentrating on the computer screen in front of him. "Excuse me!" I yelled, tapping him on the shoulder.

"What can I do for you?" he yelled back.

"Can you turn it down? I'd like for the guests to hear each other."

The DJ frowned. "Ms. Bankovic asked that I keep it at party level."

"Sasha?" I confirmed. "This is a business party, not a frat party," I said over the music. "Turn it down."

The DJ grudgingly complied, and I walked away, thoroughly satisfied. That warm, fuzzy feeling from my small victory didn't last long. Sasha had Jared cornered a few feet from the punch bowl. He looked bored and uncomfortable; she was giggling, gesturing to the mistletoe above them.

"Hi, baby," Jared said emphatically, pulling me to his side.

"Nina," Sasha said, surprised. "What are you doing here?" I raised an eyebrow. "I mean . . . Where have you been?"

"With the DJ, insisting he lower the music to an acceptable decibel. Now, if you're finished flirting, I'll save my fiancé from beneath the mistletoe so you no longer have a reason to threaten him with your dry, clumpy lipstick."

Sasha's mouth fell open, but I didn't give her enough time to fire back a reply. A slow song came over the speakers, and I pulled Jared to the center of the dance floor.

His fingers pressed into my skin, eager and anxious. "Would it be redundant of me to say that I enjoy it very much when you're jealous and mean?"

"Yes, but say it anyway," I smiled, wrapping my arms around his neck. Before long, more couples joined us, and we were lost in a sea of lovers swaying to the music.

When the song ended, Jared left for the punch-bowl line, and I stayed behind to greet co-workers and guests. Some were retirees, men and woman who had been with Titan since the beginning. Seeing them brought back hundreds of memories, and it was soon a relief to welcome the new faces of the company.

"You shouldn't be standing around when there's a slow song, peanut," Grant said. He undoubtedly wore his most charming smile.

"I'm here with Jared, Grant," I sneered.

"Oh, come on," Grant grinned. "Just one dance?"

"No."

He laughed and shook his head. "You look," he gave me a once-over, "incredible. Red is . . . wow."

"Thank you," I said, looking in every direction but his.

"Are you sure you— Jared! Nice to see you."

The pleasant expression on Jared's face as he handed me the small plastic cup faded abruptly when he turned to Grant. "I wish I could concur," Jared said, noticeably restrained. "You might have better luck with the interns." He nodded to a dark corner of the room. "They're spiking their punch and might be more susceptible to your persistence."

Grant's smile didn't budge. "Happy Holidays to you both."

"Merry Christmas," Jared said.

The people around us were beginning to stare, so I looked to the floor, attempting to downplay the spectacle Jared had made.

"What is with you?" I said, trying to keep my head down.

"I didn't want him to be under the impression that I liked him."

"You made your point. Now, can you please be the reserved, controlled Jared I know and love? I need to earn the respect of the people here."

"I'm sorry," Jared said, kissing my hair.

"Nina?" a voice called from across the room. I winced at the horrid sound and then turned to see Sasha barreling toward me with someone in tow.

"Practice what you preach," Jared said with a contrived smile.

Sasha's annoying smirk twisted her face in a way that made her already sharp features seem cartoon-like. She gestured to the brawny, dark-haired man behind her.

"I'd like for you to meet my date, Ryan Scott. Ryan, this is a fellow intern of mine, Nina Grey."

I couldn't hide the instant shock and dismay that came over me.

Ryan held out his hand. "Intern? Doesn't she run the company?" He winked.

Sasha laughed once, caught. "Er, not yet."

I took Ryan's hand. "I believe we've met."

"Oh?" Sasha said, genuinely intrigued.

Ryan glanced at Jared and then back at me. "Could I steal you for a minute?"

"No," Jared said without pause.

I chuckled nervously and then peered up at Jared from under my lashes. "I'll just be a minute."

Jared frowned, but he didn't argue.

"Well," Sasha said to Jared in her high-pitched, irritating voice, "I guess it's just you and I, then."

"I'll be *right* back," I said, staring directly at Sasha.

Ryan held me by the arm, quickly stopping in a quiet corner. "I thought we had a deal."

"A deal?" I hissed. "I agreed that I owed you for helping me fool Jared. I didn't say I would help you talk to Claire. Ambushing her is not a good idea."

He sighed. "Well, I've got a lot on my plate right now. My partner was murdered, and I think it has something to do with the other police deaths over the last year. I think they're all connected. I need to talk to her before I can get my head on straight enough to investigate this. It's big, Nina, really big, and I can't focus on it if my mind is always on Claire."

"You're investigating the police murders?"

Ryan's features were so stern I was suddenly nervous. "Not officially. Anderson and I were both on the case before he was killed. I wasn't sure before that they were connected, but now that Kit's dead, I know. Even the ones that appeared to be accidents."

"Listen—"

"No, you listen. I'm in a lot of trouble. No one else at the station knows what we were up to, and if they do, they're not going to let a rookie take the case. They killed my partner, Nina. It's personal. If I don't figure this out soon, you can kiss my ass good-bye. This is serious, and I need to be focused, but Claire's eyes above me in that hellhole are all I can think about."

"Are you finished?" I said, irritated.

"No," he said, frowning. "And just so you know, I'm really, really sorry."

"For what?" I said, returning his expression.

Ryan grabbed each side of my face and kissed me. Not just any kiss. His tongue was inside my mouth, and he kissed me so passionately that it was beyond obscene in front of everyone I worked with, not to mention my fiancé.

Before the embarrassment soaked in, Ryan was thrown across the room and slid on his side along the dance floor, stopping just before he crashed into the DJ station.

The music abruptly cut off, clearing the air for the screams and audible panic.

"Jared, stop!" I shouted, watching him charge.

I ran across the wooden floor, hoping to stop any bloodshed, but before I reached Ryan, Claire appeared in front of him, in a protective stance, facing her brother.

Jared stood motionless, breathing heavily from the angry adrenaline running through his veins. "He did it on purpose," Jared huffed.

"And you played right into his plan," Claire said lividly. She turned to Ryan. "Kissing my sister? That's how you planned to get my attention?" she said, pulling him up by his tie.

Ryan choked a bit before loosening up the knot around his neck and then smiled. "I did what I had to," he said to Claire and then looked to Jared. "I'm sorry."

"I don't care what your reasons are. Don't ever touch Nina like that again. I can't kill you, but I'll make you wish you were dead." Jared grabbed my hand and then led me from the party, down two flights of stairs, and out to the parking lot.

When we reached the Escalade, I covered my mouth with one hand. Jared was still angry, but when he looked at me, I couldn't help but smile.

"He so got you," I said, trying not to laugh out loud.

Jared smiled. "He did, didn't he?"

We both laughed aloud, uncontrollably, more than we had ever done before. By the time we were finished, I was breathless, and the muscles in my stomach were sore and tight.

We drove home, hand in hand, smiling at one another at each stoplight. Ryan finally getting face time with Claire should have been a disaster, but a sense of relief surrounded us, as if our group was finally complete. I had no idea what Claire would tell Ryan—how much truth she would really share—but Ryan being Claire's taleh, and the fact that he was now in love with her, was proof that we were supposed to be in each other's lives. Jared's prediction was wide of the mark, but he had never looked so happy to be wrong since we'd met.

The next day, I awoke to large flakes of snow falling gracefully from the sky. Each fluffy white piece drifted downward as if it were orchestrating its own symphony. Looking out the window, the ground was already covered in at least two feet of snow, and the grey clouds above didn't foretell anything but more of the same.

"It's been like that since four a.m.," Bex said from the hallway.

I tightened my robe around me and opened the door.

Bex stood before me, bored and holding a half-eaten apple. He took another bite, crunching loudly. "He's bringing coffee."

"Good," I said, leaving him to head for the bathroom.

Steam from the shower quickly surrounded me, but before I rinsed the shampoo from my hair, I heard the door open.

"Jared?"

"It's me," Claire said, shutting the door behind her.

I peered through the fuzzy glass, barely able to make out her tiny frame. "What are you doing here?"

"I've been up all night with Ryan. We talked a lot. We fought more."

"Oh? About what?"

"About what he saw in the desert and if I was there or not. He knows the men who stabbed him last year were cops. He knows a lot more than we thought. Finally . . ." She sighed, "Finally I just told him."

"Everything? You confessed about the other cops and the commissioner? About Anderson and about what you are?"

"Not yet."

"How did you explain without telling him everything?"

"I promised I would explain later." She frowned. "It doesn't feel right to tell him, Nina. We were raised on the belief that this secret kept our family safe."

"Then don't tell him until it feels right."

"What if it never feels right?"

"I don't know," I said, turning off the water. A towel flew up and over the shower door, landing on my head. "Thanks."

"Don't mention it," Claire said, shutting the door behind her.

By the time I was dressed and ready, Claire, Jared, and Bex were downstairs in the kitchen, discussing Ryan. Just by entering the room, I saw that it was obviously not a constructive conversation.

"You're such a hypocrite!" Claire growled.

Jared slammed the side of his fist on the table. "Are you in love with him?"

"No!"

"Then it's a different scenario!" Jared glanced in my direction and then took a breath, attempting a calmer tone. "You said it yourself. It doesn't feel right to tell him."

I sat down, scanning the siblings with my eyes before speaking. Outwardly, Claire was angry, but her eyes were begging for understanding. Telling Ryan anything was a huge step for her. Just as Jared struggled with it two years before, Claire was now fighting with her conflicting feelings. She needed her brothers to support her.

I took a seat across from Jared and next to Claire. The choice was meaningful, and I hoped that they would notice. "Maybe Claire is looking for your blessing, Jared," I said.

"Or just some understanding," she grumbled.

Bex stood up and walked across the kitchen, picking up a plate and then setting in front of me. It was an omelet, loaded with ham, green onion, mushrooms, and cheese.

"Thanks," I smiled.

Bex nodded and then touched his sister's shoulder. "Claire, I love you, but take a step back and think about this. Ryan is a cop. He's investigating murders *you* committed. What do you think he's going to do when you tell him you murdered his partner? You think he's going to forgive you because he saw your eyes in the desert?"

"The partner who orchestrated his kidnapping and ultimate demise," Claire said. "Listen." She sighed. "I know how it looks on paper. I may not be in love with Ryan, but he says he's in love with me. If he listens to what I have to say and I approach it carefully, I think he could be an asset."

"We can't take that chance," Jared said, finality in his voice.

Claire stood, her palms flat on the table. "You took the same chance when you told Nina, and she wasn't even an asset! Her life has spun out of control since the second you revealed yourself to her, Jared. At least let me make my own decision, as you did!"

Jared's nose wrinkled in disgust. "You were on me for months about Nina, Claire! How quickly you forget the hours I spent listening to your lectures on doing the right thing. Keep the secret. Keep the secret! That's been your mantra for years!"

Tears filled Claire's eyes as her face turned red. "Coming from you!" she screamed. "You know what it's like to have no one, and you know what it's like to finally be free of the burden of what we are, to have someone else besides your mother or your brothers to confide in! I have *no one*, Jared! You've lived it, and you still deny me the liberation you insisted on?"

Jared shifted in his seat, but I could see in his eyes he would not yield. Claire saw it too.

"Go to hell!" she shrieked before storming out of the house. She slammed the door with such force that the surrounding painting and pictures on the wall fell from their nails and crashed to the floor.

"You're making a mistake," I said, meeting Jared's obstinate stare. "Claire, wait!" I yelled, hoping she would hear it before she sped away. I ran outside, stopping at the Lotus.

Claire wiped her eyes. "Sorry. I cry when I'm mad."

"I do too," I said, offering an apologetic smile.

"He asked me to go to Anderson's funeral." Claire focused her eyes straight forward, too emotional to make eye contact.

"Are you going?"

"I couldn't think of a good enough reason when he asked, but I shouldn't. It's wrong."

"I'll go with you."

Claire's ice blue eyes darted up in surprise. "You will?"

"Yeah," I said. "When?"

"In an hour," she said, attempting to mask her hopeful expression.

I looked at my watch. "Okay. Give me a minute to get dressed."

Jared frowned as I slipped on a demure black dress. I sat down on the bed to pull up my black stockings, and he sat beside me.

"This is inappropriate on so many levels," he said.

"Kind of like you sitting next to the reason your father lost his life on the night he died?" I said, slipping on my heels. Jared helped me with my coat, and then I poked a pearl earring into each of my ears. I turned, cupping his jaw with my hands. "Your point is justifiable, but it is her choice, Jared, just as it was yours. Trust Claire to make her own decision. She's never let you down before."

"She's never wanted to tell before."

"Then that's your answer," I said, kissing his soft, warm lips. His mouth lingered on mine, and then I pulled away, knowing Claire was anxiously waiting.

I returned to the Lotus alone, slipping into the passenger seat. Claire pulled on her large, dark sunglasses and then shoved the gear into first, soaring down the drive, and fishtailing when she hit the street.

Saints Peter and Paul Cathedral was surrounded by dozens of police cruisers and even more civilian vehicles. The line at the entrance was already backed up to the next block by sniffling mourners.

"We should have come earlier," I said.

"We shouldn't be here at all," Claire said quietly. "Shit."

A knock on her window prompted Claire to roll it down, revealing Ryan in his dress blues. "You made it," he said with a reserved grin. He opened the door for Claire and then jogged around the front of her car, opening the door for me. "Thanks for coming. It means a lot."

I simply nodded, walking behind Ryan as he escorted Claire to the front steps, bypassing the endless line of weeping friends and family. As we passed them, some recognized Ryan and shook his hand. Seeing him seemed to upset some of the women, and even some of the men fought back tears as Ryan traded quiet words during a short hug. Once they acknowledged Ryan, their expressions changed to curiosity, evaluating the small young lady in the black leather dress with pointed-toe stilettos.

Each person we passed offered a pained expression for Ryan and then regarded Claire with bewilderment. Claire's dress was long-sleeved, with a respectable crew-neck line. Her skirt was short but an inch longer than mid-thigh. Maybe it was her beauty that struck them or the black stilettos that shot up from the ground, turning into a slithering snake with a shiny, turquoise eye on the stainless steel heel of her shoe.

The ensemble was something only Claire would dare wear to a funeral, but the look fit her. Ryan didn't seem to mind. Before we reached the doorway, Ryan took Claire's hand in his and led her down the aisle. She glanced back at me, unsure of how to react.

We walked to the front of the sanctuary, seated behind the family, but on the first row of police officers who served with Kit Anderson. Ryan sat between Claire and me, making the situation even more uncomfortable. The pianist worked the keys, and a solemn song echoed throughout the church. Two rows ahead, in the center of the pew, two small children sat on each side of a woman. A man sitting in front of Claire reached forward to touch the woman's shoulder. She patted his hand and then squeezed her young son closer.

My fingers touched my lips. "Oh my God," I whispered.

"Yeah," Ryan said, leaning into my ear. "That's his wife and his two kids. His little girl is three. His son is seven."

I couldn't hide the horror in my eyes as I looked to Claire. She was impervious, lowering her chin as a gesture for me to remain calm. Each second after that moment was an eternity: the eulogy, the service, and the songs. Once the prayer began, I scrambled from my seat, ignoring those I forced to stand or slide their legs over while I side-stepped to escape.

The doors pushed open, and the brisk air in my lungs felt like the first time I'd breathed in over an hour. The railing was the only thing keeping me erect while I struggled to catch my breath.

"Nina, Jesus!" Claire said. She grabbed my arm, steadying my weak knees. "You just ran—not walked—*ran* out of the funeral of a murdered Providence police officer! Why don't you just tape a target to your back?"

"He had babies! A family!" I cried.

"You have a family too," Claire said. "We just happen to have better aim."

"We should have talked to him, given him a chance to do the right thing."

Claire grabbed my shoulders. "Kit Anderson was a father and a husband, but if I hadn't taken him out, he would have handed Ryan over to Donovan's men, and Ryan would be dead right now."

"It doesn't make sense. Why would they need Ryan? If they wanted you, why not just come to you?"

"Leverage and control," Claire said. "It's a way to hold me hostage when they know they could never hold *me*."

"Are you all right?" Ryan called, running down the steps to the sidewalk. He lifted my chin. "What happened back there, Nigh?" He looked to the church and then back to me.

"I'm sorry," I said. "I haven't been to a funeral since Jack."

"Oh. Of course, I didn't realize," Ryan said, hugging me for a brief moment. "Maybe some food might make you feel better? Have you eaten?"

"No, actually," I said, just realizing that fact.

"The wives are cooking for the guys at the station and taking some food over to the family too. Let's stop by there before you two head home."

"Nina has some things to do," Claire said, slipping on her sunglasses.

Ryan's eyes met mine. His expression told me this was the moment of reparation.

"I should eat," I said.

Even through her dark glasses, I could see Claire's big eyes zero in on mine, an indication of the retribution I would receive once we were alone.

Ryan's smile spanned from one side of his face to the other. "Okay, then. You wanna ride with me?"

"Yes," I said without pause. If I was lucky, I could postpone my punishment until Jared was around. As much as I loved Claire, she was still intimidating.

The ride to the North Providence Police Station was full of tension, although Ryan babbled like a nervous teenager on his first date. Few people had left the church by the time we'd arrived, but within the half-hour, the small space quickly overflowed.

Ryan, Claire, and I retreated to a smaller room where the officers on duty were watching television and playing cards, and two in the corner were arm wrestling.

"Scotty Dog!" one of the officers said. "Which one's the ex and which one's your date?"

"Stow it, McCarty," Ryan said. "Claire, Nina, this is Matt, and that's Pat." He gestured to the officer wrestling Matt's hand to the table. Finally, Pat succeeded.

"I was distracted!" Matt said.

Ryan laughed. "You're such a baby, McCarty. Take the loss like a man."

Matt tapped the table. "Come on, then, Scotty. Put your money where your mouth is."

Ryan watched Matt pull out a fifty-dollar bill, slamming it on the table. Claire's body language was notably different. She raised her hand to her mouth, subtly trying to cover the slight grin that touched the corners of her mouth.

Ryan saw Claire's expression as well, prompting him to sit, and then roll up his sleeves. "Let's do it."

Their hands and arms shook as they pushed against the other. Matt's face was red, and a vein had popped out on his forehead like a pulsating worm slithering under his skin.

"You gonna let the rookie beat you, McCarty?" Pat said, smiling at the spectacle.

A few moments later, Ryan slammed Matt's hand to the table. "Yeah!" he grunted, standing up in celebration.

"Oh, brother," Claire said, rolling her eyes. "I thought you invited us to lunch, not a pissing contest."

"You wanna stab at it?" Ryan asked, returning to his seat.

Claire stiffened. She was competitive, and being forced to lose to Ryan to protect her identity was not something she would handle well.

"Don't do it," I whispered.

"I won't be easy on you just because you're a girl," Ryan said.

Matt laughed. "I don't know. She's got some eggs on her arms."

By the look on his face, Ryan knew exactly what he was doing. He had experienced her strength before, and he was going to test his theory.

"I don't want to hurt you," she said, uninterested. "You're still healing."

Ryan shrugged. "Then I'll use the other arm. I'll still beat you."

Claire sat in the open chair.

"Claire, no," I said.

Ryan held up his hand and Claire took it. She lowered her chin, glaring into Ryan's eyes.

"She's feisty," Matt said, intrigued.

"Shut up, McCarty," Pat said.

"Say, 'Go,' Nina," Claire said.

"This is stupid." I said, attempting a last chance to avoid the only two products of their ridiculous stand-off—neither of them good.

"Go!" Matt yelled.

Their arms turned rigid, and then their hands began to tremble. I knew the shaking was on Ryan's part; Claire looked bored.

After fifteen seconds, the officers around the table began to harass Ryan. "I thought you said you wouldn't go easy on her, Scotty Dog?" McCarty smirked.

"Come on, Scotty. Quit foolin' around," Pat said.

Ryan's face turned several shades of red, and then beads of sweat formed on his brow.

Claire raised an eyebrow and then pushed a bit, leaning Ryan's hand closer to the table.

McCarty laughed out loud. "She's gonna beat him! Scotty's gonna get beat by a girl!"

Ryan took a deep breath and then pressed his lips together, holding his breath and straining so hard I thought he might pass out.

Claire looked at Matt and then back at Ryan. She rolled her eyes, and the slight tension in her arm gave way. Ryan slammed her hand to the table.

The officers all cheered, and Ryan stood, rubbing his arm.

"You're not serious," Matt said, doubtful.

Claire patted the empty table space in front of her and smiled. "Have a seat, sweet pea."

"This is bad, bad idea," I said. "Claire, it's time for us to go."

Matt put up his hand and Claire took it.

I turned to Ryan. "Don't let her do this. It's going to draw attention."

"To what?" he asked, focused on my eyes.

I recoiled from his stare. "Nothing."

"Go!" Pat said.

Matt's arm stiffened against Claire's. Before long, his face was as red as Ryan's had been just moments before.

"Holy God, you're strong!" Matt grunted.

"Claire, please," I said. "We have to go!"

"Okay," she said, slamming his hand to the table, immediately bringing it back to the start position. "Officers," she nodded.

It was hard not to sprint to the car. Jared's reaction was at the forefront of my mind. "Stupid! That was so," I wheeled around, stopping Claire in her tracks, "stupid!"

Claire kissed my nose. "No, it was fun. Let's go."

15. THE TRUTH IN SIXTY SECONDS

Jared shut the curtains, allowing me to relax a bit. The morning sun hurt my eyes, and the ache in my head throbbed every time my heart beat. I turned another page of my textbook, trying to catch up to classmates who hadn't missed the last two days.

I pressed my fingers against the skin between my eyebrows. "The computer guy didn't know what he was talking about," I said. "I said simple. This laptop is impossible."

Jared rubbed my back. "Not impossible. You just have to adapt to change."

I slammed my book shut. "That's all I do, Jared, adapt to change. The only thing that is constant is the fact that everything keeps changing."

Jared smiled, kissing my shoulder. "I'll leave you alone to finish your paper, and then we're going to get out of the house for a while."

"Thanks," I grumbled, opening my book again.

My eyes passed over the words, but nothing sunk in. Wedding plans, Kit Anderson's children, Ryan being in danger, dead birds, and the whereabouts of the book danced around in my mind. Each thought lingered only for a few seconds, and then I flipped to the next one like the channels of late-night television. When I caught myself wandering from the topic of my paper, I would force my focus back to reality. Each time that happened, I grew more frustrated.

Two hours and six pages later, I pulled on my boots and met Jared outside. The crisp air surrounded me as I walked down the drive, and I buttoned my coat to ward off the cold.

The Escalade was left running so I wouldn't have to shiver while the cab warmed to a tolerable temperature. Jared helped me inside with a smile, kissing my red nose before shutting the door, and then we made a new set of tracks down the street. The sky had dropped another six inches of snow on the ground, but only after a few hours of sleet had laid down a solid bed for the snow to stick to.

Jared had no trouble navigating through the ice and powder, but red and blue lights lit the inside of the cab, and the Escalade came to a stop next to a nine-foot snow drift.

"Can't he just *call*?" Jared said, gripping the steering wheel.

Ryan knocked on the window, and Jared lowered it. Ryan began to speak, but Jared let his finger off the button, stopping the window halfway. Ryan waited patiently, and then Jared lowered the window again. When it was at chin level, Ryan addressed me, but Jared, once again, let his finger off the button.

"Funny," Ryan said. "Where's Claire? I haven't heard from her today."

"It's possible she's not going to pick up the phone every time you call, Ryan," Jared said, amused.

Ryan's eyes focused on me. "Have you seen her?"

"Not today. If she's not answering, then she must be busy."

Jared sighed. "If you pull me over every time you can't get Claire on the phone, we're going to be seeing a lot of each other."

"I just . . ." He shook his head. "I just came across some information I wanted to share with her about the investigation."

"Like what?" Jared asked, annoyed but curious.

Ryan narrowed his eyes. "Walter Graham was the man who tried to rob Nina outside the pub. Ronnie Studebaker, whose friends called him 'Stu,' was the man who stabbed me. Robert Benson was with them. They were never caught or charged."

"Yeah. So?" Jared said, impatiently.

"They were all detectives of the Providence Police Department. Now they're dead. Graham was killed while answering a robbery call, Benson stopped breathing in his sleep, and Stu went missing. His body has never been found. I can't account for the fourth man involved in the attack."

"Do you have a point, Ryan?" Jared said.

"Commissioner Johnson and six members of state government, in addition to seven police officers, have come to untimely deaths in the last eighteen months, including Kit Anderson. Graham was killed the same night twenty-three deaths were reported in Rhode Island and Massachusetts. All GSWs."

Jared laughed once. "You're not telling me anything I don't know, Ryan."

"Exactly. How do you know this information unless you are responsible for forty-one deaths?"

"Whoa! You are way off, Ryan," I said, shocked at his conclusion.

Ryan leaned into the window. "You know what I think? I think the cops were dirty and that the cops and those dead officials are part of some sort of crime ring and Nina got mixed up in it somehow. There's no way you could have killed twenty-three people at the same time in two different states, so I think they lied about what happened. You with me so far?"

Jared grinned, amused with Ryan's story. "I'm with you. You're full of crap, but I'm with you."

"I think everyone who's dead is a threat to you somehow because they know too much about whatever it is that you do. The question is how much is too much? And how much more can Claire tell me before you take me out?"

Jared laughed out loud. "You should ease up on the cop shows, Ryan. Now, if you don't mind, my fiancée and I have wedding shopping to do."

"Wait," Ryan said, "you're not married yet?" He looked to me, genuine surprise on his face.

"We've been busy," I said, embarrassed.

Jared's jaw tensed. "The date has been set. June first. We'll be sure to send you an invitation; that is if I haven't taken you out yet."

The wheels spun against the wet snow, but the Escalade didn't move. "Damn," Jared said.

He pushed open the door, forcing Ryan to jerk back, and disappeared behind the vehicle. The snow drift kept me from getting out on my side, so I climbed over the console, and Ryan helped me to the ground.

"What are you doing?" I asked Jared.

"Digging the truck out. It'll be just a minute, sweetheart," he assured me.

"Do you want help?" Ryan asked.

"No," Jared said quickly.

I turned to Ryan, crossing my arms. "You don't really think Jared is responsible for your partner's death, do you?"

"If he is, Kit's not the first cop he's killed. There is a single connection tying every single one of those deaths together. Maybe you could talk your boy into keeping his gun in his holster until I figure it out. Or maybe you could just tell me."

"I don't know anything," I said, feigning offense.

"I saw what Jared is capable of the night I was stabbed. I've experienced firsthand what Claire can do. They aren't normal. I know Graham and the other cops were dirty, but Anderson was a good man. He didn't deserve to die. Quit treating me as if I can't keep a secret and just tell me."

I looked past Ryan to see Jared stand up, look around, and then lean against the Escalade, freeing it from the ruts without effort.

"Okay, baby. We're out. Let's go."

Ryan walked to the Escalade, evaluating the slide marks the tires had made. He craned his neck at Jared. "I'm going to figure this out. It would save us all a lot of time and energy if you'd just tell me."

"Let's go, Nina," Jared said.

I nodded, climbing into the cab.

"Maybe I could help you. Have you thought about that?" Ryan said.

Jared took off, leaving him in the snow-buried street.

I pulled my coat tighter around me and stuffed my hands under my arms. "It wouldn't hurt to have a connection in the police department."

"Not Ryan," Jared said.

"You sure talk a lot of smack to Claire about thinking with your emotions. You're not being objective at all!"

Jared ignored me, instead, pulling over when he noticed a woman trying to dig the snow out from under her buried tires.

A short drive around town turned into a three hour-long aid mission to free stranded motorists from the ice and snow. I would pretend to help, and Jared would pull or push cars and trucks out of snow drifts, ditches, and the side of the road.

It felt good to use Jared's abilities to help others, even if it was something small.

When we returned to the house, Claire's Lotus was in the drive, along with a police cruiser.

"I don't believe it," Jared said, helping me from the passenger side. He carried me through the snow to the side entrance and then stomped through the house until he found them.

They sat in the kitchen at the breakfast table, laughing. Claire seemed genuinely happy for once, and I smiled at the sight.

"How long have you two been here?" Jared demanded.

Claire's smile faded. "Don't worry. I waited for you. I told Ryan you'd tell him what you thought he needed to know."

"No questions asked," Ryan promised.

Jared's hand balled into fists at his side, and the tendons in his neck were strained. It took every ounce of willpower he had not to charge.

"I'm not telling him anything," Jared growled. "Leave before I do something we'll all regret."

He turned his back to Claire, and she jumped up to stop him.

"Wait," I said, landing the palms of my hands on Jared's chest. "Sit. Calm down. We'll just talk," I said, nodding to Claire and Ryan. "Let's just sit down and hear them out, and if you still feel the same way, we'll go."

Jared took a deep breath and then nodded, taking a seat across from Claire. I sat beside him, placing my hand on his knee.

Claire mimicked his sigh, turning to Ryan. "Anything Jared tells you is privileged information, Ryan. Nina has lied to you, to her best friends, and to her family. Are you sure you want to know?"

Ryan glanced at me.

I leaned forward. "It's not fun knowledge to have. In this case, ignorance *is* bliss. I recommend you walk away, but it's your decision."

Ryan met Claire's eyes. "I'm sure."

"Okay," Claire said. "First thing's first." She grabbed his shirt and ripped it open, popping off the buttons.

"Hey!" Ryan said, holding up his hands.

"Standard procedure," she said, pulling up his white undershirt, baring his chest. She ran her fingers down each side and then around his back.

"Come on. You think I'm wearing a wire?" Ryan said, looking at each of us.

"I killed your partner," Claire said, expressionless.

"What?" Ryan said. His eyebrows turned in, and he shifted nervously in his chair.

"Just get right to the point, Claire," Jared said, shaking his head in disapproval.

"Why would you kill Kit? He was a good man. He was a good cop . . . ."

"He set you up. He asked you to meet him so men working for someone named Donovan could kidnap you and ultimately use you as bait."

Ryan shook his head. "No, Kit wouldn't do that."

"Then he was forced. He has kids. They probably threatened to kill them if he didn't cooperate."

Ryan's shoulders fell. "So you were protecting me."

"That's my job," Claire said.

Ryan's once confused expression metamorphosed into suspicion. "W-What do you mean it's your job?"

"Here we go," I said, covering my mouth with my hands. I remembered the moment Jared had told me the truth about what he was, and I knew Ryan wouldn't believe her.

Claire was stoic. "I'm your guardian angel. My father was an angel; my mother is human. When my father fell in love with my mother and decided to stay with her, he was cursed by Heaven so he would continue to protect his taleh, his human."

"My dad," I added.

Claire continued, "The curse is carried throughout the bloodline for a few generations, so Jared, Bex, and I also have taleh. We have trained our entire lives to be able to protect you, and we have superhuman speed and strength. Nina is Jared's. You're mine. I killed Anderson to protect you. I killed everyone else to protect Nina so Jared could stay with her while she healed. I've watched you throughout your entire military career, and, yes, I pulled you out of the desert."

"I thought you said you were going to let me tell him," Jared said, displeased.

"I don't have all day," Claire answered.

Ryan was silent.

"You forgot the most important part," I said.

Claire rolled her eyes. "Oh yeah, and because of the curse, I can't die unless you do."

The room was silent. I squeezed Jared's knee, thankful he hadn't dropped the truth on me the way Claire had just done with Ryan. We all waited for him to breakdown, yell, or try to leave. He just sat in his chair, letting it soak in.

I took my hands from my mouth and slid them across the table. "Are you okay?" I asked, touching his hand.

"Yeah," he blinked. "Just trying to get it all straight in my head."

"If you tell anyone, I'll end your life," Jared said in a low, frightening voice.

"Not likely, since you'd also be killing your sister," Ryan said.

"He was paying attention," Jared said.

One side of Ryan's mouth turned up. "So you would literally take a bullet for me."

"No," Claire said, with zero emotion.

"No?" Ryan said, surprised at her answer.

Claire rolled her eyes, annoyed that she had to answer. "If I have time to stand in the way of a bullet, you have time to move."

"True," Ryan said, nodding.

"So the question is," I said, "what will you do with the information now that you have it?"

Ryan paused in thought and then fastened the few buttons left on his shirt. "Find Donovan."

"Welcome to our club," Bex said, plopping into the chair beside me. "I just talked to Kim. They're on the move."

"Kim. Our Kim?" Ryan asked, his eyes darting to me.

"Yes. She's sort of the opposite of a demon magnet."

Ryan left that one alone, turning to Claire. "It sounds like you left a lot out."

She stood, pulling Ryan with her. "Yes. This is going to be like on-the-job training. Can you handle it?"

"So far," he said.

"That's the hardest part," I said, turning to Bex. "Where are they now?"

Bex traded glances with Jared before he spoke. "We have to move. They have an entourage, so it will take all three of us."

"Okay," Jared said, nodding as he was lost in thought. "Where is Kim?"

Bex twitched. "Outside."

Jared nodded. "Kim stays with Nina."

"Jared!" I protested.

Claire pulled on her coat. "Did you hear Bex, Nina? The three of us are going. We don't need Kim."

"Ryan," Jared said. "I'll need you to stay with Nina. The only things you can't handle will be protecting what we're going after."

Ryan nodded. "I won't let her out of my sight."

"You have your gun?" Claire asked.

Ryan patted his side in confirmation.

I threw my arms around Jared and squeezed, shutting my eyes tight. "Don't stay away long."

"In and out, baby. In and out." He smiled.

"And don't come back full of bullet holes this time!" I called after him.

The door shut, and the sound of the Escalade's engine faded as everyone I loved most in the world traveled farther and farther away.

"Bullet holes?" Ryan asked.

"Come on," I said, pulling him into down the hall. "Let's find more comfortable chairs. This is going to take a while."

16. IF I TOLD YOU EVERYTHING

The rain beat against the window of the classroom, prompting Professor Sawyer to speak louder than her small voice could accommodate. Words squeaked from her throat as she struggled to lecture through the snickers and murmurs of the students.

Her words blurred together as I stared at the blank page of my laptop monitor. The nightmares were absent the night before, but only because sleep never came. The Ryels didn't return home until just before the sun rose, and even if I could have ignored the worry long enough for my eyes to close for a moment, Ryan's incessant questions kept me awake.

"So what if she gets shot in the head?"

"If I die and then Claire dies, does she go to Heaven?"

"What if I don't die but I'm a vegetable?"

"Can she get knocked out?"

"So her dad was an angel? Can he see me right now?"

"Can Gabe hear my thoughts? Because that would be no bueno."

His curiosity was insatiable. I finally lost my temper and yelled at him to shut up, but he only smiled and sat quietly long enough to think of more questions. For the first time, I was glad that Ryan was no longer enrolled at Brown.

I twirled the diamond ring around my finger, trying to block out images of what Bex and Claire had described earlier that morning. Their clash with Isaac and Donovan was short-lived, but had the Ryels been human, it would have been lethal. The vision of Isaac was so vivid and frightening in my mind, and the thought of coming face-to-face with him terrified me. He and Donovan had been commissioned to protect the *Naissance de Demoniac*, and because they were faced with all three of Gabe Ryel's children, they decided retreat was the prudent option—but not before sinking four bullets into Bex's chest.

The kitchen was a bloody mess by sunrise, and although Bex's eyes were wide with excitement, seeing Claire pluck the remnants of bullets from his flesh left me, well, unsettled.

"Oh, to hell with this! Class dismissed," the professor said in defeat.

I blinked, seeing the other students pack up without pause and leave the classroom. Once the doorway cleared, Kim stood with a smirk on her face.

"Why didn't you come back to the house with the others?" I asked.

She shrugged. "Two papers due today. I still go to class, you know."

"So how did it go?" I asked, following her down the hall. My feet scampered along her wide strides.

She shook her head, clearly troubled.

"Don't do that, Kim. You're the impervious one."

"Taking Shax or Donovan and Isaac head on isn't working. We need to think of another way to get the *Demoniac*. They know when we're coming. We can't distract them because they want nothing else more than that book."

I frowned, wary of Kim's uncharacteristic concern. "I still say we don't need it. Your family had the book all this time. You have to know what it said. Didn't you open it?"

"No," she said firmly. "I was never allowed to open it."

"What about your uncle? Your father? Between them and Father Francis, can't we just get enough information for Jared to work with?"

Kim lowered her chin. "I guess you didn't catch the part about how we weren't allowed to open the book."

"You said it yourself!" The words were louder than I'd meant for them to be. I looked around and then lowered my voice. "We can't take it when they know we're coming."

Kim nodded, but her somber expression melted away as an idea lit her eyes. "There is *one* thing they would want more than the book."

I shook my head. "No. No way, Jared would never go for it."

"We need them to come to us. We need bait."

"Think about it. He's not going to risk my life to save me, Kim. And I kind of hate you for even mentioning it."

"Hey, guys!" Beth yelped in her southern drawl. "Ew. That's a horrible face," she said, mirroring my expression.

Kim pulled a cigarette seemingly from nowhere and popped it between her lips. "We were just discussing how we would use Nina as bait to lure demons," she said flatly.

Beth's face morphed into revulsion. "What class are you guys taking?"

The corners of my mouth turned up, and I wrapped one arm around Beth's tiny waist. "Come on. I don't want to lose our table at the Ratty."

The three of us carried our trays to the corner spot, and I couldn't help but smile when I saw that Ryan's chair had been filled. His friends surrounded him with wide grins on their faces. They all talked and laughed, making the dead silence upon our approach that much more noticeable.

"Look who's back in town, babe!" Chad said, standing to greet Beth.

Beth's tray slapped against the table when she dropped it to throw her arms around Ryan.

"Hi, Bethy," Ryan said, giving her a squeeze.

"Yay!" Her pageant-smile stretched to its limit, showing every one of her teeth.

To the others, lunch with Ryan was a celebration, but as the questions about his last days at war, how he got hurt, and why he'd waited so long to tell them came, I grew nervous. So did Ryan.

He stood. "Well! I have to go home and get the old uniform on."

"I bet you look great in it." Lisa smiled. "I love men in uniform."

Kim rolled her eyes. "I'm out too. Let's go, Nina."

"Where are we going?" I asked, looking up at her.

"Yeah. Where're you going?" Ryan said.

Kim tugged on my arm until I stood. "To class, Detective," Kim said. "That okay?"

Ryan glanced at me and then shrugged. "Just asking."

Kim gestured for me to follow, and we walked to the parking lot. She glanced up once but didn't stop to explain why. Her long legs and quick strides had me struggling to keep up, and I was panting by the time we reached the Sentra.

The light sprinkles still falling from the grey clouds gently disturbed a large puddle near Kim's car. She barreled through it, splashing my jeans with dirty water.

"What's your hurry?" I asked, annoyed.

"I'm taking you to Quincy. We can talk to my father to see what he knows, and if he knows what I think he does—nothing—we present my idea to Jared."

"But I have class!" I protested.

"Jared doesn't show it around you, Nigh, but he's desperate. He knows something is coming. They're planning something, and we've got nothing. We have no idea how to protect you when we don't know what we're protecting you from."

"Demons," Ryan said. "Isn't that all we need to know?"

"No," Kim said. "And you're not invited."

"Well, that's too bad because I'm coming," he said. He opened the car door behind the passenger side and slammed it behind him.

Kim looked to me.

"Jared will follow us," I warned.

"So?" Kim said. "He'll want to know what my dad has to say, if he says anything."

I looked around; the Escalade was notably absent. "I haven't heard from any of them all day."

"Does being in the dark make you feel better? You should know by now why they keep things from you."

"It's bad, isn't it?" I said, afraid of the answer.

"Just get in the car," Kim said, settling in behind the wheel.

The drive to Quincy was silent, but when we slowed to a stop in front of a large gate, Ryan and I shared a collective gasp.

"This is your house?" Ryan asked, staring in awe at the looming mansion ahead.

"Yep," Kim said, keying in a code.

The gate opened slowly, and then Kim accelerated slowly. The gravel drive crunched beneath the Sentra's tires.

"No way," Ryan said, his mouth hung open.

"Yes, way," Kim said, turning off the engine.

Ryan and I leaned against our windows, amazed at the colossal building in front of us. It wasn't a home; it was a fortress.

Ryan glanced at Kim. "If you're so rich, why do you drive this piece of shi—"

"The Sentra serves its purpose."

I stepped onto the gravel drive. It snaked all the way to the large detached garage. Her house was bigger than mine and far more equipped with security. Cameras were mounted on every corner, and the black iron fence blocking general traffic from entering the drive spanned the entire estate.

Two large dogs ran with great leaps, barking wildly until they reached us.

"Hey boys!" Kim said, giving them both loving, vigorous scratches. When the reunion was over, she turned to us. "This is Zeus, and the little one is Hera."

"Neither of them is little," Ryan said.

The dogs led us to the front entrance, wagging their tails with such fervor that their entire back half wiggled with the movement.

Kim opened the door, revealing a vast foyer. A small round table stood in the center of the room, boasting an incredible vase that held beautiful long-stemmed flowers.

"Charlie!" Kim bellowed into the air, causing the dogs to bark. "Charlie!" she said again. Her voice echoed across the marble tile.

Two men entered the foyer, both no less than six feet, six inches tall. They were nearly equal in their massive size and so intimidating that I realized I was unconsciously cowering behind Ryan.

The larger of the two had a full brown beard. When his eyes focused on Kim, he held out his arms, and a wide smile broke across his face. "Boo Boo!" he said, his booming voice reverberating throughout the house.

Kim made her way to him quickly, and as tall as she was, the massive arms that encircled her made her seem tiny. Kim's feet came off the ground as the man arched his back and then returned her to earth after a few sweet moments.

"Nigh, Ryan, this is my dad, Charles Pollock, and this is my uncle Bruce."

"Nice to meet you," I said, watching as my hand disappeared into each of theirs when I shook them.

Ryan did the same, but he didn't seem intimidated at all.

"How's school, Kimmie?" Bruce asked.

"I'm not really here to catch up. I brought Nina to meet you."

"Oh?" Charles asked, suddenly suspicious.

Bruce reached behind him but stopped, looking beyond me.

"Let's all just relax, here," Jared said from behind me. I turned to see both of his arms outstretched in front of him, his Glock securely between his hands.

Bruce glanced at Charlie, me, and then at Kim, grudgingly pulling his sidearm slowly and carefully from behind him and placing it on the ground.

"It's okay, Bruce," Kim said.

Jared released the hold he had on his weapon and then stood beside me, placing it on the table next to him.

Bruce pulled another gun from his back, pointing it at Jared's face, but then his shoulders dropped. "How many of them are there?" he said.

"Three," Claire said. I turned to see her in the same stance as Jared. "And if you pull a weapon on us again, I'll blow out your knee cap."

"Bruce," Kim said, shaking her head in warning.

Bruce put the second gun down and then pulled up his pant leg, revealing another gun. He set all three side by side on the ground and then stood.

"You sure you don't want to check the other leg?" Claire asked, her weapon still drawn.

Bruce sighed and then reached down, pulling a rather large hunting knife from a holster. "That's all of it."

"Kim," Charles said, stiffly and nervously. "What's going on here?"

Kim reached out to her father. "Nina is my friend, Dad. And she's important. These people are here to protect her. They're not here to harm us."

Charles nodded slowly and then touched the arm of his brother. "Easy, Bruce."

Bruce relaxed, and Claire stepped out of her rigid stance, replacing her gun in its holster.

Jared turned to me. "What the hell are you doing here?"

"Don't cuss at me," I said, immediately defensive.

Anger lit Jared's eyes. "You . . . You have no idea how dangerous it is for you right now."

"Maybe I would if you would just *tell* me."

"If I told you everything, you wouldn't want to leave the house. And I don't want that for you," he said, his eyes dark. "But you can't do certain things, Nina, and running off with two humans without telling me where you're going is one of them."

"I'm sorry." I huffed. "I thought you'd just follow."

"Oh," Jared said, taken aback. "You did?"

"Oh, Christ, let's hear what Kim has to say and get out of here," Claire snapped.

I peeked at our audience, embarrassed about the outburst. "Sorry," I said, clearing my throat.

"The book," Kim said to Charles.

"Kim!" Bruce said. Charles made a small gesture with his hand, and Bruce immediately conceded.

"They know," Kim said.

"You're the son of Gabriel, aren't you?" Charles said, clearly in awe.

"One of them," Jared answered.

Bruce's face turned red. "Thief. If he hadn't taken the damn book, none of this would be happening."

Claire took a step forward, and Jared gripped her shoulder. "You call my father that again," Claire seethed, "and it will be the last word that comes from your mouth."

"They're going to help me," Kim interceded.

"What?" Charles said, confused.

"Jared promised to help me return the *Demoniac* to the Sepulchre in Jerusalem."

Charles' eyes darted to Jared. "Is this true?"

"Yes," Jared said. "I need time to study it, but after that, you have my word."

Charles took a step back and then walked several steps away with Bruce right behind him. They conversed in low whispers and then returned.

"We can't trust them," Charles said, finality in his tone.

"None of that matters now," Kim said. "We've all got some history here; that's apparent. But we need to focus on the problem. Dad, Nina is the woman in the prophecy in the *Naissance de Demoniac*. Does that mean anything to you?"

Charles' eyes shifted to mine, and then he scanned me from my hair to my shoes. "No," he paused. "*Who* is she?"

Kim turned to me. "I told you. We're not allowed to open the book. He knows nothing."

"Is that why you came here?" Jared said, livid. "I could have told you that! If Charles knew anything, Gabe and Jack wouldn't have taken it in the first place!"

"It was worth a try because our next option is the last resort."

"What are you talking about?" Jared said.

I looked at the crowd of people around me, feeling the negative, hostile energy in the air. It was in that moment that I recognized we had finally come to the last leg of the journey. Getting the book back into our hands had always been the only choice, which was why Gabe and Jack had come to me with the answers at night.

"I have to distract Shax long enough for you to get the book," I said softly.

Jared turned to me, his eyebrows squeezed tightly together. "Are you serious?"

"No, Jared, she's trying to be funny. Of course she's serious," Kim said.

"Bad idea," Ryan said.

I reached out to Jared, touching his cheek with my fingertips. "It's the only way you're going to get the book.

Jared glanced at Claire and then back to me. "We've been trying to get the book to save you. It doesn't make sense to put you in danger in order to get our hands on it."

"This is stupid. Let's go," Claire said.

Kim held up her hands. "Wait. Just wait. We all know she doesn't have much time left."

Kim saying aloud what everyone else knew—and had hoped to keep from me—felt like a bittersweet release, but the siblings' expressions were ashamed.

Jared's eyes hit the floor.

"Did I miss something here?" Ryan said, shifting his weight. For the first time since we'd arrived, he seemed uneasy.

Kim's eyes met mine. "Both sides are talking. You know too much, Shax wants revenge, and you pose a threat to Hell just by being alive. We could pluck out your uterus today, and they would still end your life to prevent a miracle. You're going to die anyway, Nina. It's time we resort to desperate measures."

"Christ Almighty," Charles whispered.

The air was absent of sound. Everyone's eyes were on me, but I couldn't reply. I could barely breathe.

"I'm not going to let that happen, Nina," Jared said. "We can figure out another way."

"Is it true?" I said, looking up at him.

His eyes fell away from mine, and I knew the answer.

"Why is this happening?" I cried, pulling away from his grip.

"Nina," Claire said as I passed.

I ran outside into the rain. Since the day Jack died, my life had spun so far out of control it was hard to remember what my life was like when I was just like any other girl. It wasn't fair. Eli had instructed me to be strong and not to mourn the normal life I once had, but I didn't want to die—especially for a choice I didn't make.

Jared was immediately behind me, encompassing me in his warm arms. "I'm sorry," he whispered, his voice pained. "Let me find another way."

"No," I said, wiping my nose. "Let's just get it over with."

A few moments later, the rest of the group joined us. They all waited patiently for my answer.

Charles fidgeted. "I wish there was some way we could help you."

Kim hooked her arm with her father's. "I'm helping them," she said, her eyes strangely soft and sad. "I won't leave her side until it's finished."

Charles nodded, squeezing his daughter to his side.

"Okay," I said, shaking off the fear. "How are we going to do this?"

"This is crazy!" Ryan said. "Tell her, Jared! There's no way we're using her for demon bait!"

Jared cringed, but he didn't speak.

Claire grabbed my hand. "We choose our own fate, right, Nina?" she said, managing an encouraging smile.

"Yes," I said. "If it's going to happen, I want it to be on my terms."

"You're all insane!" Ryan said, horrified. "I feel like I'm watching you all sentence her to death!"

Kim opened the door to the Sentra. "Now all we need is a plan," she said.

Jared tugged on my hand. "Ride with me."

I squeezed his fingers in mine, knowing he faced the same fate as I. The ride home was quiet: no radio, no talking, just the noise of the road under the tires and the rain pounding against the windshield.

The window wipers danced back and forth, clearing the rain drops long enough to let the next droplets splash into their place. Headlights from oncoming cars whizzed by, but they were driving slowly because of the weather. It was Jared who was disregarding the speed limit by at least thirty miles per hour.

The decision to use me as a distraction was mine, but the plan was up to Jared. He would be forced to map out our every move, hoping that it was perfect enough to spare our lives.

"We can do this," Jared finally said, lifting my hand to his lips. "It's going to work, and we'll have the book, and then we can save you."

"I know," I said with a small smile. "I trust you."

"Sweet potato fries," he said, his cloudy eyes glossing over.

"Sweet potato fries." I smiled back.

17. THE ROOF

Jared paced, brooded, and once in a while, when his thoughts were particularly tormented, he winced. The color had long left his face as he played back the different scenarios in his mind. Back and forth, he paced so many times that I watched the floor, wondering when he would wear a trail. His inner turmoil could have set the room on fire. It was unbearable to watch, but I couldn't leave him, not when he was planning my death.

Claire sat next to me, holding my hand, suffering Jared's torture as I did. Jared had the most to lose, so the plan was his alone. Each decision, from the moment we left the house until the book was safe within its walls, fell on Jared's shoulders. Watching that responsibility slowly tear him apart was agonizing.

I did not envy his position. Just the thought of doing the same made me feel sick to my stomach.

Jared stopped mid-step. "Ryan?"

"Yeah, man?" Ryan said, standing. He had never been a fan of Jared, but we all shared a common thread. Whether we liked it or not, if one of us was hurt, we would all fall. A loss would affect all of us differently, but it would change our lives in the same horrific way.

"Come with me," Jared said, leaving the room.

Ryan glanced at Claire and then followed Jared into the hallway. Claire's grip on my hand tightened.

"You can hear them," I said.

She looked down at our hands and then closed her eyes. "Don't ask me to tell you, Nina. Let Jared do this his way."

"Okay," I nodded, trusting her judgment.

Ryan returned with a solemn expression. Uncomfortable at best, afraid was a more honest description, he took a few steps toward Claire and me and then held out his hand.

"Feel like going to the pub?" he asked me.

My eyes veered to Claire, and my head turned slightly unintentionally. "Um, I guess," I said, looking back to Ryan.

"Good. Give her something shiny, Claire," he said, pulling me to stand.

Claire reached behind her and held out her pistol. "Take it," she shrugged, trying too hard to seem indifferent. "I have seven more at home."

My first instinct was to ask a dozen questions, but something told me time was an issue. Jared wanted this to be over.

I took a deep breath. "On the bright side, if I die, I don't have to worry that I didn't study for the test I have in the morning."

"You're not going to die," Ryan said. "This is just a test run."

"A test run," I said, looking at the gun in my hand. "Okay. Let's see what they've got."

I followed Ryan into the hall, passing Jared along the way. He didn't meet my eyes, so I grabbed the sleeve of his shirt.

"You don't exactly exude confidence. Can you just pretend?"

He forced a smile. "I'll see you soon."

"Good job," Ryan said dryly, pulling me behind him.

In Ryan's truck, we took the short trip to the pub. Every bump, every pot hole, every street light seemed especially big or bright, as if my mind wanted to record every second of my last moments on earth.

The truck slowed to a stop in the parking lot across the street, and I looked out the window to the pub. College co-eds meandered on the sidewalk, congregating in small groups, laughing and chatting without a care in the world. I had seen a few of them in the halls of Brown, and I wondered what they would say when they heard the news and what the news would even be. Would the newspapers call it an accident? A murder? A suicide? I shuddered at thoughts of myself post-mortem. Would demons allow me any dignity or mercy at all?

"Ryan? If it comes down to it, don't let them take me, okay? I don't know what things a demon is capable of, but I don't want to . . . ." I struggled to say it aloud. "Don't let me suffer, okay? Take care of it. You know what I mean?"

"What?" he said, his nose wrinkling. "You mean you want me to issue a mercy shot before they drag you off to torture you to death?"

I didn't remember Ryan being so blunt before. Perhaps the desert had taken every bit of sensitivity he had left.

"I don't want to be alone with those things even for a minute. If they take me, I'm giving you permission."

"Stop," Ryan said. "I won't let anything happen to you, and I know Jared, Claire, and Bex are all watching. You act as if you've never been bait before."

I sighed. "Can't say that I have. Let's get this over with."

Ryan stepped out and then walked around, opening the door. We walked into the pub hand in hand, and Ryan scanned the dozen or so faces, picking a spot on the corner of the bar. He ordered a shot and two beers and then rested his elbows on the dark wood in front of him. The music was blaring, and the loud, variable tones of conversation blurred into one another.

"So what's the plan?" I asked over the music.

The bartender set our drinks on the bar, and Ryan tossed him a twenty. "I don't know. I'm just following orders. So far it's to drink, but not too much where I can't aim straight or it affects Claire."

"Aiming's not going to help," I grumbled. "Why do you get a shot and I don't?" I asked.

He threw the liquor down the back of his throat with one bend of the wrist. "Jared said you get one beer."

"Just one?" I picked at the label on the bottle. "I guess he drinks when I do."

We didn't bother to toast to anything. I tried my best to forget that I was terrified and sipped on the bitter, dark liquid until it was gone. Ryan ordered another round, but when the bartender placed a full bottle in front of me, Ryan grabbed it with his other hand, drinking from them both. So much time had passed since I'd had any alcohol at all, just the one round helped to drown out the laughter in the background, which became increasingly annoying as time dragged on.

When Ryan finally stood, I couldn't help but breathe a sigh of relief.

"That's it? We're done?" I asked.

Ryan shook his head. "No, we're just starting. Zip up your coat. We're going for a walk. Once we hit that door, I need Oscar-worthy drunk, giggly college kid on the sidewalk, okay?"

"Well, I've never felt so giggly in my life, so this should be a breeze," I deadpanned.

Ryan pushed open the door, and I hooked my arm in his. We walked a block and then made a turn. After two blocks, we turned in a different direction.

"This is obvious," I said, noting the dark street.

"Sshh, we're being followed," Ryan whispered.

"Goody," I said, trying to keep my steps in line with his.

Before we reached the corner, two men stepped onto the sidewalk from the alley. Ryan stopped, pushing me behind him.

"Hi there, boys," Ryan said.

One of the men smiled. "That's a pretty little girl you got there."

Ryan was clearly irritated. "Thanks. Tell your boss I'm insulted."

"And why's that?" the other man said, amused.

Ryan smiled. "You're smaller than I expected," he said, looking up at the ominous man looming over him.

Without warning, Ryan head-butted the first goon. The man stared into Ryan's eyes, stunned. Blood suddenly streamed from his nose, and then he stumbled back, finally falling to the ground.

The second man pulled his weapon. His small smirk quickly faded when Ryan and I traded glances and then pulled ours. Every nerve in my body was on edge. Instead of fear, I was fighting back a smile. Pointing a gun and being on the offensive were so empowering that I had to work to keep from giggling with excitement.

"He set us up!" the man said, kicking at his partner. He shook as he kept his gun pointed in our direction.

"Get up, Lenny! We got set up!"

"Put your gun on the ground!" Ryan growled. His voice sounded different than what I was used to, no doubt residuary from his tour in Afghanistan.

The man did as Ryan had commanded and then scampered off, pulling his friend with him. I clicked the safety on the pistol in my hand, habit from my lessons with Jared, and then stuffed it into the back of my jeans.

"That was the plan?" I asked.

Ryan put his hands low on his hips, spitting on the ground. "No. That was most definitely not the plan. They were supposed to take you."

"*Take* me?"

"Well, not *take* you, take you. Try to take you, I guess. I really don't know."

"That makes me feel a lot better!" I huffed.

Ryan froze when a clicking sound echoed in the alley behind us. Donovan stood just feet away, pressing the barrel of his gun to Ryan's head.

"So they're trusting humans to watch their talehs now, are they? I don't care if you are some sort of hero. I ain't buyin' it," Donovan said, looking around.

I reached for my gun, but a warm hand encircled my wrist. "She's a brave little pistol, isn't she?"

If it weren't for the voice, I would have expected to turn and see Jared standing behind me. The same warm skin, the smell, the blond hair—but his eyes were a lighter blue than Claire's—almost white. He was so tall I had to take a step back just to get a good look at him.

"Isaac?" I whispered.

He smiled and then smirked at Donovan. "I'm famous."

"And dead if we don't get the hell outta here. They wouldn't leave her alone."

"Of course not," Isaac said calmly. "But we'll play."

Isaac and Donovan led us down the alley to a waiting car. Isaac wasn't nearly as gentle as the other celestial beings I'd met. It shouldn't have surprised me; a hybrid that protected a man who worked for demons had to have been so far detached from his origins and core beliefs. I didn't dare attempt to let my mind linger on what he was capable of.

After tying our hands behind our backs, Donovan hit Ryan on the head with the butt of his gun, and after a short *crack*, Ryan fell limp. Isaac slipped a black cover over his head and then tossed him into the back seat of the car. Ryan's head fell against the door on the other side.

"Don't!" I said, recoiling.

Isaac smiled and then shoved the same black covering over my head, tenderly helping me to a spot next to Ryan.

"I don't tolerate violence against women," Isaac said.

A part of me was relieved, but knowing they meant to kill me, I obsessed about the meaning behind Isaac's words for the entire trip to our destination.

Still blinded by the fabric over my face, I was pulled out of the car and then escorted up a short flight of stairs. We paused for a moment but quickly continued after the sound of a creaking door.

"More stairs," Isaac said, patiently waiting for me to find my footing. Our footsteps echoed against a hardwood floor, and then I was seated.

The fabric was lifted from my face. Instinctively, I studied my surroundings. The room was large, and as my eyes scanned over the axes and swords that hung on the walls, absolute horror struck me.

"This is Shax's building," I gasped.

"Yes," Isaac said. "The last place you'll ever see."

I swallowed hard. Isaac's voice was so pleasant, almost maniacal. His soft tone, coupled with the absence of all humanity in his eyes, was beyond frightening.

"Nina?"

I rotated my neck to its limit to see Ryan sitting in a chair directly behind me, his back to mine. "Are you okay, buddy?" I said.

Blood saturated his hair line just above the temple. "Besides my head throbbing so hard my eyeball feels like it's going to pop out? Peachy."

He squinted, obviously in pain.

"You didn't have to do that," I growled at Donovan.

"That's the beauty of it." Donovan smiled.

"Where's Shax?" I asked.

"Whoa there, cupcake. Don't be in such a hurry to die," Donovan said, scribbling something on a notepad sitting on the desk. "He'll be here soon enough."

Isaac stood before me and then crouched just a few inches from my face. "I knew Jared as a child. Did he tell you that? I remember the way he spoke of you. Now that I see you," he said, gently touching my cheek, "I can't fathom what he sees in you that is so special. You are such a plain little thing."

"Ow!" I yelped, looking down.

Isaac had dug his thumbnail into my wrist, and blood oozed from the half-moon-shaped gouge.

"Leave her alone!" Ryan said, jerking in his seat.

Isaac licked the crimson liquid from my arm. "I thought maybe it was something I couldn't see. Merovingian and nothing to set you apart from the rest of them. Very disappointing."

I lowered my chin and glared up at him. "As you must be to your father. With all of your amazing talents and abilities, you're nothing but a sellout—a sycophant for the other side."

Isaac reared his hand and let it fly, back-handing me so hard I fell over onto my side, crashing to the floor in the chair I was tied to.

"You son of a bitch!" Ryan screamed, wildly struggling to get free.

"So much for not tolerating violence." I groaned.

"That was just a warning," Isaac said, setting me upright. "I have less tolerance for disrespect." He slowly leaned in, kissing my forehead.

"Let's go," Donovan snapped. "They'll be here soon."

Isaac nodded, and then they were gone.

"You okay?" Ryan said, scooting his chair until I was in his line of sight.

"I'm not going to lie. That hurt."

Ryan leaned in, inspecting the bump quickly rising above my eyebrow. "Jared's going to be pissed."

"I'm sure he already is."

"They should be here by now. Something's wrong. Jared said if they weren't here within a few minutes that I should get you out of here."

I looked around. "We can't leave. There's a safe behind that desk in the wall. The book is in there."

"How do you know?"

Ryan's wrists and feet were tied to his chair like mine, and he pulled and twisted his arms, ineffectively attempting to escape.

"Jack told me. We have to get into that safe."

Ryan raised an eyebrow. "Did Jack tell you how to do that if you're tied to a chair? Because I got nothing."

I sighed. "Didn't the Special Forces teach you anything?"

Ryan smiled. "Yeah. Keep a knife with you at all times." He wiggled his right leg. "In my boot."

The chairs complained against the wood as we positioned ourselves so that I could reach the knife. After several minutes of grunting and groaning, I finally felt the handle.

"I think . . ." I grunted again, straining against the tight restraints. "I think I've got it!" I said, grasping the hard plastic between my fingers.

"Don't drop it," Ryan said too late, watching the knife fall from my fingers to the ground.

"Crap," I huffed, blowing my bangs from my face.

"Okay," Ryan said, taking a deep breath. He jerked to the side until his chair tipped over and then maneuvered his body until his hand was within inches of the knife. "Nothing's ever easy when I'm around you, Grey."

"Shut up," I said, un-amused.

"What the hell is going on in here?" Claire said. She stood in front of the half-open windowsill, arms crossed, with her hot pink duffel bag over her shoulder.

A wide grin erupted across Ryan's face. "Better late than never, gorgeous."

"Shut up," Claire said.

"Wow, I'm getting it from every angle," Ryan said, letting his entire body relax and fall against the floor in protest.

"Where's Jared?" I asked.

"Behind me. We don't have much time," Claire explained, tearing the cloth around my wrists and feet with a flick of her finger.

"I'm on the floor, bleeding, and you save her first? I'm hurt," Ryan said to Claire.

Claire freed him and then lifted Ryan to his feet. She pushed back his head to inspect his wound, overly rough. "You'll live."

Ryan winced. "Thanks, honey, I love you too."

I walked over to the window, searching through the dark for Jared. "I thought you said he was behind you."

Claire chomped on the large wad of gum in her mouth. "He had to calm down. When he sees that knot on your head and that hand print on your cheek, he's going to freak out all over again. Back up."

I took a step back, and Bex appeared in the window, barely making an effort as he pulled himself through. "You smell like beer," he grimaced.

"Nice to see you too," I frowned.

"Where's the safe?" Bex asked.

"Where is *Jared*?" I said with an impatient tone.

"Right here, sweetheart," Jared said, crawling into the window behind Bex. "I'm right here." I didn't wait for him to crawl all the way into the room before I grabbed him. After a few awkward maneuvers to stand while encapsulated in my arms, he kissed my forehead and then inspected the remnants of my brush with Isaac. His jaws fluttered under his skin. "I'm going to enjoy killing him."

"The safe!" Bex said.

"Behind the desk," I said, pulling Jared with me. "It's there." I pointed.

"But," Claire said, bending down to touch the wall. "It's just wall."

Bex twitched and then closed his eyes. "They're coming."

Claire ran her hands over the drab paint. "I don't feel anything." She knocked. "It doesn't sound as if anything's back there."

"Are you sure? Maybe we're in the wrong room?" Ryan said.

I looked around, seeing the same paintings on the wall. "No, I'm sure. I've seen this a million times; the safe is right there."

Bex looked to Jared. "We have two minutes."

Jared sighed. "Claire? Move."

Claire obeyed, and Jared rammed the wall with his fist, pulling back broken sheet rock. Claire helped him, and within seconds, the entire panel was open, revealing the safe, three feet inside the wall.

Thousands of dust motes flurried in the air.

"That explains why you always saw them waist-deep in the wall," Jared said.

Claire held up her hand. "Quiet." She leaned her ear close to the safe and then moved the dial back and forth, nodding intermittently. Within moments, the safe clicked open. Claire seemed stunned. "That was too easy. It's rigged with explosives or something."

Jared shook his head. "I don't smell anything, do you?"

"No," she said.

"Shax is notoriously pretentious, Claire," Jared said. "I'm not surprised."

She stood. "This whole thing is too easy. They take our bait, sit Ryan and Nina in the room with the safe, knowing we would come after them, and then leave?"

Bex pulled out the book. "Got it!"

"Make sure it's the real thing," I said.

Bex flipped through the pages. "It's real, all right."

Jared grabbed my hand. "They left because Shax is bringing his legions to end us, Claire. They wanted us to come here and give them a reason to take us all out. Heaven can't step in if we provoke them."

Bex took a few steps toward the door, his head jerking in every direction. "Legions is right. I think the whole of Hell is coming. We should leave. Now."

"The roof!" I said. "They always used the roof!"

"Who did?" Ryan asked.

"We don't want to repeat what Jack and Gabe did, Nina. That leads to the same end," Claire said, looking out the window, planning an escape.

"Maybe not," Jared said, looking up. "Maybe she had the dreams to show us how to get out."

"Fine," Claire said, grabbing the book from Bex.

Screeching from below echoed throughout the halls, turning my blood cold.

Ryan's eyes darted in every direction. "Is that . . . ?"

"Yes. Let's go," Claire said, shoving the book into her hot pink duffel bag. "Bex?"

Bex nodded, running across the room and diving out the window.

Ryan's expression was a mixture of disgust and alarm. "It sounds like a dying animal—a thousand dying animals."

Claire pulled her sidearm from its holster. "You should hear one when you send it back to Hell." She gestured to me. "Show us the way, Nina."

The howls and screams of Shax's minions grew louder. Jared turned to me, cupping his hands on each side of my face.

"This is it, isn't it?" I said.

Jared looked deep into my eyes, as if he wanted to pass the truth through them instead of just saying the words. But he said them, anyway. "I won't let them touch you."

"I'm afraid," I said, shaking. The fear was so intense I felt powerless to control my own body. As the screeching grew closer, it became a physical effort to avoid slipping into a full-blown panic. I looked to Ryan. "Remember what we talked about."

Ryan nodded once. "I remember."

I grabbed Jared's hand, and we fled, climbing the staircase and then sprinting down the hall.

"This way!" I yelled. I stopped in front of a closed door at the end of the hallway. It was pointless to whisper, with the deafening shriek of the demons filling the air. I pulled on the knob, but it was locked. Jared moved me aside and then landed a lethal blow with his foot. The door swung open and hit the concrete wall, wooden pieces splintering and then falling to the ground.

"Come on," he said, pulling me up the crumbling staircase.

On the roof, the wind mercilessly whipped all around us, and the night sky crowded even the brightest lights below.

Jared ran to the edge. "Which building?"

I lifted my chin in the right direction. "That one."

Ryan frowned at Claire, unsure. "You're going to jump the length of a football field?"

She smiled. "Yes. And you're coming with me."

Ryan shook his head. "I'll take the fire escape."

I grabbed his coat and then pushed him into Claire's arms. "Thousands of those things are going to swarm this roof in about seven seconds. You won't make it to the landing."

Jared wrapped his arms around my waist and then took three long strides, grunting when he leaped from the edge. My fingers locked around his neck. I didn't dare look down, afraid the second I realized we were doing something impossible his powers would fade and we would fall five stories to the ground.

He made the same grunting noise to land as he did when we departed, but the landing was not as rough as I had anticipated.

I could hear Ryan's yells somewhere between our building and Shax's. His voice grew louder as they approached, and when Claire's feet hit the ground just ten feet away, she let him go.

He fell to the ground, rolling onto his back. "Let's never *ever* do that again." Ryan puffed.

Claire grabbed his hand and yanked him to his feet. "Don't be a baby." She grinned, pulling him to the roof access.

After two flights of stairs, my lungs begged for air, but the adrenaline surging through my body made my legs feel they could go on forever.

Jared stopped and looked above us. A second later, a loud crash sounded on the roof, followed by the sounds only demons on the hunt could make.

"We're not going to make it," Jared said, looking to me and then to Claire. "Take Nina and Ryan out."

"No!" I said, gripping his arm.

"There are too many, Jared!" Claire said. "Half of them will slip past you."

They both looked to Ryan, and then Jared grabbed Ryan's coat with both fists. "Get Nina out of here. Get her to the alley." Ryan looked at Claire, and Jared jerked him again, demanding his full attention. "Get Nina out! We'll hold them off."

Jared pushed Ryan back, pulling two Glocks from their holsters. Claire threw the duffel bag to me. "Make sure he doesn't get himself killed, all right?"

"Okay," I said, tugging on Ryan's coat.

We descended the stairs, leaving the Ryels behind. Ryan didn't take his eyes off Claire until she was out of sight, and then he focused, taking two steps at a time.

The screeching grew louder, more excited, and then the gunfire began.

Ryan stopped, held his pistol to his chest, and then slammed his back to the wall. "Shit!"

"We can't stay here! We have to go, Ryan. We have to go!" I pleaded, tugging on him with each word.

"I can't leave her," he said, looking up.

"The only way you can help her now is to stay alive!" I said, emphasizing each word.

He closed his eyes tightly and then grabbed my arm, pulling me down the last two flights of stairs.

"This is the door to the alley!" I said, pointing.

Ryan tugged on the handle a few times. When it wouldn't open, he aimed his gun, shooting a few rounds into the handle. I looked away, protecting my eyes from splinters flying in every direction.

Ryan rammed his shoulder into the door, forcing it open. I ran out into the alley, struggling for breath. The darkness outside was so quiet, as if we had entered a new world. The normal sounds of Providence were all around us: car horns in the distance, motorcycle engines revving as they pulled away from a stop light, the last bit of rain water falling into the gutters—it was as if I were caught in one of my dreams.

"Wake up," I whispered, closing my eyes. I focused on my bed and Jared's warm body next to mine. I opened my eyes, but the same scene was before me. I shut my eyes tighter this time. "Wake up!" I screamed.

Ryan gripped my shoulders, startling me. "It's not a dream this time, buddy. We need to move!"

Something dark and swift caught the corner of my eye. Not smoke, and not a shadow, but thicker than the night air.

"What the hell is that?" Ryan yelled, shooting once. The bullet ricocheted off the brick of the building.

"Watch out!" I screamed as the cloud rose above both of us, positioned to attack.

Ryan shoved me out of the way, and I landed hard on my knees and hands. His body flew backward, hitting the building on the other side of the alley, and he then fell the fifteen feet to the ground.

"Run, Nina!" Ryan said, stunned.

I scrambled to my feet, but before running off alone, I hesitated. Ryan was human, and I promised Claire to keep him safe. The blackness focused on me, and Ryan shot another round to return its attention to him.

"RUN!" he yelled, shooting again. The invisible enemy dragged him back into the building by one foot, and he held his gun in front of him, shooting at what he couldn't see.

Everything inside me wanted to stay, to try to help somehow, but I held the duffel bag close and dashed down the alley, into the street. Tears filled my eyes, blurring my vision, finally spilling over my cold cheeks.

Another alley was ahead, dark and forbidding, but it seemed the right way to go, so I kept running.

When my lungs couldn't take in enough air, I stopped, hunched over and puffing. Whatever it was that had Ryan couldn't be far behind, so I leaned against the back entrance of the building, working up enough courage to move. A bus stop was just a half block away.

"Take a step, Nina," I said to myself, willing courage to move my feet. "It's right there," I breathed, "Go!"

The door opened, causing me to lose my balance and fall back. Something grabbed me from behind, wrenching me inside with so much force that my hands, legs, and head all fell behind, jutting straight out in front me.

"Shhh!" Bex said, covering my screams with his hand.

More tears streamed down my face, and I threw my arms around his neck, sobbing with uncontrolled relief.

He held me at bay, searching my eyes. "Where is everyone else?"

I shook my head. "I don't . . . I don't know," I choked out.

"The book?"

I held up the duffel bag.

"Okay," he said, hugging me to him. "Okay, let's get you out of here."

He led me to his Ducati, which was parked around the corner, and we sped off, fishtailing down the street. As Bex took roads that would lead us to Woonsocket, I fantasized that Jared, Claire, and Ryan would be at St. Anne's waiting for us.

I replayed what happened over in my mind, wondering if I could have done something different or if I should have tried to help Ryan. Risking his life—and ultimately Claire's life—to steal a book that would save me was the epitome of selfishness, until I remembered that it would spare Jared as well. Even knowing that, I wasn't sure I'd made the right choice. Even if I were part of some kind of prophecy, our lives weren't any more valuable than Ryan's or Claire's.

Father Francis held open the door, waving for us to come inside.

"Are they here?" I asked, already knowing the answer.

The priest closed the door and then shook his head sadly. "Not yet. You have it?"

"I do. It's here," I said, opening the duffel bag. I handed the leather-bound book to Father Francis, and he held it gingerly, as if he were holding a bomb.

He retreated to the front of the cathedral, sitting on the first pew. "The *Naissance de Demoniac* of Shax the Duke," he whispered. He completed the sign of the cross and then prayed over the book.

Bex closed his eyes and then smiled. "They didn't like that."

18. THE MISTAKE

It was my turn to pace.

Father Francis and Bex poured over the pages, searching for something to present to Jared upon his arrival. But it had been almost an hour, and we were still the only ones who had made it to the church.

Every parishioner who entered the large, wooden door was politely turned away by Father Francis. It was harder for me to be polite, because each time the door opened, my heart stopped.

After my hopes had been dashed for the sixth time, anger took over. An older woman pushed her way through the door, only to be startled by the sight of me charging down the aisle. "Can't you see the sign? The church is closed!"

The woman scrambled to reach the door handle to escape.

"We need a bigger sign," I said, crossing my arms.

"Patience, child," Father Francis said, approaching me with a look of understanding. "He will come."

"When?" I said emphatically. "He should be here by now. I feel like I'm going crazy."

Father Francis gently guided me back to my pew, patting my shoulder. "Faith is what you need."

"I used to have faith. It's hard when everyone tells you that your death is inevitable."

"Death is inevitable for us all," the priest said.

Bex looked up, his eyes narrowing.

"What?" I asked. "Is it Shax?"

"No," Bex said, his eyes fluttering. "They've been crowding us since we got here, but they are," he opened his eyes, "all gone."

"But why?" I said, incredulous. The theme of the night had been that Shax had let us get away with his precious book far too easily. Their retreat only set me on edge, wondering when he would decide to put up a real fight.

Suddenly the door opened, cracking against the wall. Bex stood up, pulling me with him, using his body as a shield.

"You got a bathroom, Father?" Kim asked.

Father Francis scurried down the aisle, shutting the door behind Kim. "Of course, child, just through there," he gestured.

"Not funny," Bex said, frowning at her as she walked past.

"What?" Kim said, oblivious. "Just because you're being chased by hundreds of demons, a girl can't pee?"

Bex just shook his head, laughing once, absent of humor.

I collapsed into the pew, exhausted. "Something's wrong. They should be here by now."

Bex glanced at me and then turned a page of the book, choosing to ignore my words.

"I should have helped him. Ryan was dragged to his death, and I just ran away," I said, feeling the sting of salty tears well up in my eyes.

"I'm trying to read," Bex grumbled.

A door slammed down the hall, and then Kim's loud footsteps announced her arrival before she came into view.

"Oh, geez. Are you crying?" she asked. "And where is everyone? They go out for ice cream or what?"

I dried my tear-stained cheeks with my sleeve. "Jared and Claire stayed behind to give me and Ryan time to get out. When we got to the alley, something took Ryan."

"Something?" Kim said, as her eyebrows rose. "Like what?"

"I don't know. I couldn't see it. It was kind of like a shadow, but it was more. . . ." I trailed off, unable to find the appropriate word to describe it.

"Shadowy?" Kim said, unimpressed.

I rolled my eyes. "Not everything's a joke, Kim. Ryan's dead."

"No, he's not," she replied, confident.

Her words piqued my attention. "Why do you say that? Have you heard something? Do you know where they are?"

Kim nodded to the door. "He looks like crap, but he's right there."

I turned, gripping the top of the pew. Ryan, Claire, and Jared all stood near the entrance: dirty, blood-stained, and badly beaten. Before I registered that I was moving, my legs were carrying me down the aisle at full speed, and I crashed into Jared's chest. He wrapped his arms around me tightly and sighed with relief.

"Easy," Jared smiled, returning my repeated kisses as best he could. He kept his weight on one leg, and his pants were torn.

"What happened?" I said, crouching down to get a better look.

"We won," Claire said with a tired smile.

Ryan limped slowly down the aisle, his arm around Claire. Blood trickled from the outside of his eyebrow, and he was favoring his bad shoulder. They settled into a pew behind Bex, and Father Francis scurried away, waving back at them.

"I'll get the first aid kit!" he called to them as he disappeared down a dark hallway.

Jared smiled down at me. "We did it."

I leaned up on the balls of my feet to touch his lips to mine. Jared's words were empty. Winning that small battle was only part of the war we had just started.

Jared led me down the aisle, sitting beside me in the pew behind Ryan and Claire.

Ryan leaned back, holding a folded piece of fabric against his eye. "Next time we get into it with Hell, I get dibs on Mr. Puff."

Claire smiled, licking her split lip. "Your effort was impressive, even if that thing did hang you in the air by your ankle and use you to open two doors and make you scream like a girl."

"I didn't scream like a girl," Ryan protested.

"Maybe I was just hoping you would." She grinned.

"Thanks," he said, reaching out to touch her dirty face. His thumb gently grazed her cheek. "Again."

Claire's eyes met his for a moment, and then she pulled away. "Just get used to it. You don't need to thank me every time I save your stupid ass."

Ryan nodded and then relaxed against the pew.

I watched Claire for a moment, as she desperately attempted to feign indifference. I could recall that expression well; Jared used it many times in the beginning. Unfortunately for Claire, Ryan was far more confident than I was stubborn, and he was certain she would come around.

My eyes settled on Jared's beautiful, dirty face. His eyes were tired, but bright blue, excited, and amazed that we had the book and our lives. Seeing his expression only made it more real that he didn't expect any of us to make it to the church alive—a fact that, to me, was more unsettling than relief.

"Did you find anything?" Jared asked Bex.

Bex handed Jared the book. "Not yet. It keeps talking about the birth, the birth, over and over. How it disturbs the balance and how Hell will stop it and prevail."

Jared flipped through the pages, increasingly frustrated with each one. "Every prophecy has a loophole. That is why the Nephilim were created, to try and stop the bloodline from King David to Jesus." He slammed the book shut. "What did Father Francis say?"

Bex's eyes shifted toward me for just a moment, and then he shook his head, looking down. "He doesn't see anything either. But we've only looked at it once. We could have missed something."

"You know my vote," Claire said.

"Which is . . .?" Ryan said. His eyes remained closed.

Kim stood and stretched. "Jared, I know you want to find something, but we had a deal."

"I know," Jared growled.

I touched his arm. "What is Kim talking about?"

Jared didn't look up from the pages. "The promise I made her. If she helped us get back the book, then we would go with her to Jerusalem to return it to the Holy Sepulchre to set her family free."

I couldn't argue, but Jared had just begun to look it over. Kim was being uncharacteristically impatient.

"What's the rush?" I asked.

Kim waited for Jared to answer, but when he stayed focused on the book, she sighed. "Shax holds my family responsible. He'll retaliate."

Claire laughed once. "He'll do that anyway when you return it and it's out of his reach. Your family's held him off this long. You can wait a few hours, Kim."

"You don't get it," Kim said.

"Just let him read the damn book," Ryan groaned.

Questions formed in my mind, and I swallowed, always hesitant to get the answer. No matter what she might say, at that point I couldn't afford not to understand anything. The days of keeping me in the dark were over. "What doesn't Claire get, Kim?"

After a short pause, Kim took a breath. "I'm not there," she said in a low tone. "I've always been twenty minutes away; Shax knew that. He could have sent an entire legion to my father's house, and within minutes I would be there, and they would have to leave. We need to get on a plane, return the book, and then I need to get home before Shax realizes what we've done. Right now he just thinks you're looking for a loophole to the prophecy. He has no idea he's about to lose the book forever."

Claire put her elbow on the back edge of the pew and rested her head on her hand. "You don't think Jared finding a loophole to the *prophecy* is more concerning to Shax than losing the book?"

"No," Kim said, matter-of-factly.

"And why's that?" Claire snapped back.

Quiet overcame the group, until Jared closed the book with a clap. "Because there is no loophole."

I smiled hopefully. "Stop it, Jared. You haven't even read the whole thing yet."

"I just did," he said, his eyes focused on the black seal that branded the cover. "They aren't going to stop until they prevent the birth of our child."

Kim sat beside me, lowering her chin. "This entire cat-and-mouse Jared's been engaged in has been a game to Shax. The fact that Ryan is still alive should tell you he's just toying with all of us."

I shook my head. "If that were true, why the dreams? Why did Jack and Gabe push us to get the book?"

Jared stood. "Because they knew that is exactly what I would do, and the dreams were their way of helping us complete a fool's errand alive."

"No," I said, standing next to him. "I don't believe that. If that were true, they would tell me to stay away from the book, not how to get it. Gabe wouldn't have helped my father if it was pointless."

"Maybe you're right," Jared said. "Maybe we need a little more time with it."

"Jared?" Bex said.

Kim held up her hand in frustration. "Shax is a Duke of Hell, Jared. You pretty much walked into his house and slapped him, and he let you just walk out? Do you really think that's how it works?"

Ryan pulled the fabric from his eye, revealing a deep, bloody gash. "We didn't just walk out, Kim. Trust me. They put up a fight. I've never seen anything like that in my life, and I hope I never do again."

"Jared," Bex said again.

Jared frowned at Bex and then returned his attention to Kim. "Nina is your friend. Are you telling me you're not willing to wait for us to figure this out before we take it somewhere that we can never get it back?"

"She is my friend, but this is my family we're talking about. We've been dealing with this for lifetimes. It's time to end it. It's time the Pollocks are free of it."

Jared looked down at the book in his hands and then back to Kim, his expression stern. "I understand your plight, but you're not getting this back until I'm satisfied there's nothing in it that can help Nina," Jared said, shoving it under his arm.

Kim took a step forward. "We had a deal."

"I haven't forgotten that," Jared answered.

Father Francis came in with the first aid kit, taking quick steps. "I'm afraid it wasn't where I thought it would be. . . ."

"Jared!" Bex yelled. "They're coming!"

"Oh my God," Kim whispered, her eyes slowly rising to the ceiling.

A deafening boom surrounded St. Anne's. Every window burst inward, covering the ground with shards of colored glass. Jared took me to the floor, covering me with his body.

Even after the explosion, it sounded as if a tornado were hovering above the church.

"Not in the House of the Lord!" Father Francis yelled over the noise, his arms extended to the sky.

The priest was lifted high in the air by an invisible assailant, his legs kicking until he was blown back, smashing into the beautiful mural high above the stage. Pieces of the painting came down with him when he fell to the floor.

Bex rolled into the aisle and then took off toward the priest, so fast his body was a blur. He took Father Francis, limp and lifeless, into his arms.

The wind rushing through the broken windows blew Bex's platinum hair wildly as he felt for a pulse on the priest's neck.

"He's alive!" Bex called.

Another explosion shook the building, and pieces of the ceiling fell in large chunks onto the pews, sending sheet rock and plaster into the air.

"We have to move!" Jared yelled, pulling me to my feet.

The large wooden door blew open, forcing another strong pulse of wind across the room. Had Jared not kept his arms around me, I would have fallen over.

I held my hand to my face to shield it from the blast. When I lowered it, Shax was standing in the doorway.

He wore an all-black suit, shirt and tie, matching his cold, obsidian eyes. A small smirk was on his face. He was finally ready to fight.

Jared stood his ground, positioned in front of me. Claire stood on the other side, guarding her taleh.

Shax looked to each side of the church in dramatic fashion. "Where is your Samuel now, Jared?"

"He's around," Jared said, his body rigid.

"I'm afraid you've made yet another mistake, and Heaven won't intervene this time."

Two shadows, which had been lurking behind Shax, came into view under the dim light of the church. Isaac and Donovan stood on each side of their demonic master, their expressions anxious and ready. They had come to murder us all.

Jared shifted. "Isaac, listen to me. You don't have to do this."

"Shut up," Donovan said.

"I don't want you to die," Jared continued, "but if he comes near her, I'll kill him."

Isaac smiled. "Not if I kill her first. And I will."

"You're outnumbered," Claire said, her small yet frightening voice somehow carrying across the room.

Shax grinned, and the long clawed hands and feet of the night filtered into the room, covering the walls and ceiling. I looked above me, seeing grotesquely malformed bodies of demonic minions scale the crumbling rafters.

The smell of burnt flesh and sulfur was overwhelming, and I could feel bile rise in my throat. Shax's servants weren't screeching this time but making strange, excited, cooing and whistling noises, waiting for the order to attack.

"Give me the book," Shax hissed.

"No," Jared said, tossing the leather bound pages to Kim.

"I dare you to come and get it." Kim smiled.

Shax slowly turned his head to Isaac, and then Isaac's smirk turned into a satisfied grin. He pushed the far pew with both hands, slamming it into the pew before it, creating a domino effect. As the heavy benches toppled over and blew forward with the speed of a freight train, Jared and Claire reacted, jumping to the other side with Ryan and me in tow.

Kim simply sidestepped to the center aisle, remaining calm as thousands of pounds of wood roared by, narrowly missing her body.

"You're going to have to do better than that," Kim said.

Isaac leaped the hundred yards to Kim's position and then wrapped a hand around her throat, lifting her off the ground. "I'm not a demon. You can't control me."

With a grunt, Isaac threw Kim back, but Bex moved quickly, catching her before she collided with the podium. The demons concentrated in the area closest to Kim scattered, afraid of being too close.

Bex looked Kim in the eyes, and after she acknowledged that she was okay, he scrambled to his feet, taking off full speed, slamming into Isaac. When they collided, a loud crack echoed throughout the cathedral.

My human eyes couldn't make out who was hitting whom, until Bex hit Isaac so hard that his body sailed across the air and he landed in the exact spot he started, next to Shax.

"It's like people tennis," Ryan said, in awe. "Everyone keeps flying across the room."

Isaac wasn't about to quit. He engaged Bex again, but this time Isaac got the upper hand. Bex was on the ground, and after the second time Isaac landed a blow that would have been fatal to a human, Jared's arm tensed.

"Do something!" I said.

"I can't leave you," he said. "If I take my attention off you for a second, they'll attack."

Donovan walked down the center aisle with purpose, dodging the falling chunks of ceiling. Claire pulled out her firearm, aiming right at his face. Isaac's attention was distracted, then, and Bex head-butted Isaac and then threw him against Donovan. They both slid across the floor.

Isaac stood, pulled out his gun, and aimed directly at Ryan.

"No!" Claire said, throwing herself in front of him.

Ryan and Claire were face-to-face when Isaac's gun discharged. Claire's body jerked twice as it was hit, and Ryan's horrified expression matched hers.

Stunned, Claire looked down and then turned to Jared. "They went through me."

Claire and Ryan fell to their knees at the same time, and Jared rushed to his sister's side. He pulled me with him, and I fell to my knees just behind him.

Ryan's head fell back, and he coughed, blood spraying up and spattering across his cheek.

"Oh, God, no!" Jared cried, pulling off his shirt and wadding it up, pressing it against Ryan's wounds.

Isaac's maniacal laugh seemed to be all around us. "I always wanted to see that smug smile wiped off your face, Claire."

Bex glanced at the bloody scene and then focused on Isaac, his hands balled into fists at his sides. He lowered his chin, then, and his expression morphed into something one might see from a demon rather than an angel.

Claire looked up at her brother, expressionless. "End this."

Horrified, I watched Claire tend to Ryan's wounds, but within moments, Jared pulled me to my feet.

He took my hand in one of his and then pulled out his side arm with the other. He pointed it directly at Isaac, shooting one round after another, walking toward him as he fired, forcing me to follow.

Isaac jerked with each hit, stumbling backward. "You son of a bitch!" Jared screamed. His eyebrows and lips pulled in so tightly the skin around them was white.

"Jared!" Bex cried, but it was too late.

Donovan had his gun to Jared's temple. "I suppose it'll take you a while to heal from this one," Donovan said.

An abrupt blast resounded in the room, and Donovan fell to his knees, finally falling over, succumbing to the bullet hole I had just shot into his brain.

"Shawn!" Isaac said, struggling to reach his taleh.

It was too late for both of them. Shawn Donovan's life had already spilled onto the floor.

Isaac fell back, already feeling a weakness in his body.

Jared's eyes were wide as he processed what had just happened. "You killed him," he said softly, looking at me.

"He was pointing a gun at your head," I explained.

Jared laughed once, momentarily forgetting that we were still surrounded by the enemy.

A quick wind passed by, and Bex and Shax were suddenly in a ball. The sounds coming from their scuffle were horrific. Distracted, Shax lost his control on the demons clustered on the walls and ceiling, and they began descending from their position and swarming around us.

"Run to Kim!" Jared said, pushing me in her direction.

The hundred yards down the aisle to where she was protecting the book seemed a mile away, but I took off without hesitation.

Seeing my pitiful effort to run to her, Kim scrambled to her feet, sprinting down the aisle to meet me. I turned, seeing Jared and Bex attacking Shax and recognizing that his minions were quickly crawling to the floor in endless numbers. Adrenaline kicked in, and my feet moved faster, desperate to reach Kim before the demons caught me.

"Run, Nina!" Kim screamed. The horror on her face told me that in moments I would be crushed and torn apart by the Hell so closely pursuing my flesh.

Their screeches were almost on top of me when Kim's long arms reached out, encompassing my body as she brought me to the ground. I curled into a ball, and Kim wrapped her body around me. I could feel her being nudged forward over and over as the demons tried to knock her away with their sheer numbers. The wailing of the minions experiencing what Kim was capable of was deafening, but the individual howling resounding farther away was most definitely the sound of Shax losing his fight with Jared and Bex.

I covered my ears. The frightening medley of violence and pain was too much to bear.

And then it was quiet.

19. WAITING

I peeked out from under Kim's arms, seeing Jared and Bex slowly making their way down the aisle. Kim helped me to stand, and Jared wasted no time pulling me into his arms. His hands were trembling, and he was uncharacteristically shaken.

"Are you okay?" Jared asked, evaluating every inch of me for any signs of trauma.

"Yes, I'm fine," I said, shivering as the adrenaline soaked back into my system.

Bex carried Ryan in his arms, leaping and maneuvering around the ruins of St. Anne's to the entrance.

With the inordinate level of noise just moments before, the night seemed eerily quiet. The crumbling concrete, wood, and sheet rock grated against each other under my feet with every step. Those tiniest sounds echoed, even though the church seemed to be torn open and vulnerable, a contrast to the silence outside.

"We're going," Claire said. Her voice was distant and emotionless.

"Right behind you," Jared said. He led me quickly out of St. Anne's by the hand.

I turned to take one last look at the rubble, and saw Kim help Father Francis to his feet. She threw his arm over her shoulders, hobbling along herself beside him as they followed us to the Escalade.

Time passed in slow motion. Although everyone was desperate to get Ryan to the hospital, the distance to Jared's SUV seemed like miles, and getting everyone, bruised and bleeding, settled into their seats was a slow, frustrating process.

Claire rode with Ryan in the hatch, holding his head in her lap as he was nearly sprawled out. She seemed lost as she held pressure on his wounds, watching his face intently.

Bex sat in the back seat with Kim and the priest, but his focus was on Claire. He reached back, gripping his sister's shoulder. Bex's expression was heartbreaking, as the worries in his mind played out across his face.

"The closest hospital, Father," Jared said.

"Landmark Medical Center. Two minutes away. Stay on this street and then turn left on Cass Avenue."

Jared blew through the stoplight and then weaved in and out of traffic, making a hard right turn into the hospital's ambulance bay.

"We need help here!" Jared yelled, jumping out of the driver's side.

I ran to the back, watching Jared open the hatch. Bex helped the priest into the emergency room, and Claire let Jared place Ryan on a gurney.

Jared was gentle, as if it were Claire he was holding. A small cry escaped my throat, drawing Jared's attention away for just a moment. His eyes were dark, and suddenly, I felt an overwhelming sense of déjà vu—but more of an out-of-body experience. Watching Jared and Claire hover over Ryan's limp body was like seeing my last trip to the hospital from a different, more real perspective. It was cruel for both of them to have to suffer through it again.

Ryan was pale, but he had stopped coughing up blood. I wasn't sure if that was a good thing or not.

He managed a weak smile for Claire. "How about a kiss just in case?" he said; his words were broken and hoarse.

Claire tenderly touched his forehead. "I'll tell you what, cowboy. You come out of this alive, and I'll kiss you."

"You promise?" he said.

"I promise," Claire said, letting go of his hand. A frown barely touched her face before she turned around. "He's going to be fine."

"He is," Jared said, nodding.

Claire took a deep breath and nodded back, A million thoughts and worries scrolled in her eyes.

The minutes ticked by, and as more time passed, Claire grew increasingly restless. It was difficult to watch. I could only imagine the same scene, in the not-to-distant past, when Jared was pacing the floors waiting to hear news about me.

Jared opened his phone and pecked out a few numbers.

"Don't call Mom," Claire said.

Bex touched Claire's back for a brief moment. "Claire. She'll want to be here."

Claire shook her head. "Not yet."

We congregated in the emergency department's waiting room. Jared sat on the sofa next to me, Kim kept to herself, alone in a chair, and Claire stood with Bex in the corner. No one spoke; further discussion was unnecessary. We were waiting for someone to tell us if they had saved Ryan or if Claire would die.

Claire kept her eyes closed, concentrating on everything she felt from Ryan. Her clothes were ripped and filthy, and her platinum ponytail had given up holding her hair in place hours ago. Once in a while she would twitch, and I wondered if she could sense when they used the scalpel, or if it was difficult while he was under anesthesia to sense anything at all. Jared would have answered my questions, but it was hardly the time.

The tension in the room was unbearable, but the waiting was worse.

I watched the faces of the people walking by. Some noticed our ragtag group, some didn't. Glancing around the room, passersby would no doubt wonder if we'd been in some sort of large accident. The news of the wreckage that was once St. Anne's would soon spread, and I worried that the hospital would be crawling with police officers soon.

The random thought occurred to me that those staring had no idea that the pretty platinum blonde they couldn't help but notice could be dead in the next forty-eight hours. Claire was the strongest, most amazing woman I had ever met, and she looked so helpless in that moment—so hopeless.

Finally, she broke the silence. "That's it," she snapped, stomping her way to the door.

Bex stopped her. "Whoa. Where do you think you're going?"

Claire shoved at her brother, fighting to get free. "I can help him. I have to do something; I can't just sit here!"

Bex grabbed her face, cupping her cherubic cheeks in his hands. "They won't let you in there, and if force your way in, you'll just distract them from what they should be concentrating on."

Claire slammed the side of her fist into Bex's chest. "Let me go!"

Bex maneuvered his hands to get a better grip on Claire's arms, but she stopped struggling. Her eyes grew wide with fear.

"He's fading. They're losing him," she said, her voice sad and frightened.

Claire's body bent backward, stiff and unnatural.

I stood, cupping my hands over my mouth. "What's happening?" I cried.

Jared stood with me, restraining me with his hands on my shoulders as Bex cradled his sister and then helped her to the ground.

Claire relaxed and then stiffened again.

"Help her! She's having a seizure!" I said.

Jared turned my head, refusing to let me witness Claire's body writhing on the floor. "No, she's not. They're shocking him with a defibrillator."

"What?" I said, pulling away from him.

Claire lay in Bex's arms, limp. "He's dying," she whispered, a single tear falling from the corner of her eye, down her temple, into her ear. Her eyes were nearly vacant, fixed on the ceiling.

"No," Bex said. He closed his eyes. "Don't take her," he said softly. "Please don't take her too."

A sob escaped my throat, and I buried my face in Jared's chest. "They can't do this to us," I said. I pushed away from him then, raising my fists to the ceiling in a rage. "You can't do this to us! We are the good guys, and this is what we get? How dare you! How! Dare! You!"

"Nina," Jared said.

"It's not fair!" I screamed.

Jared enveloped me in his arms and kissed my hair. His fingers pressed into my skin, and I suddenly felt guilty, knowing Jared was suffering the agony of losing his baby sister and then feeling my sorrow as well.

"I'm sorry," I said, holding him tightly. I took a breath and focused on numbing all of my emotions.

"Don't do that," Jared said, sensing my efforts. "You don't have to do that," he whispered.

"I don't want you to hurt any more than you already are," I said, tears spilling down my cheeks.

"Claire?" Bex said in a strange tone.

I closed my eyes, terrified to peek out from Jared's arms to see Claire's lifeless body. There was still so much I didn't know about hybrids and the curse. Jared had prayed for Gabriel to take him quickly; maybe Samuel had taken mercy on her and couldn't bear to see her suffer.

"Nina," Jared said, nudging me. "Look."

Claire sat straight up, looking herself over, and then stared at the doorway. She didn't speak; she just waited. Finally, a nurse walked in, slightly confused by the spectacle on the floor.

"Er, we just stabilized Ryan. We had to remove his spleen to stop the bleeding, but he's a fighter. I'll come back when we know more."

I looked up to the ceiling, stunned. "Um, I'm sorry. Th-Thank you."

Out of the corner of my eye, a black figure appeared next to me. I jumped and recoiled, grabbing at Jared until I realized who it was.

"Samuel," Jared breathed.

I frowned, and Samuel smiled in response. "You are unhappy with me, young Grey."

"You haven't been much help," I said, too angry to hold back.

He smiled, his white teeth a stark contrast to his rich, dark skin. "It appears to me that the situation is under control," he said, making his way to Claire. He leaned down, touching the top of her head with his massive hand. "Ryan will be fine, I'm told."

Claire smiled, another tear falling from her eye. "Thank you, Sam."

Bex and Claire embraced each other with raw relief. For the first time, I heard Claire giggle. Her wet eyes were bright, and the sound of her laughter chimed in the air, reminding me of Lillian. Bex laughed along with her, wiping the tears from his eyes as they celebrated together.

Jared squeezed me to his side, and Kim's mouth widened to a large grin. It was as if we could all breathe again.

"He's going to make it?" I said. The question was redundant, but I had to hear it again.

Samuel nodded once. "Yes."

He returned to my side, and I wondered if any of the passersby could see him. No one seemed to notice the half-dressed giant in the room.

"We still need your help," I said. "We've read the book. We've all come close to death more than once trying to get our hands on it to find a loophole. Jared didn't find anything."

Samuel looked to Jared, who shook his head with a frustrated expression.

"I think you already know the answer," Samuel said.

Jared sighed. "I was kind of hoping that would be a last resort."

Samuel touched Jared's shoulder. "It's a means to an end, isn't it?"

With his last words, Samuel blinked from the space he had once occupied. Jared sat in the chair, pulling me into his lap, lost in thought.

Bex helped Claire to her feet and then walked her to the sofa. "He's right. It's what you should have done all along."

"Stop," Jared said.

The nurse returned, this time with a smile. "He's in recovery now. He's doing well."

"When can I see him?" Claire asked.

"Soon," the nurse said, offering a comforting smile before leaving the way she came.

Claire collapsed against the back of her seat. "That was close."

"Too close," Bex said, hugging her against his side.

"What is Samuel right about?" I asked.

Bex glanced at Jared, waiting for his brother to answer. When he didn't, Bex began, "We just started a war. The only way to win is to convince Heaven to fight with us."

I shook my head. "But we've tried. They won't help."

One side of Bex's mouth turned up. "They will if you give them something to fight for. They won't let Hell destroy the baby once it's born. We just have to protect you until it gets here."

"What baby?" I said.

Jared peeked at me from under his brow. "The baby you're carrying."

Everyone in the room stared at me, waiting for my reaction.

"Me?" I said, touching my palm to my chest. "But I'm not pregnant. We haven't—"

"Ew! Ew! Stop," Claire said, shaking her head.

"Just once," Jared said, looking up at me sheepishly.

I remembered the night I begged Jared to help me forget about the chaos surrounding us—the night he said it wasn't a good time to tempt fate. I didn't realize at the time he had spoken literally.

"How long have you known?" I said, taken aback.

"The following morning I knew something was different. It took me a week or so to pinpoint exactly what."

"I'm—"

"With child," Bex said. "Expecting. Bun in the oven. Knocked up."

"Hey," Jared said, disapproving of Bex's last choice of words.

"Pregnant," Claire said, as her eyes brightened.

Kim sighed. "You totally ruined my spring break. Just saying."

I took internal stock of my body, waiting to feel different, but it never happened. "No. I mean I don't *feel* pregnant."

Kim raised her hands, letting them fall with a slap on her thighs. "Seriously. How are we going to travel to Jerusalem with Preggo over here?"

"She'll go," Jared said, letting a small smile pass over his lips.

The nurse knocked on the window, gesturing to the gurney she was wheeling down the hall. It was Ryan. She whispered into his ear, and he lifted his hand, giving us the thumbs-up.

Claire stood to follow, pausing at the door way. "We'll all go."

"Looks as if we'll be waiting until Ryan is better before we're going on our trip," Jared said, pulling my hand to his lips. "We could tend to a few things while he heals."

"What's that?" I asked, feeling a bit overwhelmed.

"There's a pretty little chapel on an island I'd like to take you to."

I couldn't help but smile. "I guess we'd better."

"What are you doing Saturday?" he asked.

"Homework." I heaved a sigh and frowned. "Mountains of homework."

Jared frowned. "Sunday?"

I mirrored his expression. "I guess you're busy tonight?"

Jared's brows shot up. "You want to go tonight?"

I nodded.

He bobbed his head with a big grin. "We can go tonight if you want. We can go now."

"I'm ready," I said.

Jared grabbed each side of my face, pressing his warm, wonderful lips to mine. "How is it possible that I just went from almost losing everything I've ever loved, to getting everything I've ever wanted all in the same night?"

"Do you believe in guardian angels?" I asked, kissing him again.

EPILOGUE

"One bathing suit, one white dress, and a few undergarments—that's what I've packed for my wedding getaway," I said, watching as Jared effortlessly clicked shut the buckle of my seat belt.

"That's all you need, sweetheart," he smiled, checking the buckle one last time.

The stewardess went through her routine, and then the pilot came over the speaker, informing us of our place in line for takeoff and the current weather in Nicaragua.

"Should be a pleasant flight, Mr. and the soon-to-be Mrs. Ryel," the pilot said.

Jared's grin stretched the width of his face. "I might have paid him extra to say that."

"I figured as much," I teased. I looked out the window to the dreary Providence weather. In just a few hours, I would be lying on my favorite Caribbean beach with my husband. It didn't seem real but, at the same time, it was expected. We had earned this moment a thousand times over.

The chartered jet taxied to the runway and, within moments, gained momentum. The fuselage shuddered until the wheels left the ground, taking off in graceful, weightless flight. The lights of Providence became smaller, until they were just a cluster, separated from other cities by the dark countryside.

I relaxed against Jared, my eyes heavy.

Jared kissed my hair. "Do you think you'll have good dreams?"

"Yes," I said without pause. "Maybe I'll dream about the baby. Maybe I'll see what she'll look like."

"She?"

"Yes, it's a girl," I assured him.

"And what if it's a boy?" Jared asked, playfully nudging me.

"It's not. It's a girl."

"Blond, of course," Jared said.

"With blue-gray eyes," I sighed.

"No. She'll have your eyes," Jared insisted.

"You could have told me," I said, nuzzling against his arm.

"I thought about it. I went back and forth so many times about telling you or letting you find out the normal way."

"Nothing about us is normal." I smiled. "Why start now?"

Jared planted a sweet kiss on my forehead. "I don't have a preference. I just want him or her to be . . ." He trailed off, worried how his next words would affect me.

"It's going to be a long nine months, protecting us until the baby gets here."

"You worry about all the normal pregnancy stuff. You leave the rest of the details to me."

I frowned. "You talk as if it's crib assembly and child-proofing."

"I wish." Jared smiled.

"Me too," I said, resting my head against his warm skin. He wore a short-sleeved, white t-shirt in anticipation of the warmer weather of the Caribbean, but the light clothing allowed me more access to his soft, heated skin. The feeling of his skin against mine was a natural sedative.

Before long, I dozed off, sleeping deeper than I had in months. I didn't dream of our baby or of Jack or Gabe or of anything at all. I closed my eyes and was lost in a peaceful darkness until Jared kissed me awake when the plane was about to land.

The pilot made his announcements on the intercom, and Jared checked my seat belt one last time.

"It's fastened," I said, smiling.

"I just want to make sure. . . ." he said, laughing once to himself.

We landed without event, and once we set foot on the pavement, I grinned. "It hasn't changed a bit, except for the number of people waiting on us this time."

"We only have two suitcases and no tech cargo. It's been an easier trip for me this go-round."

"I'd say so." I laughed. "It even smells the same."

"And the last time we were here, you were only *pretending* to be Mrs. Ryel."

An instant grin lit my face, and I followed Jared out of the terminal to the waiting men outside.

Jared carried our suitcases to an old, rusty pick-up truck and then spoke in Spanish to the men as they loaded our belongings. Taking my hand, Jared helped me into the truck and nodded to the driver to proceed.

After a short drive, our island chauffeur slowed to a stop beside the pier. As we boarded the small boat Jared had secured for us, it occurred to me how unlikely it would have been for anyone else to have made arrangements at such late notice, and so early in the morning. Jared, however, had enough connections to do whatever he set his mind to.

"It's awfully dark to be wandering around in the ocean, isn't it?" I said, unsure as the boat captain steered in the general direction of the island. The boat was quickly swallowed by the night, and the cool air off the water won over the thin fabric of my jacket.

"Cold?" Jared said, wrapping his arms around me.

"Not now," I smiled.

"He's made this trip enough times, I'm sure he could do it blindfolded."

"When it's this dark, he pretty much is," I said, a bit anxious.

The salty air whipped by as we shot across the black water, a stark contrast to the turquois blue I remembered. Jared could hardly sit still, and had I not been so nervous about a possible head-on collision, I might have been just as excited to be back to the only place we had ever been able to be normal.

A half-hour later, the boat docked at the small pier of Little Corn. I sighed with relief. The waves had just begun to rock the boat a little more than I was comfortable with, and lightning had started to spark across the horizon.

We met another small truck with our luggage, and a small, sleepy man by the name of Jose drove us to the same *casita* we'd stayed in during our previous trip.

Speaking above the distant thunder, Jared spoke kindly to Jose in his native tongue and then pulled our suitcases from the back of the truck, opening the door for me.

It had just begun to rain when he set our suitcases on the floor beside the bed, and the smell of the rain combined with the sound of raindrops tapping on the roof and bouncing off the palm fronds took me back to a not-so-distant past when everything seemed innocent and exciting.

Inside were the same simple accommodations, with only two differences: every surface was adorned with glowing candles, and a tall fan waited at the end of the bed. It stood stationary, ready to serve its purpose while I slept next to Jared's feverish body in the Caribbean heat and humidity.

I covered my mouth with my hand as I yawned. My long, undisturbed nap on the plane left me feeling groggy. "It's beautiful! Better than I remember," I said, trying to muster the appropriate excitement in my tone. Speaking through a yawn dampened that prospect, but thankfully, Jared could feel what I couldn't adequately express.

"We're finally back." Jared sighed, a content smile on his face.

I returned his smile. Time had stopped for us here, and I had a feeling that once the wedding was over I wouldn't want to leave.

Jared lifted me off my feet and carried me to the bed. He lay on the bed, his face just inches from mine. His blue-gray eyes were bright and soft at the same time. I didn't want to close my eyes and miss a second of that expression on his face, but exhaustion had settled in.

"You should rest, Miss Grey. We have work to do."

"Work?" I asked, sleepy. "What kind of work?"

"We're changing your name tomorrow," he whispered in my ear.

ACKNOWLEDGMENTS

I would like to thank my sister, best friend, cheerleader, and number-one fan, Beth. You know exactly what to say at the best possible moment, and your encouragement always seems to turn into reality. Without you, there would be no Providence.

Thank you to my daughters for understanding they are more important than Mommy's work but that sometimes creativity keeps strange hours.

Thank you to Brenda for her time and being excited for every unit sold, and to Mandy Morris for being a Super Fan! You are always willing and eager to fly the flag and share the story.

I would also like to thank Dr. Ross Vanhooser for his unending generosity and faith.

Thank you to Ben Scroggs for his selflessness, flawless work, and patience.

Thank you to Trisha Johnson of Shutter Full of Dreams photography for your generosity and talent.

Thank you to Bobbi Washburn for her generosity.

Saving the best for last, I would like to thank all *PROVIDENCE* fans! The positivity you bring to my daily life is invaluable to me. Your unwavering passion for Nina's story drives the completion of every chapter. You are the reason *Requiem* came to be, and you are the reason the *PROVIDENCE* series will continue with a third book! Thank you all!

ABOUT THE AUTHOR

Jamie McGuire is the author of the New York Times bestsellers *Beautiful Disaster, Walking Disaster,* and The *Providence* trilogy.

She and her husband, Jeff, live with their children on a ranch just outside Enid, Oklahoma, with three dogs, six horses, and a cat named Rooster.

Please visit www.jamiemcguire.com

Made in the USA
Coppell, TX
07 February 2021